ANA LEE KENNEDY

NIGHTSHADE'S FLAME

WEREWOLVES OF REBELLION

BOOK ONE

For more information contact:
Riverdale Avenue Books
5676 Riverdale Avenue
Riverdale, NY 10471
www.riverdaleavebooks.com

Design by www.formatting4U.com
Cover by Scott Carpenter
Digital ISBN 978-1-62601-316-2
Print ISBN 978-1-62601-317-9

First edition, November 2016

Chapter One

Frank hated the heat. The sun beat down on the Wraithkillers' MC with vengeance and the aroma of pig shit, cow manure and hay, cut and drying in the fields, bombarded his sense of smell. Sweat trickled through his hair, caught by the black-and-white bandanna rolled into a long strip and wrapped around his head. He watched Crow, president of the Wraithkillers, for any signs of deceit, wishing he could just kill the man, piss on him, and walk away. He blinked several times and willed those thoughts to pass. Their days of Claiming and Maiming—as the old timers of their clan called it—were over. He had to control his urge to spill blood. They all did, humans and werewolves alike.

"It's a fair trade, Frank," Crow stated, bringing Frank back to the problem at hand.

"You stole one of our women," Frank growled, furious with Crow, "and you call it a fair trade?"

"Sure." The man smiled, revealing perfect white teeth that looked ten times brighter against his dusky skin. Some said Crow was part Native American and part African American. Others swore he was of Jamaican descent, and some even said Crow had

1

Japanese in his bloodline. Whatever his nationality, he was shrewd, smart, strong, conniving, and women gravitated to his good looks and charm. Men admired him and desired what their president had, but they knew better than to challenge him.

To Frank, the man's grin hinted at a panther preparing to attack. However, this one appeared to have had one too many hits of something today, so Frank would have to be doubly careful not to piss him off.

"You have our crate of guns and we have one of your women,"—Crow glanced over at a prospect— "who is Beastman's old lady, I believe." When the prospect nodded to confirm the woman's identity, Crow continued. "Return what is ours, and we'll give back what is yours."

"Dammit, Crow!" Frank thundered.

Crow's men all reached for knives or pistols.

Frank prayed he could curb his temper. "My men didn't steal anything from you. They found the crate sitting half-busted in the road with 9 millimeters and AK-15s spilling out of it. You're lucky we found the box at all. The Wraithkillers are known for dealing weapons. If the pigs had come across it, you know they'd be sniffing around your club to tie you to that crate. We did you a favor."

Crow shrugged. "It doesn't matter. You still took what doesn't belong to you." He swept one hand toward the woman at the back end of a tractor where a couple of Crow's prospects had bound and gagged her. "I like to keep things even."

Frank looked over at Phil, his second-in-command, who shook his head and sighed.

"Might as well swap for what's ours," Phil said. "You know, if Beastman doesn't get his old lady back he'll break protocol, and come in here to Crow's compound and take her. Probably start another war, too."

"Listen to your second-in-command," Crow urged, his tone smug.

Frank wanted to throat-punch the bastard. He curled his right hand into a fist, his claws beginning to slice into his palm, and willed them to subside.

"What he says is the truth," Crow added. "You don't want anything to destroy the tentative peace we've had for the last six months, do you?"

Frank fought with his inner animal. It would feel so good to let his claws grow, then rip out Crow's throat while watching the arrogant expression on his face fade away, along with his life. But Frank was a better man than that. He was the president of the Wolves of Rebellion, and he'd battled for a long time to create a haven of sorts for his people in the Appalachians. No one but those of the utmost integrity knew of their true identities, and after warring with the Wraithkillers for the last two years they'd finally established some semblance of peace between the two motorcycle clubs, although Crow liked to rattle everyone's chains and stir shit whenever he could.

Frank let his gaze sweep Crow's compound, touching on the barn, which had been converted into the gang's clubhouse. A small, ramshackle farmhouse sat off to the left at the edge of the tree line. About 30 motorcycles, most of which were Harleys, sat parked between the two buildings, and an array of old John Deere equipment—from tractors to a combine and all the attachments—were stored around the barn, or at the back of it. Next, he assessed the Wraithkillers present. Most right now were prospects, but he spotted Crow's second-in-command, Firewater, off in the doorway of the clubhouse. Four of the gang's "sheep" stared out at them, their breasts barely contained in their bras, hair rumpled, each woman curious to see how events would play out. He'd give Crow credit. The man took care of his biker family—provided for them, watched over them. Crow was only doing what was best for his club—and that's exactly what Frank would have done, too.

With a dissatisfied grunt, he settled his attention on Luella, who sat with her hands tied to the tractor's hitch, her feet bound and a red bandanna stuffed into her mouth. And what a beautiful mouth it was, Frank mused. Before she'd become Beastman's old lady, Luella had given him some mind-boggling blow jobs. He still had a fond spot in his heart for the woman. And Phil was right—Beastman would storm into Crow's place and slaughter most of the Wraithkillers before any of them even had a chance to draw a weapon. If Crow knew that he was staring back at six werewolves—real werewolves—he'd piss a puddle between his feet.

"All right," Frank said, motioning for a couple of his prospects to bring the repaired crate. He waited until the men had set it down halfway between his men and Crow's. Once Steven and Ass Crack backed away, Crow indicated for his guys to investigate the box. They confirmed everything was there, then picked the crate up and carried it into the barn, yelling at the sheep to stay the hell out of the way as they entered.

"Come," Crow announced. "Everything has been settled. Untie the woman. We're back to being friends, so have a drink with us."

"Take Luella home," Frank told Johnny, a loyal prospect. "Make sure Beastman stays *there* with her too." He leaned over to whisper in Johnny's ear. "Tell him that if he even attempts to come here to Crow's compound, I'll put him on protection duty for a month."

Johnny smirked. "He hates protection duty."

"That's the point," Frank said.

Chuckling, Johnny put his arm around Luella's waist. "Come on, honey. Let's get you home to your man."

"Frank?"

Frank turned.

"Thank you," she said. "I mean it."

"Hey, baby, no sweat. You're family. We take care of our clan."

At that, she offered him a huge, watery smile, her big, round blue eyes filling with gratitude. She nodded, then let Johnny lead her over to his Yamaha Midnight Special.

Joining Crow in his clubhouse for drinks was the last thing Frank wanted to do, but he knew if he refused, Crow would be affronted. He had to leave here with the peace between the clubs still intact. "Boys, let's go have a beer."

Inside the converted barn, the aroma of sex, weed, stale beer and unwashed bodies assaulted Frank's nose. The same smells resided at the werewolves' clubhouse, but he knew those odors. They were familiar and possessed the wild perfume of everyone's true identities—and they were residual scents. The stink in the Wraithkillers' crib offended his senses. Humans always smelled like food or sport, but when their odors were mixed with other unsavory elements such as dirty ass and armpits, it might as well have been wolf repellant.

The days of hunting humans were long gone, so he gulped down rising bile and tried to focus on other things. For a moment he stopped to admire the work that the Wraithkillers had done in switching the place over to a real clubhouse. Although the inside was modern, someone had gone to great pains to retain a barn-like atmosphere, right down to the floorboards, the hewn rafter beams and the stalls that had been turned into offices, and a gambling den. From what he could see through a partially open door, the last one was a master bedroom, complete with a king-size bed and a naked woman kneeling on it, her ass in the air as she enjoyed two men going at her in the same hole.

On the left, four pool tables and two electronic dart machines created a recreational area. A few bikers and their sheep companions were engaged in a loud, drunken round of cricket that Frank heard clearly over the low pulse of country western music, filtering through a hidden sound system. One of the women, a blonde with a huge tattoo of a tropical scene on her back, hit the triple 19 spot and squealed so shrilly that Frank thought his lykoi ears might explode. The man next to her cheered, picked her up, then carried her up to the loft and slammed a door shut.

"That bitch cheats," a shirtless man said.

"How the hell do you cheat at darts?" his companion asked. "We used house darts, so we know they're not weighted."

"I dunno," the shirtless man replied, "but no bitch should be able to play darts like that...."

Frank snorted at the conversation, detouring around a couple fucking on one end of a leather sectional that encircled a large stone fireplace. The woman met her partner thrust for thrust; her long, skinny legs wrapped tightly about the prospect's driving hips. Frank detected that all her sounds were fake. Then again, the sheep, or "sweet butts," as some MCs called them, were there to be used as the guys wished. The biker screwing her let out a low moan and stiffened as Frank and his men passed. Frank was glad that each member of his club had a purpose and truly meant something, but that was the way of most lycanthropes. Well, all but one clan. He pushed that thought away and subdued a shiver of distaste that tried to jiggle down his spine. His immediate family swore that the Waterleaper Clan were extinct.

"How can Crow afford all this for his clubhouse?" Phil asked quietly.

"He deals weapons. And with meth so rampant in the river towns," Frank added, dropping his voice even lower, "I imagine business is good—*really* good."

They finally reached the bar: a simple but beautiful oaken counter, lined with high stools. Behind it, oak shelves held cheap to high-end liquors. Instead of mirrors behind the shelving, shadowboxes had been wood-burned with designs of crows and apparitions. Frank raised his eyebrows at the craftsmanship. He'd bet there was a least a grand wrapped up in those boxes.

Maybe Phil had a point. Why would Crow invest so much money into his clubhouse? Sure, luxury—

such as new pool tables and furniture—was fine, but if he had money like the Wraithkillers seemed to have, he'd be more worried about providing health insurance, living spaces and homes for his members, not wood-burned designs and top-shelf liquor. He wondered how else Crow planned to flaunt the obvious cash flow coming into his gang.

Someone placed a bottle of beer in front of him. He looked up to meet the eyes of a man he'd never seen before. He was big—really big. Frank veiled his surprise. The bartender was probably pushing seven feet, easy, with powerful shoulders and arms that looked like they could bend steel. The only other biker Frank knew of who compared was Beastman, and he was smaller than this dude. Other than the bartender's size, the guy didn't stand out. No ink, no scars, no body alterations.

The man nodded, once, then turned his attention to setting beers in front of each of Frank's men. Frank dismissed him as a new recruit.

Movement at the stairs drew Frank's attention, and his mouth dropped open. He'd seen many redheads over the years, especially since his clan had made their home in an Irish-settled area, but the woman—flaming-red hair, tiny, voluptuous—coming down the stairs, rocked him. Drool pooled at the corners of his lips, and he snapped his mouth shut tightly. What the hell? He liked blondes, not gingers.

Every man in the joint paused to watch her as she arrived and headed to the end of the bar. The sheep in the club, bent on keeping the attention of their bikers, clung to the guys. The disdain and jealousy in their expressions spelled trouble for the redhead. Once she reached the bar, Frank tensed. The last traces of bruising encircled her eyes and decorated her mouth as if she'd been drinking purple, blue and green Kool-Aid. Someone had either beaten her or she'd been in one hell of a fight.

Crow walked behind the bar and set a 9 millimeter on the countertop. "Here, a gift. One of the best 9 millimeter in the crate, just to say no hard feelings."

"That's a pricey weapon," Frank replied, trying to keep his attention on Crow instead of the woman.

"We've had enough bloodshed between our clubs, Frank." Crow's voice rumbled low and deep. Frank couldn't detect any deceit in it. "Things were tense outside for a few minutes. You did the right thing, and I want to show my thanks."

The redhead motioned to the barkeep, who listened to what she said, then fixed her a whiskey neat and handed it to her. She sipped from it, her eyelids closing, facial muscles relaxing.

"Whose woman?" Frank asked, casually dipping his head in the ginger's direction.

"No one's," Crow replied. "Her name is Bernadette Kelly. She came to us by way of a prospect who met her through a prostitute in Columbus. The whore said that this ginger wrote a book on the lives of three hooker friends, so the prostitute put her"—he inclined his head in the redhead's direction—"in touch with the prospect, and the dumbass brought her here. She swears she's a writer doing research for a book on motorcycle gangs." He glanced over at her and whistled low. "I'd love to fuck that gorgeous piece of ass, but the last thing I need is a rap for fucking a cop."

"What makes you think she's undercover?"

9

The way Crow looked at the woman sent a frisson of irritation through Frank. It was as if Crow wanted to actually eat her. The ginger caught Crow's scrutiny. She raised her glass to him, offered him a half-smile, briefly flicked her gaze over at Frank, then turned away and headed back upstairs.

"Bernadette is way too smart for her own good," Crow explained. "It's the way she looks at you, the way she pays attention to everyone and everything. She's cop smart. At the very least, she's probably a journalist. You get me?"

Nodding, Frank said, "Yeah, I get you. Who did she get into a fight with?"

"Hey, dude." Holding up his hands palms out, Crow shook his head. "None of my guys touched her. No one the pigs snooping around here. That ginger was cornered by two of my sheep—nasty cat fight. It took me and Bloodbath here"—Crow jerked a thumb over his shoulder at the huge bartender—"to break it up. The sheep who messed her up look just as bad, though. Bernadette is a hellcat, that's for sure. My girls say they don't trust her, so they decided to beat some information out of her, but I think there was more jealousy involved than anything else."

"Did she tell them anything?" Frank asked.

"Nope. She stayed true to her story about being a writer."

Frank watched the delicious way the ginger sashayed up the last few stairs, her round ass begging to be bitten. "How 'bout I take that ginger off your hands instead of the gun?" Frank looked directly at Crow. *Where the fuck did that idea come from?*

Crow blinked. "Seriously?"

Frank shrugged. "Why not? We could use some new girls, and if this one doesn't work out, I'll have some of my wolves take her back to Columbus."

"Take her." Crow slid the top of a cooler back and withdrew a lager. "I hate to let something that beautiful slide through my fingers, but better your ass in a sling with a potential cop than mine."

Frank pushed the pistol toward Crow. "Deal."

Leaning over, their shoulders bumping, Phil asked, "Boss, you're letting your pecker think for you. She's fucking gorgeous, but you don't know who she is."

His second-in-command had a point, but Frank couldn't shake the draw he felt when he looked at Bernadette. "We seldom know who any of the women are when we pick them up, or when they come to us."

"But Crow already suspects that one is tied to the cops. At the very least, she's one of those pain-in-the-ass journalists."

"Then we'll contact the Monroe County Sherriff's Department and ask." After chugging his beer, Frank set it on the bar top. "And if she *is* a journalist, we could use her to our advantage."

Phil stared at him for a long moment then a smile broke out on his face. "How?"

"To paint the Werewolves of Rebellion in a good light."

Phil smiled. "It's your club, Boss."

"I'm ready to head out, Crow," Frank said and held out his hand. "I'll be outside waiting for the woman."

Crow gripped his hand and shook is vigorously. "I'll send her out once she's packed her stuff."

11

Chapter Two

Bernadette had barely opened her laptop when one of the Wraithkillers threw open the door to her room.

"What the hell?" she snapped from her chair. "Don't you know how to knock first?"

"Our club, our rules," the man barked. "Crow's sending you to another club."

She sat up straight and shut the lid on the laptop. "What? Why?"

He crossed his arms, the tattoos winding around his forearms blending with all the ink on his chest, and let his gaze wander over her body. His attention settled on her breasts the longest. Finally, he met her eyes. "Because Crow says so. Now pack your shit. You're going with the Werewolves of Rebellion."

Bernadette didn't have much, just a backpack with her laptop, a high-end digital camera, her cell phone, two changes of clothes, her toiletries bag, sneakers, which she now wore, and a pair of flip-flops. She started to follow him, but spotted her good pen on the stand. She reached for it, but it zipped into her hand. On reflex, she curled her hand into a fist before she dropped it.

"What the fuck?" The biker stared at her in disbelief, and fear. "How'd you do that?"

She shrugged. "Just a parlor trick I learned when I was little."

He stared skeptically at her, then accepted her explanation with a nod. Bernadette had seen that expression time and time again. People feared what they didn't understand. Hell, she didn't understand the strange little things that she could do.

"Let's go." He motioned for her to follow him downstairs.

"Stay gone," the blonde with the tropical tattoo snapped. She sat across a guy's lap, his hard dick gripped loosely in one of her hands. "Or I'll have to mess up that pretty face again."

"Yeah, and with that fat lip and the travel brochure tattooed on your back you're definitely a runway model," Bernadette retorted, trailing the biker outside. Behind her, the men burst into laughter. The blonde let out an enraged scream. Bernadette's escort shot her a sidelong glance, but Bernadette caught the amused glint in his eyes.

She checked out the group of bikers standing next to their motorcycles. All but one of the steel horses were Harleys. The man who had been talking to Crow at the bar kept his gaze on her as she traversed the lot. She'd been fascinated by him earlier, his colorful sleeves drawing her eye yet again, but she tried not to stare at him too long. Each Werewolf of Rebellion stood a good head taller than Crow's men, but the president of the werewolves looked rougher with all his tats: more dangerous, and oh so delicious, with his coal-black hair and piercing blue eyes. She shook away the thought. She couldn't let anything deter her from getting the research she needed for her book. *I can't let a handsome face and tattooed muscles distract me.*

With resolve, she walked the last few feet to the group waiting for her. The sun beat down ferociously, and a gentle breeze brought the aroma of livestock, but did little to ease the stifling heat. Between the windburn she was liable to get from the bike ride, and the sun's ultraviolet rays, she was sure to reach the other clubhouse looking thoroughly cooked. Mentally, she added sunscreen to her shopping list.

"Ms. Kelly," the president said, holding out one very large, callused hand. "I'm Frank Nightshade, president of the Werewolves of Rebellion."

She accepted his hand, which enveloped hers. "Please," she stated. "Call me Bernadette."

He nodded, his gaze direct, curious and… interested?

"Why am I being sent to you?" she asked.

He blinked, as if her question surprised him. "I'll explain everything later. Right now, the sooner we get out of the Wraithkillers' compound, the better." He straddled his bike and placed his hands up on the monkey bars. "You'll ride with me, Bernadette."

The way he'd said her name, deep and rumbling, like a deliberate caress, forced a delicious tremor up her spine. She allowed Frank to help her step up on the foot peg, her gaze instantly drawn to a realistic wolf head baring its fangs that someone had airbrushed over the bike's gas tank. She then swung her leg over to sit snugly behind Frank. She studied the emblem on the back of his cut: a large full moon with the silhouette of a half-man, half-beast, its head thrown back, howling. Something dangerous danced down her spine again.

"Hang on," he ordered.

Bernadette leaned forward. The instant her breasts made contact with his cut, the leather of it warm from both his body and the sunshine, heat settled in her pussy and pulsed there, creating an incredible ache that almost had her writhing on the seat. When he started the powerful machine the vibrations of the motor penetrated the padding and intensified the throbbing in her folds. She'd only just met this man, but oh, what a man he was. She placed her hands on his waist, thinking to merely steady herself, but when Frank pushed off and started down the dirt lane, she pressed closer to him, wrapping her arms about his waist. *Damn...he feels fine. Hard, all hard muscle....*

To her surprise, he released one monkey bar and patted her hands, lying flat across his belly. His stomach, flat with defined abs, moved subtly beneath her palms. Heaven help her, she now understood why some women loved biker men. If the men were all similar to Frank Nightshade she'd have a tough time concentrating on her new manuscript. Of course she knew that not all biker men treated women well, or even fairly, but somehow she sensed Frank was different.

Frank maneuvered the Harley down the long drive just fast enough that he wouldn't have to duck-walk it. She glanced from side to side at the men flanking them, then over each shoulder at the ones bringing up the rear, and realized that they were trying not to kick up dust and choke one another.

Frank paused at the end of the road, looked both ways, and pulled out onto SR 800. The others followed, and soon they were roaring down the state route, taking the hairpin turns with ease. Bernadette's brothers had owned a few motorcycles over the years, so she knew enough that she needed to relax behind Frank, but the speed with which he took some of the curves scared the hell out of her. On a straight stretch, he patted her hand again. The action helped relax her, and despite her reservations, she molded herself to Frank's back, and tried to become one person with him as he maneuvered the Harley.

They roared up a twisty hill and passed the Midway Community Center, its entrance in the center of a wide 'L' bend, then up a second part of the slope until they reached the top and sped up and down the gentle knolls of the plateau. They slowed through the sleepy village of Antioch, but just as Bernadette began to feel she could sit up and look around at the lush summer scenery, they entered another area of sharp turns and steep inclines. She snuggled against Frank's back and waited until the ride became less zigzagging. Finally, they raced along another plateau down into a valley and up what locals called Steed's Hill. Minutes later, they rumbled into the town of Rebellion, population roughly 2,300.

In the town's square, Frank pulled into a parking spot. Some of his men parked nearby and two others had to go around the corner to find places for their bikes.

"What are we doing here?" she asked Frank.

"I have to go talk to someone, but if you need anything, I'll have one of the men escort you."

She frowned. "I need an escort?"

"Honey, until I know more about you, you don't go anywhere alone."

"Ah, I see. You don't trust me."

"Do you trust me?" he countered.

"I don't know you."

"Exactly my point."

She nodded. Fair enough. If it helped him feel better, she'd humor him. Plus, if she played along, she could glean information about Frank and his club.

"Tom, will you escort Bernadette wherever she needs to go?" Frank asked.

"Sure, Boss." The 30-something man removed his shades, revealing lighter skin in the shape of the sunglasses around his eyes. As he began polishing the lenses, he asked, "Need anything?"

"Nah, I'm good. Meet me back here in about 30 minutes." He jerked his head in Tom's direction, indicating that Bernadette should go with him.

With a last glance at Frank, she joined Tom on the curb. She remained still and watched Frank cross the square, waiting at the midway point where locals had told her that there used to be a capped off well once upon a time; then proceeded over the other half to the sidewalk. He disappeared down the hill leading north out of town. She guessed that he was going to talk to someone in the county sheriff's office to see if anyone knew anything about her. *Smart guy. Damn sexy too.*

"Where do you want to go first?" Tom asked.

The others had wandered off in various directions. Two had already entered a small hole-in-the-wall pub.

She stared up at the tall, thin biker. "I guess Family Dollar. I need sunscreen and a couple other things."

"Hell, there's no sense walking in this fucking heat." Tom offered her a charming smile that made her grin back. "We'll ride down to the store."

"Thank you." After he'd settled in front, Bernadette climbed on behind him, then placed her hands on his hips, careful to keep space between their bodies. Already she discerned a big difference between the Wraithkillers and the Werewolves of Rebellion. If her instincts were correct, she'd learn a lot about Frank's gang.

* * *

Frank strode along the sidewalk, passing the large, imposing courthouse with its red and yellow brick, its huge clock tower looming high overhead. Frank's family, whether blood or sworn, had been there since Archibald Woods founded Rebellion in 1814, when the family had helped him clear the trees to make way for Rebellion. Archibald had known what Frank's people were, but he also knew they weren't like the others who prowled the wild, untamed country. As a result of their labor, loyalty, and Archibald's gratitude for both, Frank's werewolves owned a large amount of acreage toward Graysville, a place they could forever call home.

Now the town bustled with oil and gas industry people, each one bent on buying property owners' energy rights. He'd thought of selling the MC's rights, but the more he thought about it, the less he liked the idea of all the disturbances—earth moving equipment, drilling, the loud roar of burn-off, the big sand cans and water bottles coming and going, the brilliant lights of the pad that would be seen for miles around. No, there were already hundreds of fracking pads all over the landscape employing numerous people, including several of his MC guys, but the Werewolves of Rebellion loved Mother Nature, and she'd always treated them well. She deserved the same from them in return.

Frank walked across an alley and entered the narrow hall that led to the inner door of the Monroe County Sheriff's Department. He pulled the door open and stepped into a room paneled in light wood and carpeted in gray. The usual state flag and other emblems for Ohio and Monroe County, including a few small township maps, adorned the walls. Each workspace possessed picture frames of family members, whether on desktops or hanging on a dividing wall. Deputy Sheriff Craig Williamscot, resplendent in his black and gold uniform, reclined in a comfortable chair in one corner of the office. Filing cabinets lined the wall behind him. A new state of the art computer system sat on one end of his desktop, and framed photos of the man's wife and little girl perched on the other side of it. "What can I do for ya, Frank?" he asked.

Frank waited as the office dispatcher passed between him and Craig's desk. She grinned up at Frank and winked. "Frankie, it's good to see you, honey."

"Nancy," Frank greeted her. He caught Craig's smirk at Nancy's use of 'Frankie,' but she was the only woman besides his mother and grandmother who got away with using that particular moniker. "How are those grandbabies doing?"

"Katie Bug is walking," she announced, her round face beaming her love for her granddaughter. "I can't believe she's already 14 months old, Frankie. And the other three are growing like weeds."

"Good to hear, hon," he replied, meaning it. "Nothing like spoiling them and sending them back to their mamas, is there?"

"Exactly!" She giggled, a laugh that sounded so much like an exuberant teenage girl that it forced

Frank to chuckle too. "Just you wait, Frankie, you'll have one or two kids one day and then you'll really know what all the fuss is about children."

"I'm nearing 40 now, Nancy. I don't know that I'll—"

"It's back to work for me," she singsonged as she walked to the far side of the office.

He laughed. Any time Nancy refused to enter the debate about whether or not he'd have any children, she'd cut him off.

Deputy Williamscot shook his head and grinned. "Put you in your place again, didn't she?"

"She always does," Frank stated.

Nancy reached for the ringing phone, shifting from happy grandmother persona to efficient dispatcher.

"That woman has ten times more energy and enthusiasm than I could ever hope to have."

"She's a special person, Craig. Treat that lady right and she'll stand by you, the sheriff and all the other deputies, through thick and thin."

"Don't I know it." Deputy Williamscot pointed to one of the two chairs in front of his desk. "So, what brings you in here today?"

Frank glanced around to see what ears might be listening, then realizing that everyone except Craig and Nancy had gone to lunch. He sat in the proffered chair and lowered his voice anyway. "I need some information on someone."

"Such as?" Craig quirked his blond eyebrows and steepled his fingers together, as he leaned forward and braced his elbows on the desktop.

"Have you heard of a Bernadette Kelly from Columbus?"

"Actually, I have. I met her one morning at The Lunchbox. Ms. Kelly seems to be a really nice lady, quite a looker too, and intelligent. Writes nonfiction, particularly true crime novels. She said she'd like to pick my brain one day about MCs, but I told her that it's pretty quiet around here, especially since the two MCs in our area"—he dipped his head toward Frank—"have finally reached a truce of sorts."

"Let's just hope that truce lasts," Frank said gravely. He let that tidbit of information sink into Craig's head, then asked, "Is this Kelly woman really a writer?" He hated that Bernadette's identity was so important to him, but he just didn't feel right about bringing her to the werewolves' compound until he was certain she was legitimate.

"She showed me a copy of her book," Craig replied. "Can't recall the title now, but it had something to do with lives of three prostitutes and their friendship." He stared hard at Frank. "You looking to take her as your old lady?"

Franked placed his forearms on his knees and met his friend's gaze with confidence. "Hell, no. I took her off Crow's hands."

Frowning, Deputy Williamscot sat back in his chair. "Why would Crow give her to you when she's so beautiful? I'd think he'd want her for himself."

"He was afraid she was an undercover cop or a reporter."

"So you decided you wanted to take the chance for him and potentially expose your people?"

"I just… Well, I wanted…" Exasperated, he sighed. "Aw, fuck! I have no idea why I did it, Craig. I know that we don't need someone snooping around our compound, but when I saw her, the next thing I knew, I was offering to take her with me." He flopped back in the chair and raked one hand through the top of his wind-tangled locks. "You and Miranda are the only ones who know the truth about my club, but after I had Bernadette on the back of my bike, I realized how stupid I was for taking her with us." He paused, gathering his thoughts. He sure as hell wasn't going to mention that her body pressed to his had created the worst raging hard-on he'd had in a long time. "I thought I'd put my mind at ease by checking with you about her."

"Sounds like you got an instant woodie when you saw her," Craig stated, trying not to laugh.

"Yeah, maybe." Frank let out an amused snort. "She's probably the most beautiful woman I've ever laid eyes on."

"I might be married," Craig said, "but I'm not dead. You sure you're just not thinking with your pecker?"

Frank shrugged. "I don't know what came over me, Craig. I saw her and the next thing I knew, I was offering to take her off his hands."

"Yeah, sounds like pecker trauma to me," Craig mused.

They sat silently for a long moment as Frank mulled over Craig's words. The phones rang intermittently, and Nancy answered each call in a soothing, business-like voice. She'd listen, ask pertinent questions, then dispatch the information to the closest deputy in the area.

Finally, Craig sat forward and leaned on the desk again. "What do you want to know, Frank?"

"Is this Bernadette Kelly an undercover cop?"

"Not to my knowledge."

"You're sure?"

"Yep."

"Is she a journalist?" Frank fired at him.

"That, my friend, I don't know. She could be. You know how they are in the news industry."

"Shit. At times a journalist can be worse than a cop." He glanced up at Craig, then grimaced. "Sorry, but you know what I mean."

Grinning, Craig said, "Yeah, I do."

Frank stood. "Can you see what you can dig up about her, if anything, and let me know?"

"I'll do my best, you know that." Deputy Williamscot stood too.

"Thanks, Craig. Tell Miranda and Shayla hello for me."

"That reminds me," Craig began, "Miranda said for you to stop at your mama's store. She left a few jars of treated honey there for you."

"That's great. We were almost out of it, so let her know I appreciate it." He removed his wallet from his back pants pocket. "What do I owe her?"

As they settled up the bill, several calls came into the office. Nancy scrambled to answer each one. She dispatched to the deputies, shut off the mic, and stared open-mouthed at Craig. "A body was found out on Plainview Ridge, Craig. Three different people called it in and all of them said the same thing." She gulped as the color drained from her face.

Frank and Craig both made it over to her in three long strides. Taking her by the elbow, Craig helped her sit before she passed out. "What did they say, Nancy?" he urged.

"Two people, a father and son. Both ripped to

shreds, blood everywhere… There were even entrails hanging in the tree branches."

Frank jerked away and straightened.

Nancy leaned her skull back on the head rest. "The one caller said that there's a wallet and a hunting license lying by the bodies, but he was afraid to look at them and disturb the scene." She gulped again, but the pink was slowly beginning to return to her cheeks. "The sheriff will have to cut his vacation short."

The phones lit up and began ringing like alarm bells. Frank bid Nancy and Craig farewell as he left the office. The deaths, whether murders or animal attacks, left a cold lump of dread wedged in his ribs. There was always the chance a black bear had killed the men, but unless it was a rogue or a mama bear with cubs, black bears avoided confrontations with humans. And bears didn't throw guts into tree limbs. Frank sensed something sinister about the deaths, something that hinted at darker days ahead. However, until the county and CSI decided what had happened, there was no sense in jumping to conclusions.

He'd have to hold an MC meeting, calling in everyone who didn't live in the commune, too…just in case.

Pushing his unease aside, Frank strode up the hill past the courthouse until he reached the corner. The guys should be waiting at the square for him. He'd stop at his mother's store on another day. Right now, he wanted to get Bernadette to their MC where he could find out more about her, and where he felt she would be safe.

Where the hell did that thought come from? There was no reason for him to feel protective of her—he didn't even know her.

The light finally changed so he could cross. On the other side of the square, Tom had returned with Bernadette, and the men sat on their Harleys. Upon spotting Frank, Tom threw one hand up, then straddled his bike. When Bernadette started to get on behind him he pointed at Frank's, where she got on instead.

The fact that she'd even want to ride with Tom had Frank balling his hands into fists. Then Bernadette turned on the passenger pillion and watched him as he jogged through the square. She smiled at him and patted the seat.

Fuck, she was beyond beautiful.

And if he didn't control his cock, he would be in big, big trouble.

Frank straddled the seat, then kick-started the machine. The engine roared to life and, for an instant, all was right with the world as he revved the motor and checked both ways for traffic. As he duck-walked the Harley out of the space and onto Main Street, his men to the left and right of him, he lost that sweet feeling of preparing for a ride, and the worry returned. It was urgent he got Bernadette to the MC. Once she was there, maybe he could relax.

Maybe.

Chapter Three

The ride to Frank's MC along SR 800 south to SR 26 was long, but beautiful. Having been born and raised in Columbus, Bernadette was accustomed to the flat terrain around Ohio's capital city. Here in the Appalachians, the hills stretched to the sky, creeks and streams crisscrossed the land like basket weave, trees encroached on the roads, and animals, from cows to turkeys, coyotes, deer and even a bobcat—which ran across the two-lane forcing them to slow down, revealed the wildlife teeming within the mountains.

The last bit of the drive ended with a snaking route up another hill, until they reached a small village named Graysville. They made a left, and started along a narrow paved lane that hugged a ridgeline. The view across the treetops enchanted Bernadette, but as she lost herself in the display, Frank turned onto a well-used gravel road that led downhill again. Soon the lane began to widen until meadows skirted either side. Someone drove a tractor running a hay rake, its tines spinning the cut hay into fluffy windrows. The aroma of the drying timothy and clover fell over Bernadette in a warm, comforting cloud that inspired a couple of sneezes. Frank's shoulders shook as he laughed at her.

The motorcycles rumbled through a few yards of short trees, the last traces of their blossoms still clinging stubbornly to the limbs. On both sides people ran large mowers back and forth beneath the low-hanging branches.

Leaning up, her breasts smooshed firmly to Frank's back, Bernadette asked, "What kind of trees are those?"

"Apples on the right. Cherries on the left."

She sat back. *This is an MC? How big is it, really?*

Another minute or two had them riding into what appeared to be a small community. Ten houses lined the lane as if they'd been settlers' homes. They had been well cared for and remodeled periodically, over the years. Beyond those, homes, and even a couple house trailers, sat here and there throughout a short, shallow valley. On a knoll at the end of the lane stood the largest house of all, a two-story Victorian that was straight out of the 1800s. Staring at it in awe, Bernadette was delighted to find that it was their destination, as they rode slowly up the driveway.

Frank drove around to the back of the home and parked on a large carport. The others coasted over to a big, ground-level building with a big bright sign over the double doors, then again over to what appeared to be an office that read "Nightshade Wolves." Realization hit Bernadette. She'd heard of Nightshade Wolves through her brothers. Nightshade Wolves built specialty motorcycles from the ground up.

The screened porch erupted with chatter and a few happy whoops an instant before the door burst open, spilling out several men and women. One

Bernadette recognized as Luella, who strode straight over to her, and, to Bernadette's surprise, gave her a warm hug.

"Are you okay?" Luella asked, her bruised and swollen lip making it difficult for her to speak.

"I'm fine. Why?" Bernadette replied.

"That bitch, Daffi, and her two minions beat you up pretty bad."

"If you mean the skinny, booby one with the tropical travel ad on her back? We weren't ever formally introduced."

Laughter exploded from Luella. She quickly placed her fingers over her split lip, grimacing. "Yeah, that's her, but you sure thrashed Daffi just as badly, if not worse. The other two didn't want to mess with you after you kicked Daffi's ass."

A huge man, one almost as large as Bloodbath, walked up behind Luella and put his massive hands on the woman's shoulders. Blond-bearded but bald, he boasted a long silver scar running from one side of his head a couple inches above his ear down to his temple, stopping almost dead center on his cheekbone. A tat encircled his neck. On closer perusal, Bernadette made out a strand of barbed wire with blood dripping off some of the barbs. The giant pushed seven feet tall, maybe taller, and from what Bernadette could tell, his frame and proportions fit his height. His grin widened to show several molars missing in the farthest recesses of his mouth. "My old lady told me all about how Crow's sheep jumped you. Good for you for giving it back to those skanks." He held out one of his meaty hands. "I'm Beastman."

"Bernadette Kelly." She tried not to scowl as he

crunched her fingers. "I'm an author doing research on motorcycle clubs for my new book. I want to show how good MCs get a bad reputation from the one-percenters, and tell readers that you're like anyone else in the world."

"Damn, Frank," Beastman rumbled. "This one might be a keeper."

Frank stepped off his Harley, shooting Beastman a filthy look. "I don't think she wants to join our MC. She just wants information."

"I just meant that she—"

Bernadette didn't miss the expertly placed elbow that Luella put in her old man's ribs. He shut up.

Frank held a hand out to help Bernadette off the bike. "Luella, would you take Bernadette inside and get her settled in the guestroom? I bet she'd like a shower after being out in this heat all afternoon."

Bernadette met Frank's coal-black eyes. Damn, he was a fine specimen of a man. And those eyes…like two shining pieces of onyx. They seemed so deep that she could drown in them. But he obviously wasn't as enamored by her as she was with him. She couldn't stop looking at him, which irritated her, but it had been a long, trying day, and her ass was sore from the bike ride. Hopefully, if she was around these people long enough, she'd grow used to riding on the back of a motorcycle.

Of course, I could ride Frank for hours and never tire of it. She blinked and her breath hitched. *Did I just think that? Holy shit!*

Bernadette looked at the woman, who stood waiting expectantly, her baby blue peepers sincere.

"A shower sounds divine," Bernadette answered.

"Come on, hon." Luella took her by the hand and tugged her toward the porch. "You'll feel better after you get cleaned up, and if you want a snack, I'm sure we can find something to hold you until supper. We have nightly group suppers—mostly the ones who live in the main house, so you'll get to meet a lot of us."

Before she could ask Luella any questions, the woman had already ushered her up the steps, through the screened porch, into a kitchen, through the house along hardwood floors, then up a set of carpeted stairs. Head spinning with the differences between the Wraithkillers and the Werewolves of Rebellion, she soon found herself in a beautiful bedroom for a few moments, before Luella ushered her down the hall to a bathroom.

"If you need anything, there's an intercom over there," Luella said. "I'll be in the kitchen."

"Thank you."

"Sure thing, sweetie." Luella backed out of the bathroom, shutting the door.

* * *

Once Bernadette had showered and dressed, she abandoned her usual makeup regime and applied only lip gloss and mascara. The heat and humidity would only melt it anyway. As she raked the mascara wand through her eyelashes, she compared the two MCs. The Wraithkillers were a one-percenter gang, but the Werewolves of Rebellion were the total opposite, right down to a homey clubhouse and what, if she guessed correctly, was more of a community. She started to set the capped mascara back into her makeup bag, but it gently flew out of her hand and settled in the bag on its own. Exasperated, she sighed, thankful that she hadn't done that in front of anyone as she had the pen, earlier that day. Her mother told her to keep her abilities under wraps because people feared what they didn't understand, but Bernadette had no idea how to control her strange gifts.

She turned her thoughts to her new book idea. It was obvious that she was safe here, and that Frank's MC would give her the information she needed. She'd met so many bikers who resented that people automatically assumed they were badasses and out to cause trouble, simply because they enjoyed riding motorcycles. Bikers reveled in the culture of the open road, what bike had what powerful motor, who was the best mechanic, and who had gone to what rally or charity run, and even what charitable causes they could create to help others. She wondered if Frank and his MC contributed to such venues.

All Bernadette had seen at Crow's MC was sex, drinking, drug use, fights—she touched her face, remembering how Daffi had sucker-punched her—illegal weapons and smuggling drugs.

Glad to be out of Crow's MC, she finished with her makeup, wondering why Crow had sent her away. She tugged a cami over her lacey bra, and deliberated whether to put on a T-shirt instead. Her cleavage screamed that it was about to blow, and she sure didn't want to come across like she was begging to be one of the werewolves' sweet butts—not that she'd seen any sweet butts around the place.

She smirked at herself in the mirror over the dresser. Her stay with the Werewolves, providing they allowed her to remain with them for a while, would be a major learning experience, and perhaps, through them, she'd write her best nonfiction piece yet.

She brushed her still-damp locks up into a messy bun, fastened it with a hair tie, then slipped on her flip-flops. In her denim shorts and cami tank top she was as dressed up as she was going to get, for a big community supper. Her thoughts kept straying to Frank, though, and she wondered if he'd think her cleavage too much, or if he'd like her boobs.

"Good God, Bernadette, stop it with the gutter thoughts." She looked at herself in the mirror one more time. "What is wrong with me?"

She left her room and wandered downstairs past the antiques, the numerous old portraits and new photos of people. Many men and women posed by motorcycles in the most recent pictures.

Bernadette paused at the top of the stairs and surveyed the stairwell and the first floor. Except for the more recent photos, and the occasional person who walked through the rooms below her, it was as if the house has been frozen in time. High-backed sofas and chairs, hand-crafted table runners and doilies, oil lamps, hobnail lamps and oval tea tables—it all screamed to Bernadette that she had stepped back into the 1800s.

For the second time, something eerie tiptoed down her spine.

Shaking it off, she descended the staircase, and went in search of Luella in the kitchen.

* * *

Frank waited until after supper, when the women were cleaning up, to call the men together in the main house. The stunned expressions on everyone's faces sent a pang of regret through him. He didn't want to alarm his people, but they had to be warned just in case things around Rebellion went tits up.

"What about your contact in the sheriff's office?" one man piped up. "Will he give you information?"

"Should those deaths be anything we need to worry about, my contact will give me enough information to aid us in protecting ourselves," Frank replied. He had to keep his voice even, so no one would detect how worried he was. "Right now I'm only alerting you that there could be a rogue werewolf in the area, or there's a new clan that has moved in. So, if any of you hear anything at all about the deaths, or notice that we have newcomers in Monroe County, come to me or Phil ASAP—agreed?"

Every member in the living room, standing in each doorway, up the stairs and along the balcony that Frank could see, nodded soberly.

"Good. And don't worry if you think something is trivial," Frank added. "Even a tiny detail about a potential new clan or a rogue could save a life." He surveyed the men, both young and old, confident he'd gotten the urgency of his message across to everyone. "If no one has any questions, meeting dismissed. Go enjoy your drinks and your families."

"Boss," Phil called from the balcony.

Franked caught his pointed look toward the kitchen. There, peeking around the men filing past her, stood Bernadette. Several of the guys looked directly at her and shook their heads.

"Shit," he muttered under his breath.

"What's going on?" she asked once everyone except Phil had left.

Phil moved down the stairs and sat on the second to the last step. "You're not supposed to be here," he stated none too gently.

Surprise crossed her face, then she stared straight into Frank's eyes as she crossed the room to him. "Why not?"

"Men's meeting," Phil snapped. "*Only* men."

"I'll handle this, Phil." Jerking his head toward the kitchen, Frank shot him a pointed look.

Sighing, Phil stood, but stopped next to Bernadette. Standing toe-to-toe with her, he said, "You're nice. You're built like a brick shithouse. But you're not one of us, so tread carefully." With that, he stalked out.

In seconds, the screen door slapped shut as if it were an exclamation point for Phil's anger.

"I'm sorry," Bernadette said, her gaze going in the direction of the slamming door.

The expression on her face gave Frank a horrible case of guilt. Although he didn't want to hurt her feelings, neither did he want to expose her to their clan and scar her for life.

"I didn't mean anything by coming in," she rushed on. "I thought I'd learn more about your MC, but I guess I crashed something really important."

"You did," Frank replied calmly. Why did she have to be so damn attractive? *You like blondes, dumbass, not redheads.* "The guys don't take kindly to the women poking their noses into affairs."

"Aren't they part of your MC?"

"Yes."

"Then don't they have a right to know what's going on that might affect them?" she countered.

"Yes, but it's up to the men to explain it to their families or fiancées in their own ways so we don't cause hysteria or undo worry." He waited as she thought about what he'd just said.

"I understand. I didn't mean to upset anyone." She dropped her gaze to the coffee table. "Will you tell Phil that I'm sorry?"

"You tell him."

"I don't think he likes me."

"Honey, you have to realize this isn't the city. Small communities in the Appalachians view newcomers as outsiders—suspicious and untrustworthy."

"This isn't the Middle Ages," she stated.

"In some respects, there are areas in these hills that still have the outlook of the 1800s."

"So I've noticed." She swept her hand around, indicating the décor.

"The original owners of this property were my ancestors," Frank explained. "When this house was built, we agreed to keep everything as it was back then, in respect and memory of our roots."

"We?" She offered him a quizzical look.

"My family, the Nightshades."

"Oh."

Way to go, dumbass. Why not just come right out and tell her what you are?

He recovered himself and said, "The only thing that's different is the stairs, which are carpeted now because one of the women who was expecting slipped and fell." At her startled look, he added, "Both she and the child survived."

"So each picture"—Bernadette pointed here and there—"is actual family, and MC family, all the way back to…?"

"To about 1815," he answered.

"And Nightshade," she began. "That's a lovely but odd last name."

"Because it's a poisonous plant?" he asked.

She nodded. "Most immigrants at that time took on names to hide their ethnicity or because their surname was too difficult to pronounce." She turned and fixed her vivid green gaze on him. "My mother took pride in our family history and the history of the Irish—their immigration to the US." She shrugged.

He could tell she had many facets to her personality and background, and found that she intrigued him. "At the same time, many took on names that described who they were."

"Nightshade was taken for what reason?" she asked.

"My family comes from a long line of healers," he explained.

"Oh, alternative medicine. That's wonderful."

"No, not alternative medicine," he insisted. "Healers."

She frowned. "I don't understand. Aren't they the same?"

The difference between her and his clan, and even the residents in and around Rebellion, struck him with force. Craig was right about her—she was very intelligent. Something about the way she looked at Frank told him there was more going on behind those beautiful green eyes than she let on. It sent goose flesh over his skin, a reaction he'd never experienced with a woman, ever. He wanted to back away from her, and yet he had the desire to talk with her for hours.

She was an enigma: one that could be dangerous, if he couldn't keep her from discovering the truth about him and his MC.

"So?" she said, jarring him out of his thoughts. "The difference?"

"Healers heal," he stated. "Alternative medicine doesn't always work. As for my last name, nightshade is diverse. It's a food source, and it's used for drugs. Many vegetables are in the nightshade family—or *salanaceae*—such as potato, tomato, peppers, and eggplant, and even tobacco, but everyone always thinks of belladonna and jimson weed, which are both poisonous. My family adopted the name nightshade to indicate their occupation and as a tribute to nature."

"Your MC is nothing like I expected."

Bernadette walked over to examine a few more recent photos on the wall under the stairs. Immediately, her swaying hips drew Frank's attention. His cock twitched in response, and the overwhelming urge to grab her and bend her over one of the sofas assailed him. He fought his responses to her, managed to tamp down the wild, feral need of his inner beast to take her, to claim her.

"You expected us to be one-percenters?" he asked.

"No, nothing like that."

She bent over and smelled a bouquet of wildflowers in an antique vase. The cheeks of her ass peeked from her denim shorts. Frank's cock, already half-hard, forced him to clench his teeth and exercise his willpower over it.

"It's just that you and your men looked dangerous.

But as I watched them interact with each other, saw how they were courteous to people on the street..." She shrugged. "I guess what I'm saying is that appearances can be deceiving."

If she bent over one more time, he'd show her how courteous he was by ripping her fucking shorts off and plundering her.

Fuck, where are these thoughts coming from? He crossed the carpet in two strides, pausing right behind her. The aroma of the shampoo she'd washed her hair in mixed with light perspiration and her own womanly aroma, caressing Frank's senses. Desperate for his rock-hard cock to go back to sleep, he groaned low in his throat. Shit, he'd growled, and that meant that his eyes were either changing or on the verge of it.

"Appearances *can* be very misleading," he managed to say. About to turn away from her and hide his eyes, Bernadette straightened and turned unexpectedly. She gasped upon finding him only inches from her face. He hoped the glow of his inner animal had vanished in time. Her pupils widened and only a thin ring of vibrant green encircled them. Ah, so she was attracted to him too. Perhaps that was part of his reaction to her. His wolf side sensed the pheromones she was emitting.

No, it was more than him scenting her. Something about this woman called to him, created a hunger within him that he'd never experienced. Maybe if he could seduce her—fuck her into the mattress, he'd be able to shake his responses to her—get her out of his system, so to speak.

That was another no. He wasn't that sort of man. He respected women, thought they were beautiful, no matter if they were tall, short, thin, curvy, or even fat.

Women were to be revered. They were life-givers, helpmates, confidants, witches, goddesses, and hellcats. They were complex, and yet simple. Powerful, yet delicate. If his mother and grandmother had taught him anything, it was that women wielded the real power in a family. Men just enforced it.

"The appearance thing," she was saying, "that's why I decided to write a nonfiction book about motorcycle clubs."

"That's what you were telling Beastman when we arrived this afternoon," he said. Slowly, he was managing to rein in his libido.

"Exactly," she stated with a nervous smile. She stepped back until she bumped into the side table that ran the length of the stair's wall. "I'd like to get to know you and your MC family so that I can use examples of the family ties and parts of your stories—with permission, of course—to show readers that just because someone rides a Harley or wears leathers and has a patch on their cut doesn't mean they're drug dealers, gun runners, dealing in the mafia, or any other number of criminal tags." Realization flashed across her face. "Oh...I get it! Crow must've sent me with you because he thought I was a reporter or an undercover cop posing as a writer."

"Yes," he replied. "That's exactly right, but it's also why you have to prove yourself here, too." He found himself leaning closer, his wolf side reveling in the smell of her, and his human side delighting in it too. Her pupils flared again, and he detected a slight hitch in her breath. Would she, he wondered, shatter if he palmed her crotch right now? Or would it anger her, make her shove him away?

"Don't worry." She smiled warmly.

Her glorious smile gave him thoughts of her mouth enclosed on his cock. Moving a few inches closer to her, he inhaled her sweet aroma. He shook himself mentally. *What was she saying?*

"I want to focus on how MCs are family units," she stressed and straightened her spine.

He'd overstepped her boundary line. Frank moved back a pace, cursing his inner animal's curiosity and urges. "If that's what you want to do, that's fine, but I want to see the finished manuscript, make sure that what's on paper matches your claims."

"It's a deal," she said, holding out her hand.

He clasped it, then jerked her against his body. Her eyes flew open wide, fear flashing across her face, then shifting to arousal.

"Just know, your every move will be observed by someone. We protect each other here. Whether mother, child, husband, grandparent, a member, or someone adopted into the fold, we will not tolerate anyone causing trouble—of any sort. Understood?"

"Yes, perfectly." Her breasts heaved, her breath panting.

Her soft yet firm tits, pressed to his cut chest, radiated warmth. His cock betrayed him yet again and strained painfully against his zipper. If he didn't back away from Bernadette right now he was either going to kiss her senseless, or throw her over his shoulder and carry her to his bedroom.

With monumental effort, he drew a deep breath and stepped back from her. "Get some sleep. We rise early around here. We also run a large farm that feeds many people, so there's plenty of work to do every day. You'll learn a lot by pitching in, and it'll help build trust between you and the others."

She nodded vigorously, her cheeks almost as red as her hair.

And, somehow, it made her even more beautiful.

"Goodnight," he said, and walked out of the house. A couple beers would calm his nerves and help cool not only his heated skin, but also his desire for the tempting ginger. He glanced down at his crotch. "Fucking traitor," he muttered to his cock.

Chapter Four

After checking to see if Luella needed any help with the last of the cleanup, Bernadette climbed the stairs to the guestroom. Her senses still spun from the encounter with Frank, and her nerve endings buzzed with excitement. It didn't make any sense. Bad boys had never been her type. Her mother was constantly trying to set her up with nice Irish guys. Many of them were employed in offices, with soft hands and heads full of numbers, or they worked for the pipeline, which was lucrative and created buff men, but it could be weeks to months before she'd see the fellow she was dating. By then, they'd hooked up with someone else.

She liked her men with rough hands, muscles, but not over-muscled; tall, willing to work but not obsessed with their jobs, and protective. Most of her friends likes alpha males, but Bernadette didn't want someone hovering over her, telling her what to do and when to do it. She wanted a man who would consider her an equal partner. One who would be there for her when she needed a shoulder to lean on, and who wouldn't be too manly to lean on her, when he needed it.

But a biker? And a biker president at that? One with the most colorful sleeves she'd ever seen, tats that crawled up sinewy forearms and bulging biceps? She wondered if that colorful ink reached his shoulders and crept across his chest or back. Shaking her head, she scattered those dangerous thoughts. She really didn't know what to think about Frank Nightshade, except that there was something about the man that creamed her panties. It was disconcerting. It left her vulnerable. Needy. No other man had ever rendered her speechless, dizzy, breathless, and so aroused that she couldn't wait to get her wet panties off in exchange for a clean, dry pair.

In her room she stripped out of her clothes, donned a T-shirt and fresh underwear, then stood by the window where a cool evening breeze wafted through the screen. She wondered why the home didn't have central air, but she guessed it would be expensive for a house as large as this one. In the distance, over the treetops, she caught flickers of light, as if from a giant flame. She pushed the screen up and leaned out. The back lawn sloped gently down to a big pond. Lights glowed around it, with tiki torches and lanterns around a dock. Three couples and some children in their preteen years played in the water. Between the shouts and splashes, a dull roar broke through, reaching Bernadette. A brighter but more distant light flared erratically beyond the treetops. She frowned.

"Something wrong?" a voice asked.

She glanced down and found Phil sitting on a side stoop. He looked up at her quizzically.

"There's a light way out there over the treetops," she said, "and I think I heard a faint roar."

"That would be the pad over on the next ridge,"

he replied. "They're probably burning off the excess gas on the well. Shoots flames several feet into the air and the burn-off roars. The wind is blowing this way, so that's why you hear it once in a while."

"Those pads seem to be all over the area," she said.

"Yep, lots of people have sold their gas and oil rights to pay off mortgages, buy cars, homes..." He shrugged, then Bernadette caught the red glow of what she thought was a pipe.

"Frank explained how things work with the meetings. It wasn't my intention to interrupt, or put my nose where it doesn't belong." She let her words sink in then added, "I apologize if I offended you or any of the others."

"Good to know." He tapped something on the step, and red embers skittered off into the grass. "I don't know if Frank warned you yet,"—he rose and opened the screen door—"but don't go wandering off alone around here. Stay out of the woods unless you have a chaperone. Got it?"

"Yes, got it," she answered. The club probably raised and sold pot. She knew many in the hills and mountains did it to supplement their incomes.

Without another word, he stepped inside and shut the door behind him. The big door closed, blocking out much of the light that had been spilling across the lawn. Then the rest of the feeble illumination extinguished too.

Frank wasn't kidding when he said that I'm outsider.

She'd have to work hard to gain the MC's respect and confidence. Her research into the lives of Candy

Apple, Champagne, and Jasmine had been difficult: from getting them to talk to her, let alone trust her, to dodging their pimps, to even hiding one of the prostitutes from the law—not one of Bernadette's most shining moments. But if she hadn't, Candy Apple's four-year-old son would have been left alone to fend for himself. They still texted her from time to time, though—kept in touch because she'd become their only true friend. However, Bernadette suspected her next book would be harder than climbing Mt. Everest. Instead of having to gain the trust of three people, she had to win over an entire MC and its community.

An entire community. The words resonated in her brain. Could she really earn their respect?

It was a daunting thought, but she had to do this: had to learn all she could about the Werewolves of Rebellion, and pound out another manuscript that revealed the truth behind a label; that sometimes your fate is dealt the instant you're born, and that it's what you do with that fate that counts.

Bernadette pulled the screen down, but left the window open. She padded across the soft carpet to the bed, finding it already turned down for her. Smiling, she climbed in and pulled only the sheet up over herself. Luella seemed to be a really wonderful person. She'd accepted Bernadette with open arms. She figured it was because when no one would give Luella any water while she was being held by Crow, Bernadette had gotten a bottle to give to her.

Then Daffi and her two minions had thrashed her ass for it.

At least now the bruising on her face was almost gone.

Her thoughts strayed to Frank again, the memory of his body pressed to hers still vivid in her mind. She could've sworn she'd heard him growl. Not groan, growl. And, for just an instant, she'd thought his eyes were glowing amber, but just as quickly as she'd seen it—or thought she had—the glow was gone. Probably a trick of the low lighting in the room.

Still...there seemed to be an odd undercurrent among the Werewolves of Rebellion. However, she had to admit it could just be her discomfort there. After all, she knew nothing about these people. It had been the same with her working-girl friends. The awkwardness and paranoia had lasted for many weeks before the three women began to relax around Bernadette.

But Frank was so tempting. Black hair, midnight eyes, olive-skinned...the man exuded sex appeal in a pyroclastic cloud. How did the women in the community not notice it? The way he'd heated her up, as if he'd simply flipped a switch, had left her reeling—craving. What would it be like if he kissed her? Better yet, what kind of lover would he be? Rough and demanding, as his persona seemed to imply, or the opposite, where he would worship her body with gentle licks and caresses?

"Good grief, Bernadette, get a grip." She scrubbed her hands over her face. "I'm here to write, not to screw like a depraved bunny...although that wouldn't be a bad idea...."

She shook her head, banishing thoughts of skin-to-skin contact, the way Frank's beard stubble would feel over her bare breasts... the throbbing began between her legs, and scorched its way into her lower abdomen.

"Dammit!" She punched her pillow several times and flopped onto her side, praying for sleep to arrive soon.

Staring at the dark window, she remembered that she needed to check in with her family. Her mother still relied on her, which is why Bernadette had chosen to remain in her mom's house. Their father had passed on when Bernadette was only four, so her brothers had stepped in his place, when they were able. Two of her four brothers lived with their mother too, but it was usually just Bernadette and their mom at home. She knew that while she was away her mother missed their girl talks, and their time together spent quietly working in the kitchen listening to artists such as Adelle and Melody Gardot, cooking meals together for her brothers, and sometimes inviting the next-door neighbors over, too.

Now the neighbors had moved away, replaced by a married couple who were devoted to their jobs, instead of each other. Her oldest brother, Danny, was struggling to launch his law practice, which took up an amazing amount of time. Her next two brothers, Chad and Duncan, were married with children, and Alexander, only two years older than she was, remained at home with their mom, but he was in the last few months of nursing school, so when he was home he was studying like a madman.

She missed them, and she worried about her mother. Grabbing her phone, she pressed the power button and checked the time. Too late to call. Her mom had already been in bed an hour. She'd call her after breakfast in the morning.

Finally sleepy, Bernadette settled back, enjoying the soft breeze still penetrating the screen and flowing over the bed. Soon, images of a dark-haired, dark-eyed man tantalized her dreams.

* * *

"Hey, Frank!" Tom yelled from the driveway. "Your deputy buddy is here."

Frank looked up from where he was changing dual fire spark plugs on a chopper. He finished with the second one and then stood, wiping his hands on a grease rag. The crunch of tires on gravel, switching to the smooth whir on concrete, drew his attention. Sure enough, Craig's cruiser pulled in behind the house.

He stuffed the rag into his back pocket, its end hanging out, and left the garage to meet Craig. "What brings you out here, Craig?" he asked.

Deputy Williamscot glanced around to see who was nearby. Satisfied no one was within earshot, he strode around the car to the passenger side. He opened the door then removed a small cardboard box. "Brought the honey out to you," he said. Lowering his voice, he added, "Plus it made a nice excuse to drive out here."

One of the women from the lower homes approached, nodded politely then entered through the porch. Once Craig was sure she was gone, he handed Frank the box. "There are six jars. That should be enough to hold those youngsters for…?"

"For about four months," Frank replied. "Did Miranda have trouble finding the wolfsbane?"

"She had to order it, which cost her more than usual, but she said if you're fine with it, she'll call it even for your man, Ass Crack, mending our porch swing, and buying new chain and big eye screws for it."

"That's damn nice of her, Craig. Tell Miranda I really appreciate it. I mean it." Frank glared up at the sun, then reached for the rag, using the clean side to wipe the sweat from his face and neck. "Let's go into the garage. The sun is vicious today."

"Hell, the sun's been vicious for two weeks now," Craig said, following him into the workshop. "If this hell weather keeps on like this, no one will have any gardens this summer."

"Luckily, if we need it, we can get water from the pond and the creek," Frank stated. "Otherwise, we'd be screwed come harvest time. It's hard to feed little ones when very little has been canned and frozen."

Once they were inside the workshop, Frank set the box on the work counter. He tossed Craig a questioning look.

The deputy took his hat off and reached for a roll of paper towels on the worktop. "I came out here to tell you that nothing comes up on your Bernadette Kelly. No parking tickets, no speeding tickets, nothing at all. I'd say she's a good, trustworthy woman." He shrugged as he pulled a towel off the roll, then used it to wipe his face and neck, as Frank had done. "Of course, you can never be 100 percent certain about anyone, but my guess is that you're safe with her. She writes those true crime books, so she's smart, and knows how to work people to get the information she's after—such as winning the trust of prostitutes—so if you don't want her figuring out your secret, or stumbling across it, for that matter, be very careful around her." He tossed the damp paper into a waste basket under the counter. "Also, advise your people of the same."

"What about the attack over on Plainview?"

Frank knew Craig couldn't give him details, but he might have something that would give Frank some clues as to whether or not they should worry about the occurrence. "Anything you can share with me?"

The sigh that came out of Craig told Frank what he'd already suspected.

"You know I can't tell you much, but I'd be on the lookout, Frank. Watch for anything that only you and your people can discern. Something was really weird about that attack." He paused, obviously gathering his thoughts. With worry in his eyes, he met Frank's gaze. "Forensics says it was an animal attack. The bodies were sent to Columbus, but it'll be days, maybe even weeks, before we have a full report, and if the FBI intervenes, then we may not find out much at all. You know that."

"Yeah, I know how they can be," Frank muttered glumly. "Was there a confirmation on what animal killed that man and his boy?"

Craig nodded, once. "Yeah, a wolf. An extremely large wolf."

"Fuck," Frank whispered.

"I don't want to piss you off, Frank," Craig began, "but I have to ask. Has anyone in your MC gone missing, or has anyone been acting strangely? Could one of the youngsters have lost control of their urge to transform?" When Frank started to say something in defense, Craig held up a hand. "I'm only asking because the full moon was two nights ago, and I know how the youngsters struggle with their abilities"—he dipped his head toward the box of honey—"until they mature."

Frank's surge of anger wilted. His friend had a point. The clan might call them youngsters because werewolves aged slower than humans, but from the time a werewolf turned 16 until they were about 25, they often battled the animalistic urge to hunt, especially during a full moon.

"The wolfsbane in the honey curbs that urge and their ferocity, Craig, but you know that there's always one in a group that it doesn't work as well on." He sighed in frustration and leaned his hip against the counter. "But honestly, I haven't noticed anything out of the ordinary with any of the youngsters."

"How many do you have in your commune that you're watching?" Craig questioned, his tone now purely cop.

"Six," Frank said. "Want their names?"

"I'll put them in my notes just in case something else comes up, but you know I trust you, Frank, so unless something happens that points directly here, I'm not going to worry about it."

"You're a good man, Craig."

"Hey, you rescued me at the bottom of a cliff. Thank God it wasn't any higher than it was, but when you found me in your werewolf form, I thought for sure I was a dead man." He snorted wryly. "I'll never forget how I was sure you were going to kill me, but instead, you slung me over your furry shoulder and brought me here for medical attention. Miranda and I will always be your friends. You could've left me there to die, but you didn't."

"That'll teach you not to get in a hurry to catch up with a deer," Frank joked.

"My father taught me better, but I was so excited about a 14-point buck that I wasn't watching where I was going."

They were quiet for a spell. Frank studied his

deputy friend. He and Miranda were truly good people, but the others in the sheriff's department wouldn't understand their relationship, nor would the sheriff condone Craig passing Frank information, but in Craig's defense, he never gave Frank anything confidential. Well, nothing super confidential.

Smirking, Frank said. "The current youngsters are all boys."

A grimace crossed Craig's face. "Testosterone always makes the change worse."

Frank chuckled. "Don't I know it. Thought those years would kill me when I went through them. The youngsters are David, Ryan, Sam, Albert, Marlon and Hunter."

"All of them from the Steelarmi Family, eh?"

"Yeah, the two Steelarmi sisters both got married and started families around the same time."

"Poor mamas. Bet they have their hands full with that bunch."

Laughing, Frank nodded. "That they do."

Craig put his notepad and pen back into his shirt pocket. "Use caution until we know more about what happened over on Plainview, understood?"

"Yep. Trust me, Craig, I'll be worried sick until we know what we're dealing with, but since there aren't any animals around here that would be that vicious and sick enough to throw entrails into tree branches, my guess is there's a rogue at work." He raked one hand through his sweat-dampened hair. "The question is—who is the rogue? I'm 99 percent sure it's no one from my community."

"If I have any more news I can share, I'll let you know somehow." Craig turned to leave.

"Thank you, Craig. And remember to pass my message on to Miranda."

Craig hurried out of the workshop and gave him a two-finger salute. "Will do! Enjoy the rest of your day, Frank."

Frank turned to investigate the jars of honey. Miranda had been lacing honey with wolfsbane and a few other key ingredients for his clan for several years now. After she leaned the whole story about Craig's encounter with Frank, she began researching more about lykoi people, and learned what she could from Frank's mother and grandmother, who had agreed to teach her things about natural healing. Since Miranda was a beekeeper she took the recipe for curbing the wild urges of lycanthropy in the youngsters and combined it with her honey, which tasted so much better than the bitter flavor and sulfur-like odor of the family elixir. Frank always felt that it was divine intervention that had brought the Williamscots into his life.

He looked at the clock over the side door— lunchtime. His belly rumbled in acknowledgement. He wondered where Bernadette had been all morning. Luella was supposed to keep an eye on her, so maybe she'd given her some things to do to keep her busy.

His stomach protested its emptiness again. Time for a good meal and something cold to drink. He prayed the heat abated soon. Rogues were often worse during hot, humid times, but the uncomfortable weather was enough to piss anyone off.

Chapter Five

Luella drove the late-model Suburban slowly, allowing Bernadette to enjoy the sights and breathe in the aromas of drying hay, summer phlox planted along banks and in flowerbeds, and woodbine honeysuckle, which smelled so heavenly the odor actually caused her to salivate.

In the front passenger seat, another woman, Puppy, named so because of her huge, deep brown puppy eyes and silky black hair, sat bobbing her head and singing slightly off key to Elle King's *Ex's and Oh's*. The music, the wind and its tantalizing scents all rushed through the cab. Bernadette found it exhilarating, and even joined in with Puppy's singing. Puppy glanced back at her and flashed her a bright smile, her eyes full of amusement, and kept right on belting out the lyrics.

Bernadette had a few friends in Columbus, but no one close whom she could confide in, or do any more with, than a quick lunch before they rushed off to their busy lives, leaving her to occupy herself. Her brothers and her mother had been the center of her life. The amicable silence between her, Luella, and Puppy created a nice warmth that settled in her chest.

As they entered Rebellion, the music changed to

Can't Keep My Hands to Myself. Luella hit the radio button on the stereo.

"Don't change it," Puppy protested.

"I don't like that song," Luella argued.

"Oh, come on," Puppy cajoled her. "It has a really cool beat to it."

Luella shook her head. "There might be ten years between us, but it seems like a huge generation gap when it comes to your taste in music."

Bernadette laughed.

Glancing in the rearview mirror at Bernadette, Luella smirked. "You two have got to stop making me smile, or my lip is never going to heal."

"I have lip balm in my purse, so smile away," Puppy quipped.

"Hey, Puppy," Bernadette said. "Can I ask where your family comes from?"

"We're Filipino," she answered. "My grandparents immigrated here when my dad was really young." Then, changing the subject abruptly, she asked Luella, "Oh, heck. Did you remember to collect everyone's lists?"

The light turned green, and Luella made a left heading down the hill past the courthouse and sheriff's office. "Yeah," she replied, "I got them last night at the barbecue."

"Last time we made a grocery run," Puppy explained, twisting around to look at Bernadette, "we got all the way to Reisbeck's parking lot and found out she'd completely forgotten to get everyone's grocery lists, so we had to drive all the way back to the MC and then make our rounds to each family before driving back into Rebellion."

"Hey, I handle a lot for the MC," Luella protested, half laughing. "I can't help it if my brain slips into neutral from time to time."

Bernadette couldn't help giggling at the women's banter.

A big building with a large carport for drive-through pickup with a long sign in bright red lettering appeared at the bottom of the hill. Luella turned into the parking lot and parked as close to the front entrance as she could manage. They spent about three hours collecting items for everyone, checking that all lists had been fulfilled, and making notes on lists of items that weren't available, or that they couldn't acquire in the correct sizes. The chatting between the three of them made Bernadette feel like she fit in, something she'd always had trouble doing among women.

"What's this word?" she asked Puppy.

The young woman stared at one of the lists that Bernadette held out. "It looks like Quaker Oats—the big canister."

As Bernadette searched the cereal aisle for oats, Puppy asked, "What do you think of the MC so far?"

She took down the largest can of oats available and tossed it into her buggy. "So far, I find the MC's whole setup really interesting. It's part community, part MC, and all family, even if someone isn't blood related. In my opinion, it's a shame all people can be that way."

At that, Luella turned and offered her a huge smile. "Oh, yeah. You'll fit in perfectly with us."

Bernadette wanted to ask about Frank, but her companions might find her questions too forward or nosey. She moved her cart against the shelves, allowing an elderly woman to pass with her buggy.

"You look like you have something on your mind," Luella stated.

Bernadette jerked her gaze up to meet the Luella's. Then heat rushed to Bernadette's cheeks.

"Oh, my." Luella smirked, placing two fingers over the scab on her lip. "Someone seems to have the hots for a distinctly handsome president."

"What?" The box of fruit whirls in her hand slipped free and hit the floor. "Me? Uhm, no. I just—"

"She likes Frank?" Puppy asked, her dark eyes wide with fascination. "That was fast."

"I never said that I—"

"Oh, come on, Bernadette." Luella waved a dismissing hand, as she tossed a box of salt into her cart. "I'm older than you, have seen many women come and go in the MC, and I manage so many things for the community that it's difficult to get anything past me. I'm the old lady who has the all-seeing eyes."

The heat climbed in Bernadette's face. If it grew any hotter, it might burst into flames.

Luella didn't look away. "Well?"

"He's very handsome."

The rich tones of Luella's chuckles punctuated by Puppy's higher-pitched laughter filled the aisle. Bernadette couldn't help but join in too.

"Frank isn't married, if you were wondering," Luella said. "As a matter of fact, it's been a long time since he's had a girlfriend."

"Play your cards right, prove yourself trustworthy, and maybe you'll find yourself in Frank's bed," Puppy told her.

57

The young woman said those words so seriously, her expression mirroring her tone, that Bernadette could only gape at her.

"I don't... I didn't say... I'm not after... I just—aw, hell!"

Luella and Puppy burst into more laughter. They leaned against each other, tears in their eyes, their faces red.

Mortified, Bernadette stood quietly as they tried to recover themselves. Finally, Luella, still giggling and snorting, held a hand out to Bernadette. Wary, Bernadette accepted it and Luella pulled her into a hug.

"I'm sorry, honey. We're not making fun of you."

"Really, we aren't," Puppy interjected.

"It's just that the expression on your face was priceless," Luella continued. "All I meant is that the chemistry between you and Frank is obvious."

"But we barely even spoke to each other during the barbecue," Bernadette protested. There was no way anyone could have noticed her checking Frank out...was there? "He never even looked at me during the meal."

"He checked you out whenever you were occupied," Puppy explained, laughter still in her voice. "Oh baby, is he attracted to you."

"Well, he's not my type." Bernadette began pushing her cart down the aisle.

"Is that so?" Luella said, following her. "Your eyes and the color of your face say otherwise."

"I have a book to write." This was ridiculous. So what if she found Frank attractive, for some strange reason? She didn't have time to pursue a relationship, and said as much. "Once I feel I have enough research material, I'll be headed back to Columbus anyway."

"Columbus is only a couple hours away," Puppy piped up behind her.

Bernadette groaned and tried valiantly to change the subject. "Which grocery department is next?" she asked, holding up her list. "Meat or dairy?"

Luella and Puppy exchanged amused glances.

"Meat." A mischievous grin stretched Luella's mouth and she pressed her fingers against the cut again. "It'll give us a chance to discuss Frank's as well."

Puppy gasped then erupted into another fit of giggles.

"All right, all right! He's delicious, okay?" Face flaming and with a shove to the buggy, Bernadette wheeled it around to the main aisle and headed toward the meat department, but not without snorts and squeals of laughter dogging her heels. "Hell, I'm never going to live this down," she mumbled as she hurried along.

* * *

After the groceries were purchased and loaded into the back of the Suburban, Luella drove up to Main Street and parked.

"Why are we stopping?" Puppy asked.

"Beastman said the dryer needs a new belt," Luella answered, "so he called the hardware store to have one set aside for me to pick up." She wiggled around in the driver's seat and looked at Bernadette. "Hey, I hope you're not pissed at us for teasing you.

We didn't mean anything by it. I guess, since we live in such a tight community, that we have a special ability to pick up on things between people."

"Yeah, Bernadette," Puppy chimed in, offering her a sweet smile. "We like you, so giving you a hard time is a good thing. You'll eventually realize that, the longer you stay with us."

Nodding, Luella added, "But we often forget that outsiders aren't always used to our brand of humor and friendship."

"It's all right, really," Bernadette said. "I guess my attraction to Frank took me by surprise. My mom is always fixing me up with 'good Irish lads,' as she puts it, and although most of them are nice guys, they're..." She couldn't pinpoint the right word to convey what she meant. Frustrated, she sighed.

"Vanilla?"

Shocked, Bernadette stared at her open-mouthed for a moment, then said, "Exactly. That sums it up perfectly."

"Oh, sweetie," Puppy replied. Her eyes brightened with the same brand of mischief Bernadette had seen in Luella. "There's nothing like a man from the Werewolves of Rebellion."

She shared a brief look with Luella—a look that said there was more behind her words than was obvious.

"No hard feelings?" Luella asked her.

Bernadette shook her head. "No hard feelings. We're good."

"Fantastic." With a glance at Puppy, Luella said, "I'll be right back. There's change in the ashtray, if you see the meter maid headed this way."

Once Luella had crossed the street to the hardware store, Puppy turned the key to auxiliary and turned up the radio station. *Smoke on the Water* rolled out of the speakers. Bernadette sat watching Puppy in amusement. They young woman placed her feet up on the dash, her right hand tapping out the beat of the song on the passenger door. The tune had almost come to an end when Puppy sat up suddenly and hit the volume knob, the music dropping to a faint whisper.

"Shit!" she said.

Startled, Bernadette asked, "What?"

"Wraithkillers," she whispered. "Shit, shit, shit!"

"What's the problem?" Bernadette asked, keeping her voice low. "There's a truce between the two MCs, isn't there?"

"Supposed to be, but some of Crow's men are worse than the others. Those three there"—Puppy nodded once in their direction—"are the worst. The big one is a new prospect and he's also the one who grabbed Luella." She snatched a cell phone from out of a cubby in the dash and quickly texted someone. "Just in case," she said then slipped the Samsung back into the tiny storage hole.

Although she'd spent a couple days with the Wraithkillers, the men had done nothing more than undress her with their eyes, make vulgar motions at her, and say crude things. Now she realized she'd gone to the other MC. Whether it was her decision or not, the Wraithkillers viewed her as one of Frank's people. If what Puppy said were true, the three bikers still liked to stir shit when they were out of Crow's sight.

"If they see us," she asked Puppy, "will they start anything?"

"Oh, definitely."

"Great." Bernadette's heart rate sped up. "Just what I need—more bruises."

"Don't look this way," Puppy whispered. "Don't look this way, don't look this way…fuck."

Her curse was so final, so absolute, that Bernadette thought she'd pass out from the bullet of adrenaline it shot through her system. The bikers saw them and strode straight for the SUV. Before Bernadette could even move for the door on the street's side, the men were at the passenger window.

"Well, if it isn't the Werewolves' Puppy," the huge prospect said snidely. "How old are you, baby? Twenty? Twenty-one?"

"She's legal, Bloodbath," one with a Wraithkillers patch sniggered. "Barely, not that it would matter."

The three man laughed as if it were the most hilarious thing they'd ever heard.

"Why don't you come back to our club with us, baby?" the patched biker said. "We'll all treat you really nice."

"Yeah," the third one, who sported a tattoo of a pot plant on one temple, agreed. "And we've plenty of the good stuff to relax you. Got the best booze too."

"Thanks, but I'll pass," Puppy said.

Bernadette had to give the girl credit. She didn't detect any fear or any quiver in Puppy's voice. However, Bernadette did catch the distinct click of a switchblade from the front seat.

"Aw, come on now." Abruptly opening the passenger door, Bloodbath hauled Puppy out before the girl could even draw a breath. "We just want to play with a pretty Puppy."

The guy with the pot tattoo leaned over and looked into the backseat. His eyes widened.

Oh, shit! Bernadette scooted to the other side of the bench seat.

Grinning like a jack-o'-lantern, he yanked open the back door and leaned in.

"Back off!" Luella's voice cut through Bernadette's fear and Puppy's loud cursing. "What the hell's wrong with you, Bloodbath? You think that just because Crow favors you that you can come into town and do as you please? You're nothing but a lowly prospect who can mix a decent drink."

"Aw, baby. It's good to see you too," he drawled. "You shouldn't have any hard feelings about me grabbing you for the trade. It was just business."

"Fuck you, Bloodbath. All three of you, walk away. Or I might decide to blow a hole in each of your heads."

Bernadette caught sight of the pistol that Luella drew from the back waistband of her shorts. Luella calmly opened the car door and settled into the driver's seat, all the while keeping the pistol aimed at Bloodbath's head. Next to her, Puppy leaned back and sat passively. Luella pushed the gun past Puppy's face.

"You know I'll do it," she said. "I don't have a problem doing time to protect myself or one of my sisters, so I have no qualms about putting a .45 between your snake eyes."

Gradually, the rumble of motorcycles from a distance penetrated Bernadette's consciousness. *Please, let it be the werewolves.*

"They're coming," the tat guy said. "Somehow one of them alerted the Calvary. Let's go."

63

The one with the Wraithkillers patch backed away with the tat man. In moments, they made it to their bikes, straddled them and started the motors.

Bloodbath stared down Luella. "I assure you," he said calmly, "this is not over."

"Get out of here!" A note in Luella's voice told Bernadette she was a millisecond from blowing him away. "Go while you still can, asshole."

He smiled, the expression deranged, yet bold, and walked back to his Harley.

The three pulled out of the parking spaces and made a right into an alley between two businesses, the roar of their motorcycles reverberating in the narrow space.

Once they were gone, Bernadette's heart resumed a normal pace. "You...you have a gun?" she asked, staring at Luella.

"I do," Luella stated and placed the gun in her back waistband. "I have a conceal-and-carry license, but I only carry this big thing when I know I'm going to be somewhere without one of our men."

Six Harleys made U-turns in the street, and parked in empty spaces. Beastman had barely got the kickstand down on his bike before he leaped off it and shot toward the SUV.

"Are you okay, babe?" he asked.

"Yeah." Luella nodded. "They're gone and we're all fine. I scared them off with my .45."

He chuckled, kissed her gently on the lips then said, "That fucking gun's bigger than you are."

She laughed softly. "Escort us home, then we'll tell you what happened. I still don't know everything because I got here just as two of them were trying to pull my girls out of the truck."

I'm one of her girls? An odd sense of happiness inflated her chest.

"I sent Daddy a text," Puppy offered. She placed her index finger on the end of the Samsung, peeking out from its place in the dash.

Beastman said, "Yeah, Tractor came flying out of the hayfield on his John Deere and straight up to the main house." He said something was wrong and where you were located, so we all jumped on our bikes and got here as fast as we could. He dipped his head in through the window and looked at Bernadette. "You okay back there, red?"

"I'm fine," Bernadette said shakily. "Just rattled."

"Let's get you girls home," he said.

Chapter Six

When they reached the MC the residents were waiting on their porches, watching them pass and waving to them. Some of the children, keeping safely in the grass, ran along the SUV until they reached the base of the hill leading to the main house. Two dozen or more members stood around the entrance to the workshop.

As Luella shut off the engine and opened her driver's door, Frank pushed through the men and came to her side. Beastman met him there at the same time.

"Are you all okay?" Frank asked Luella.

Beastman answered before she could. "They're fine, Frank, but three of Crow's guys shook 'em up." He drew Luella into his arms and kissed the top of her head. "Let's get you inside and I'll find you a cold beer."

She pushed him gently away. "Not now, babe. I have $1500 worth of groceries in the back. Members are waiting for their food, and the cold stuff isn't going to last long in this god-awful heat." She kissed him on his nose then strode around to the back end and opened the Suburban's double doors.

Bernadette had begun to admire Luella. It was obvious she was one tough-as-nails woman without losing her femininity or her compassion for others. She could see her becoming a fantastic friend, providing Luella would want her as a close friend.

A small, black-haired, black-eyed, wiry man appeared at Puppy's door. He'd barely opened it before he pulled her into a bear hug. "Corazon, I am so relieved that you're all right."

"Daddy," Puppy mumbled into his T-shirt. "I can't breathe."

"Sorry, sweetheart," he said.

"Take it easy, Tractor," Beastman said across the roof of the SUV. "She's okay. They all are."

"Come on home with me, Corazon," Tractor said. "Your mother has dinner cooking."

"I can't, Daddy. I need to help Luella with the grocery order. It's not fair to leave her to handle all this alone. I'll be down when we're done."

"Kung sigurado ka ba?"

She nodded to her father. "Yes, I am sure. Go back out to the field and finish baling. I'm sure Mom will text you when the food's ready."

He looked uncertain, but soon he was pushing through the men and climbing back onto his John Deere. With the sound of the loud tractor engine rattling the carport, Puppy's father headed down the hill.

The door next to Bernadette opened suddenly, and Frank was tugging her out. "Come on, honey," he said. "We need to find out what exactly happened with Crow's men."

"Not now, Frank." Luella looked at Bernadette over the groceries piled in the back. "She's going to learn how to handle the MC's purchases. Then, when we're done, and everything has been disbursed to the correct families, we'll discuss Bloodbath and the two village idiots."

"Bloodbath?" Frank questioned.

"Yeah, Crow's new prospect," Bernadette stated. "The one who bartends."

A murderous expression settled over Frank's face.

"I know that look, Frank," Luella commented as she pulled several plastic bags from the back of the vehicle. "You can get pissed and stew all you want. I'm not discussing any more with you until this chore is done." She glanced up at Bernadette. "Join me back here, sweetie. You can help Puppy separate each order."

Bernadette looked into Frank's angry face, but as they stared at each other, his anger faded and worry replaced it. He swept his gaze over her. Then something in his eyes shifted—something she couldn't quite identify.

"Are you sure you want to write this new book?" he asked.

Not expecting such a question, she quirked her eyebrows. "Yes, why?"

"You might be biting off more than you can chew."

"Don't listen to him, Bernadette," Luella said, rustling bags. "He worries too much."

"That's the pot calling the kettle black, if I've ever heard it," Frank groused.

"Right now all I'm worried about is spoiling meat and melting ice cream, Frank," Luella said, irritation filling her rising voice. A crumpling noise followed, then a wadded receipt flew past Bernadette's face and struck Frank on the chest. "Dammit, go back to tinkering with your motorcycle and leave us alone!"

He shot the woman a disgruntled look. "This evening after supper, we're discussing this."

"Frank!" Luella shouted.

Somewhere off in the crackling bags, Puppy giggled.

"I'm going, I'm going…." He paused, then offered Bernadette a wry smile.

She smiled back at him, liking the way the expression turned his dangerous façade into that of a little boy letting his guard down. As if Frank knew what she was thinking, his expression darkened, and he spun on his heel, striding toward the garage. Bernadette couldn't help admiring his ass. So many men wore baggy denims, but Frank seemed to prefer jeans that actually fit him like they were tailored for him. She wondered if his ass was as firm as it looked.

"Bernadette," Puppy whispered next to her. "You can stare at Frank's ass some other time. We need some help unloading the supplies." She giggled again.

As if someone was holding a blowtorch to her face, Bernadette cursed the heat flaring in it and kept her gaze averted as she grabbed some bags.

* * *

Frank barely remembered cutting the metal for a gas tank. When Tractor had raced up to the main house, he'd made his announcement so fast that Beastman grabbed the nearest members and prospects and had torn off before Frank could find out anything. Once Phil told him what had happened, he'd paced with the others until they'd seen the Suburban traversing the lane through their valley.

He'd feared for Luella and Puppy, but the thought of someone harming Bernadette shot such a strong rage through him that he'd almost transformed. It had been years since intense emotion had prompted an unexpected transformation. Now, with the arrival of Miss Bernadette Kelly, he found himself treading unfamiliar waters. Frank didn't like the turn of events. His senses told him that the kill in the woods was werewolf-related, but there seemed to be other forces stirring the witch's pot, and he feared for Bernadette's safety. His people could handle nearly anything, but Bernadette was human, and humans always got hurt. Worse, they ended up like that poor father and his boy in the woods.

His cell phone buzzed in his pants pocket. He fished it out and groaned when he saw Craig's number. Whenever it was something classified, he'd use his personal number so it wasn't logged on his work phone. Frank swiped the screen.

Another attack on Plainview was just called in. Closer to your MC. Keep your people in at night.

Buzzing began in his ears. Feeling sick, he slipped the cell back into his pocket and braced both hands on the workstation, leaning over as he willed himself to get a grip. How was he going to protect his MC? Sure, some lived in and around Rebellion, but most resided right here on the farm. He couldn't safeguard everyone at once.

One thing they needed to do was go on a scouting mission to see what, if anything, they could discover or learn at the kill sites. They could shift into their animal selves so that the law and investigative teams would think there was a pack of very large wolves in the area, even if there seemed to be only one doing the killing. He'd find Phil and Beastman, and they could plan a trip out tonight.

Maybe he should send Bernadette back to Columbus until this killing spree was stopped. Let her come back later, maybe in the fall, or next spring when it was safe. However, Frank sensed that Bernadette would fight him on it. She'd just have to realize that this was *his* MC. It would be for her own good, her safety.

So why did sending her back home bother him so much?

Irritated by his bizarre emotions, he left the workshop in search of Phil and Beastman.

* * *

It was early evening, and Bernadette sat at the kitchen table with Luella, as the woman made notes on a tablet and then saved the file. They had handed out everyone's grocery orders, double-checked lists, and Luella had also updated each account with whether the family had paid for the groceries in full, or if they owed a payment or two to the club. Most had paid for their food, but there were four families struggling since they'd been permanently laid off at one of local coal mines, which were slowly shutting down for good.

"I'm curious," Bernadette said. "Don't those men get unemployment?"

"They do," Puppy piped up as she retrieved a

broom from a closet. "Unemployment is only a percentage of your wages, and the government taxes it before you get your payment each week. It's not much when you're used to a steady wage, so families struggle."

"That sucks," Bernadette said. "How can it be taxed a second time?"

"It's still considered taxable wages." Luella picked up her tablet. "It's why so many folks around here supplement their incomes with more…let's say unsavory options."

"It's so difficult to get help from the state," Puppy added, "that people have to do what they must to survive, but what typically happens is that it gets out of control and they end up in the pen, and their kids go to foster homes."

"That's why the Werewolves of Rebellion are self-sustaining." Luella shut the tablet off and walked to the living room entrance. "We don't want anyone having to resort to making or selling drugs for an income—and there's a penalty if we discover anyone doing so, even pot. We also frown on poaching to put meat on the table, because we raise our own beef, even keeping a few sheep and goats. One of our members, who doesn't live in our community, raises rabbits for meat. He slaughters them every so often and distributes so many to each home. I don't care for rabbit, but it's certainly welcome when things get tight for the MC through the winter months." She left, taking her tablet into one of the first-floor bedrooms.

"Damn," Bernadette said, looking over at Puppy. "I had no idea that there were MCs like this."

Puppy, still sweeping grass and dirt into a pile

from all the recent foot traffic, paused and met her gaze. "I can't say for other MCs, but from what I've learned, they do try to take care of their own, although I've never heard of any others having property this big and the members living and working together as we do." She swept the dirt and debris into a dust pan and dumped the contents into a waste can under the kitchen sink. "Some around the area call us a commune. I guess we are—but only to a point. We allow people in and out, and the rules we have here are for wellbeing, not control." She put the broom away and looked at Bernadette. "I hope that makes sense."

Nodding, Bernadette replied, "Yes, it does. You're truly a huge family, not a mishmash of people following a controlling leader. You all work as a team."

"Hey, she's a smart one," Luella stated as she returned to the kitchen.

"I have my moments," Bernadette quipped.

They all laughed.

Four women knocked, and then walked into the kitchen. Luella introduced them to Bernadette, as Puppy bid them farewell and left for her home with her parents.

"Mom won't be happy that I'm late for supper, but she knows what grocery day can be like." She waved as she left. "See you all tomorrow!"

Farewells and goodnights followed her through the screened porch and out to the carport.

"Can I help with supper?" Bernadette asked.

"You sit and watch," Luella replied. She took some items out of the big stainless-steel refrigerator as the other women began removing pots, pans and serving bowls from various cupboards. "If someone needs some help, we'll ask. This way you can watch for a few days, and learn where things are and where foods are kept."

"Luella, did you hear about the attack on Plainview?" a short, chunky woman named Shirley asked.

The instant Luella stiffened and turned toward Shirley, Bernadette sensed the mood shifting to something dark and somber.

Shirley flicked her gaze over at Bernadette. "Damn, I'm sorry. I figured since she was staying here she knew about…" Color flooded the woman's cheeks and she returned to washing potatoes in the sink.

"Should I ask?" Bernadette asked Luella softly.

"For now," Luella replied, "I'm only going to say that something attacked a man and his son on a nearby ridge."

"Was it a bear or a big cat?" Bernadette asked, her pulse jumping, for some reason.

Luella pulled an electric can opener across a counter, and began opening several cans of apple sauce. "We don't know much about it, but it has us worried because it's so close to our home."

"That must be why Phil told me not to wander off without a chaperone."

"Well, that would be one of many reasons," an older dark-haired woman, Carolyn, answered. She filled a huge kettle with water. "You *are* in the Appalachians."

Frowning, Bernadette questioned, "What does that have to do with anything?"

"Have you ever spent any time in these mountains before?" Luella asked.

Bernadette shook her head.

"Trust me honey," Luella told her, "there's a reason there are myths and legends about these hills. I'm sure that once Frank gets a chance, he'll sit and talk with you about what he—and the rest of us—expect from you if you're going to stay here for a while. Many of the people who live back in the woods and hollows have their beliefs and practices."

"Luella, what are we making for supper tonight?" Shirley asked.

"Pot pies."

Luella gave each woman a job, including Bernadette, who peeled carrots for a while, her thoughts tumbling over themselves. She'd often heard how mountain folk could be odd, reserved, keeping to themselves and sometimes shooting trespassers, but she'd always thought that all of those stories were just—stories. Now she wasn't so sure. Also, why were the women so skittish talking about an animal attack? With black bear and mountain lions about, such attacks happened occasionally. No matter what forested area it was, people sometimes wandered into the territory of various wildlife and were attacked.

But these women seem frightened. Why? Bernadette shook it off and focused on peeling the last half dozen carrots. Maybe she could corner Frank tonight and ask him about it. After all, she was here to learn all she could about his MC. Since the Werewolves of Rebellion were so rural instead of in the heart of a concrete jungle, it would make for an excellent spin on her book.

Chapter Seven

Puppy arrived a few minutes before the pot pies were done. She took Bernadette to a door off from the kitchen and shoved it open.

"Wow," Bernadette said. "This is beautiful."

"It's where the original owner and his descendants held their big, fancy gatherings," Puppy explained, "but we use it for our daily family dinners for those who want to attend. Mostly, it's just for the ones who live here at the main house."

"How many actually live in this house?"

"Twenty-nine right now." Puppy grinned. "You make 30."

"Twenty…" She raised her eyebrows. "This house is big, but 29?"

"The basement and the attic were upgraded several decades ago and turned into rooms," Luella called out behind them. "We remodeled each one about ten years ago, but a couple of them need new carpet."

Although the huge banquet table couldn't seat 30 people, there were smaller dining tables in the room, plus, Bernadette figured, others sat at the kitchen table to eat, too. She followed Puppy to a sideboard and a dish hutch, where she helped her take out stacks of dishes and set them in the kitchen, where everyone could fill his or her own plate.

"It's easier this way," Puppy said, "but we'll set out the other things like butter and condiments, and place a pitcher of ice tea on each table, too."

As they put various things on the tables, members began filing into the house. Soon there was a line from the dining rooms and living room which joined in the kitchen, ran past the four dozen pot pies cooling on the counter and the big serving bowls of applesauce and coleslaw; then came around the kitchen table and snaked back out again.

Bernadette found herself seated at the head of the table where Frank sat. Phil sat across from her, his gaze dark and piercing. Two stately looking women, both with dark eyes and raven-black hair, studied Bernadette so intensely that she wanted to ask them what their problem was. One who seemed slightly older, her face flawless and of undeterminable age, her temples silvered, watched her even more closely.

Frank caught the exchange and leaned forward, capturing their attention. "Mother, Grandmother, this"—he waved one big hand toward Bernadette—"is Bernadette Kelly." Quickly, he relayed why she was there. "I'm sorry," he added, his tone respectful, "but there has been so much going on this week I haven't had a chance to call or stop and fill you in on things."

"Irish, correct?" His grandmother's voice came out polished, strong, and with a faint accent.

"Yes," Bernadette replied.

The mother smiled, the action lighting up her stoic face, but she said nothing.

77

Frank's grandmother assessed her for a moment. Then a smile tweaked the corners of her mouth, and she flicked her gaze to her grandson. "She is the flame to your fire, my boy. You, as you always do, will refuse to believe it, but heed my words."

"Yes, ma'am," he replied.

He shifted his attention to Bernadette. Then, when the loud, raucous chatter at the tables proved overwhelming, he leaned closer to his mother and grandmother to speak, but Bernadette heard only an occasional word with all the noise. Regardless, she enjoyed watching everyone interacting with one another.

They really are a family.

A few seats down, a young woman fed a toddler on her lap, the boy's face a mess of applesauce and pot pie. His mother grinned down at him. Beastman offered him a chunk of dinner roll, which the little guy snatched and began wallowing around in his mouth.

Frank said little to her. Often she'd glance up to find him studying her, as if he wasn't sure what he was looking at. Thankfully, his mother and grandmother were absorbed in talking to the young mother and her toddler. Once everyone had taken their dishes to the kitchen and returned with slices of white cake and chocolate icing, Frank stood and whistled so loudly that Bernadette jumped.

Beside her Luella chuckled and patted her hand where it rested on the table edge.

Once everyone had quieted, except for the toddler and a small baby in the kitchen, Frank said, "I want to introduce our latest prospect, Hudson Garsell. He's new to the area, working for a company that hauls water off the pads. He likes it here and has decided to stay. Tom vouches for him, stating that Hudson has a desire to be a part of our MC. He will reside at his home just outside of Antioch, but you'll see more and more of Hudson as he strives to help our MC and obtain his patch. Please give Hudson a big hand. Stand up so everyone can see you, Hudson."

Applause erupted in the dining room with hoots and shouts from the kitchen. Bernadette turned toward the figure that rose about halfway down the table. The man swept his gaze around the room, but when his gaze landed on Bernadette, his eyes widened. She was accustomed to the reaction men had when they saw her, but Hudson looked at her a moment longer than necessary. He appeared to be about her age, maybe a couple years older than 25, but he had an air about him that hinted he was wiser than his years. Although swarthy of complexion, his eyes were brilliant, attention-grabbing green, his hair a deep chestnut brown. His eyes riveted her. She wondered if he wore tinted contacts. The guy was nice-looking, reminding her along the lines of Johnny Depp, but taller and bulkier. Still, the way he was staring at her was disconcerting. She flicked her gaze over to Frank, who continued his speech.

"Hudson's first task of commitment to the Werewolves of Rebellion," Frank said, "will be mucking out every stall on the property by the end of the week. If he does seven tasks as part of his hazing period, without giving up or complaint, then participates in the charity poker run the end of this month, he'll earn a prospect's cut."

A long pause after his announcement forced

Bernadette's attention to Frank, whose smile had vanished. He'd noticed Hudson checking her out. Frank scowled and added, "The stall mucking includes the cow barn."

"What?" Hudson protested, but red infused his face, and he recovered by offering, "Whatever I can do to help and prove myself."

The house roared with everyone's laughter. Bernadette joined in with them, but she sensed underlying anger rolling off Frank, and found him staring at her again, his eyes smoldering with irritation. *What the hell's his problem?*

Hudson returned to his seat. Several people clapped him on the back, as they wandered into the kitchen with more dirty dishes. After that, Bernadette made sure she didn't even glance Hudson's way. Next to her, she could have sworn that Frank sat growling at his dessert, but it had to be the way the room vibrated with noise. Finished with his cake, Frank motioned to Phil and Beastman, and they left the room. Frank threw one more look Bernadette's way, one that spoke volumes that he wasn't happy with her, but what could she have possibly done wrong?

It didn't take long for everyone to file out of the house or return to their rooms. Even Frank's mom and grandmother had disappeared somewhere. Several members went in the family and living rooms to relax. Someone turned on the TV, and various programs came and went as they channel-surfed. Hudson rose with his dishes, his gaze landing on Bernadette again. He offered her a big smile and nodded, his eyes full of interest. She glanced away and waited for him to leave before she rose and took her dishes to the kitchen, too.

"Can I help?" she asked the women who were sorting a mountain of plates.

"You've helped enough today," Puppy said. "Hasn't she, Luella?"

"Oh hell, she sure has." Luella turned the spigot on and hot water filled the sink, urging a froth of dish detergent to bubble up. The liquid's green-apple scent wafted over Bernadette. "Why don't you relax for the rest of the evening?"

The stacks upon stack of dishes bothered Bernadette. "But there's so much to clean up," she said.

"Honey, the five or six of us don't do this every night," Shirley told her as she walked in with two empty pitchers. "The women who live here rotate as cooks and cleanup teams, every three days."

"You learned a lot today, and you were a great help," Luella said.

Puppy flashed her a huge smile, and handed her a slice of cake and a cup of steaming coffee. "I saw that you never got a chance to have dessert. Take these and go chill."

"You guys are amazing," Bernadette said, her heart swelling with warmth. "I really mean that."

"Aw…" Carolyn said. "Luella, we might just have to keep that one."

"Indeed," Luella agreed.

For the second time since she'd arrived, someone wanted to keep her at the MC. Did that mean she really fit in with these people?

"Go on," Shirley urged. "Get out of here before we change our minds and make you wash dishes."

Grinning, Bernadette decided to take her dessert

to her room and write notes for her book. She certainly *had* learned a lot today. As she passed through the living room, her attention landed on a threesome in the back corner, sprawled over a high-backed chaise. A woman she didn't recognize was giving a biker a blow job, his pants open, but his cock hidden by her head as she bobbed it up and down. The other woman, another one she hadn't seen before, was engaged in a deep kiss with him as he kneaded one of her large, bare breasts.

So the Werewolves of Rebellion do have sweet butts. She glanced around and noted that there were no children present. Apparently, there were times in the evening after supper that kids were removed from the clubhouse. She liked how the members were so conscientious about the matter.

As she reached the staircase, she practically stumbled over a couple humping in the shadows to the side of the newel post. The man held the young woman against the wall, thrusting into her, her legs wrapped around his waist. Bernadette rushed up the stairs before anyone approached her about sex.

In her room, she moved a small side table over to the window and placed a straight-back chair next to it. She removed her laptop from its case, plugged it into an outlet, and opened it on the table. She sat eating the cake, a mix with store-bought icing, but still delicious, and sipped her coffee. Already there were several couples and families down at the pond. Children jumped off the dock into the water, and two paddle boats made several trips around the pond's perimeter. *Well, that explains where the kids are tonight. The smaller ones are probably in bed by now, too.* Maybe she'd go down for a swim after everyone had left. She could go now, but until more of the community grew accustomed to her being there, she didn't want anyone to feel as though she was encroaching on their relaxation time.

Finished with her dessert, she pushed the plate and fork aside and focused on her coffee as she continued to watch the members frolicking at the pond. Finally, she pulled up her manuscript, which was only a few pages, but it had been a firm start. First, though, she would have to update her information and put her notes together in a way that would help her keep track of things.

Bernadette typed for a long time. Gradually, she left her writing mode and came back to herself, discovering that once again Frank was infiltrating her thoughts. She gave up and shut the laptop. Frank had seemed truly pissed off that the new prospect had been so enamored of her. Although Bernadette was accustomed to how men reacted to her, it still embarrassed her. The way Hudson had stared at her had left Bernadette feeling as though he'd actually stripped off her clothes right there in front of the entire room. It disturbed her that Frank would think she'd somehow enticed the guy, but that made no sense, either. She barely knew Frank, and hadn't spoken to him much since their encounter in the living room the night before. And today, she hadn't seen him until suppertime, almost as if he were avoiding her, but she knew that was bogus. After all, he was the president of this MC, so he had things to manage just like Luella took care of the main house.

Oh, who am I kidding? Whether she'd meant to or not, somehow she'd upset Frank further. Frustrated, she quickly jotted on a pad of paper the next couple of things she wanted to add to the actual manuscript. She would let her ideas stew on a mental backburner and then write the pages in the morning, or tomorrow evening.

It had grown quiet outside. The last family was packing up their toys and towels to leave for their abode. Making up her mind, Bernadette changed into her bikini, and then it hit her that she'd forgotten to check in with her mom that morning. She would leave a note for herself on her laptop to call her tomorrow.

Bernadette decided to grab a towel from the bathroom and refill her coffee mug on her way through the kitchen. Then she'd take it to the pond, where she could enjoy it in the quiet evening, with the calming night sounds and the cool water. Maybe a luxurious dip would extinguish her thoughts of Frank. Determined to wash him from her mind, she left the room.

Downstairs, only one couple was screwing, the others having left long ago. The sweet butt straddled a guy that Bernadette recognized as Ass Crack, dubbed so by the way his jeans always slid off his hips, and his refusal to wear a belt. The blonde bounced on his lap, her cries growing steadily louder the more she bumped up and down. Ass Crack caught Bernadette's gaze as she hurried by, his smile wide as his eyes rolled back in his head and he let out a loud groan.

Bernadette hurried into the kitchen.

"Sweet Butt night," Luella said from where she sat, nursing a glass of iced tea.

"Thanks for the warning," Bernadette replied.

Luella's laughter trailed her outside.

* * *

"Are Tom, Frank, Tractor, and the others coming?" Frank asked Phil.

"Yeah, they're all on their way."

Beastman crumpled a beer can and tossed it into the waste barrel. "Did Deputy Williamscot give you any more information?" He moved over to the mini-fridge and withdrew another can. "It would help if we had more information about what we're dealing with."

"That's why I've decided to go on a scouting mission," Frank said. When the others joined them in the workshop, he waited until they were sure no one would interrupt them. Then he explained what they were about to do. "What worries me is how tightly the lid is on these incidents," Frank finished having explained that there had been another kill. "Deputy Williamscot hasn't given me any additional information. Has anyone heard anything at all? There's always someone who leaks details. Granted, it always gets blown out of proportion, but there's generally some truth in them."

"Not me, Boss," Phil answered.

None of the others had heard anything either.

"Well," said Frank, "let's wait until it's fully dark. Then we'll walk into the woods toward Plainview and shift there."

The others gave him strange expressions.

"I don't want Bernadette to see us." He answered their unspoken questions.

"Shit," said Tom. "I forgot about her being here."

Frank raked a hand through the top of his sweat-dampened hair. He sighed and said, "If Bernadette hasn't gone to bed by the time we return, I plan on telling her to go back to Columbus. I figure she'll argue, but it's my MC, and she's not safe here if we're dealing with a rogue werewolf."

"If our new prospect has his way, he might convince her to stay," Beastman stated, a chuckle in his words. "I saw the way they were looking at each other."

"Nah, it was *him* ogling her," Phil replied. "I think his attention made her uncomfortable. She turned red as a chapped ass."

"Are you talking about the new guy, Hudson?" Johnny asked. "I didn't get off work until late tonight, so I missed eating with everyone."

"Yeah," Phil said, "He's a good guy. But when he laid eyes on Berna—"

"Enough of this shit!" Frank bellowed. "What's wrong with you guys? We're here to investigate a possible rogue killing people, not talk about a prospect's hard-on!"

"Damn, Boss." Phil offered him a wounded expression. "Is it the heat that's getting to you?"

"Yeah…the heat." Making a show of his discomfort, Frank used the hem of his shirt to wipe his brow, then pulled the garment down again. "It's freaking mid-July, but it feels like it's the height of August."

Thankfully, the men dismissed his crankiness, and then launched into a discussion about the weather, and if there would be a good harvest to get them through the winter months. Frank let them talk as he walked over to the mini fridge. *What the hell is wrong with me? I never snap and growl at my people unless pushed well beyond my patience, and that's not often.*

He took a beer from the refrigerator, popped the tab and guzzled the entire contents. The cold brew gave him instant brain freeze. He cursed the pain, letting loose repeated 'F' bombs until it passed. However, he also welcomed the pain, since it diverted his thoughts about a voluptuous ginger who was oh so tempting. His grandmother's cryptic announcement had irritated him even more. Then, when he'd gone in search of her to ask for an explanation, he'd discovered that she and his mother had left early. Flame to his fire? What the hell did that mean? With a snarl, he crunched the can, then threw it toward the garbage barrel.

"It's dark enough," he groused. "Let's go. It'll be full night by the time we reach the tree line."

His men cast dubious looks at him, but said nothing as he passed them on his way outside. They filed out of the workshop behind him and headed around to the back of it, where they couldn't be seen by anyone from a window, or any part of the lawn.

The hike across the field to the tree line was accompanied by crickets chirring in the hay. It was the only pasture that Tractor hadn't mown and baled yet. Tree frogs sang their nightly song, the intensity of the noise often overwhelming everything else. Somewhere in the hollow to the rear of the property the yips of coyotes reached Frank's sensitive ears. A cow bawled in the barn.

At the woods, Frank walked into the trees without a backward glance, knowing his men would follow him without comment. He strode in far enough that the farm disappeared, and then stripped off his clothes. The others did the same.

The tree frogs continued their punishing *scree-scree-scree* in the surrounding pines, oaks, and elms. Frank let himself be one with nature, allowed himself to absorb the noise, enjoy the darkness and the half-soft, half-prickly sensation of pine needles under his bare feet. Tingling assailed his skin. It began softly at first, growing steadily stronger until it became painful. Although used to the feeling, Frank still gritted his teeth against it. The tingling turned into a fiery sensation that flowed through his muscles, into his joints, up into his face and scalp, until his hair follicles tightened and it felt like the top of his head would pop off.

More tingling assaulted his skin as fur sprouted from it. Then the one thing that hurt like seven kinds of hell took its turn—the actual transformation from man to man-beast. His muscles shifted to accommodate a larger body. His legs twisted into the semblance of a canine's, feet transforming into paws. He grunted and moaned as the pain claimed him. Dimly he detected the same sounds coming from Phil, Beastman, and the others.

Many years ago, shifting from man into werewolf had pulled agonized screams from his throat, but now he could manage the discomfort of morphing. Now he could keep his animalistic side from overtaking his human mind. Whoever the rogue was either enjoyed killing or couldn't defeat the primal instincts of lycanthropy.

Frank fell to the ground as the last vestiges of his human side changed. Fangs protruded from his mouth, and claws split the tips of his fingers with a fiery sensation, eliciting a hiss from him. A howl of anguish rent the night. It sounded like Johnny, the youngest of their group, still young enough to struggle with battling the urges and torments of being a werewolf.

Eventually the sounds and scents intensified. The noise of the very bugs scurrying beneath the pine needles reached Frank's ears. The pungent smell of pine tar, earth, and a variety of animal and plant life tantalized his muzzle-like nose.

"Fuck, I hate how bad shifting hurts," Johnny said, his speech guttural.

"You'll eventually manage the change," Tractor told him.

"That day can't come soon enough," Johnny replied as he shook his fur coat.

For a moment, Frank lay on the ground staring up through the canopy at the twinkling of stars. Why couldn't life on earth be as simple as it was out there in the great beyond? Or was it? Were there people out there who suffered, who loved, who believed in something greater than themselves and raised their offspring to believe it too? He snorted at his philosophical thoughts, then the snort turned into a sneeze, and he jumped to his feet. His enhanced night vision revealed his fellow lycanthropes in clarity.

"Ready?" he asked, his way of speaking just as guttural as his men's.

They each bobbed their heads, their tall, pointed ears twitching as they captured all manner of sounds. Although Beastman towered over everyone else, they all mirrored one another, except for fur color, patterns and eye color. Their legs looked like the furry thighs of men, but had turned into the triple-jointed ones of a canine's. Their long, paw-like feet were tipped with shiny claws. Fangs protruded from their muzzle-like mouths, and heavy fur covered everything including their genitals. That was one thing that Frank was always thankful for when hunting or running through the briars.

"Remember," Frank stated, twitching his ears, "this is only a recon. Don't disturb anything at the crime scenes. Our footprints will look strange, so try not to step in anything soft or wet. It'll only confuse the investigators and create misidentifications." He stooped over with the knuckles of his paw-hands flush with the ground. "Use your heightened senses. If you come across something unusual, point it out." With that, he launched himself over the log where he'd laid his clothing, and loped into the woods on all fours.

Yips and growls trailed him. Beastman, his fur a deep tawny color, kept pace with him as did Phil, but both remained a couple of feet back, in respect for Frank as their leader. Tractor, Johnny, and Tom brought up the rear of their pack.

In minutes they were off the MC's property, with Frank leading them across wooded private land, then through parts of Wayne National Forest and around the edges of the huge gas and oil pads. As Frank ran he kept fixating on Bernadette. If he'd been a youngster when Hudson looked at her like he had, Frank would've launched himself over the table—but why had he felt such rage at the new prospect? He couldn't blame Hudson for eyeballing Bernadette the way he had. She was gorgeous, and had curves that made a man's mouth water.

He led the way down a steep incline to the Little Muskingum River, the 'creek' where locals enjoyed swimming and fishing, and then hurried over Foraker Covered Bridge to cross over a fence line and run uphill over pasture fields. If Bernadette knew what Frank was—what most of them were at his MC— she'd run screaming into the night. Few humans could comprehend that lycanthropes were real, and, when a werewolf revealed him or herself, humans reached for the nearest weapon, usually something with bullets. She could never know what they were. Beyond a good fuck in the sack, having a relationship with her wasn't an option, so there was no point in feeling as though Hudson was infringing on Frank's territory.

On the plateau Frank and his pack skirted a couple of private properties until they crossed a stream and ascended another steep incline to a heavily wooded area with thick undergrowth. It was a favorite place of hunters, especially during deer season and for rabbit hunting.

Panting, they paused for a few minutes to catch their breaths. Willing his heart rate to slow, he struggled with more images of Bernadette smiling at him, the way her eyes flashed greener when she was amused or flustered, the way her juicy breasts strained against the low-cut tank top she'd been wearing today…

"Frank? Frank!"

He jerked his head up to look at Phil. "What?"

"I asked how you want us to proceed." Phil frowned at him, his bushy eyebrows knitting, but his human eyes showed concern. "Are you okay?"

"I'm fine, just a bit distracted—and worried about what we'll find at the kill sites." He drew in a breath, filling his lungs to capacity and then letting the air out in a big gust. "Let's do this."

He crept forward, eyes keen for any unusual movements or clues, nose twitching in the breeze that bore the scent of stagnant water, mice, nesting birds, and deer bedded down several yards away. Frank listened for any signs of someone or something in the forest that didn't belong. Behind him, and to either side, the sniffing from his men seemed too loud for the still environment.

Still. It's too quiet. He held up one forearm, flexing his hairy, clawed fingers. His pack stopped. He looked from one to the other, sending his worries airborne with the scent of his musk. They straightened their stances, ready for a fight.

Off to their right, a ground squirrel chittered, voicing its irritation with their intrusion into its world. Somewhere in the distance, dogs barked.

Frank led them into another pine grove. The wind passed through the boughs, the swishing noise haunting. A pinecone fell, bouncing from branch to branch, and landed at Tractor's paws.

Jerking his head toward the north, Frank indicated that they should follow him. Several yards ahead, the area opened up to a scene of devastation. Shrubs and undergrowth lay mashed flat against the ground, and crime scene tape cordoned off the area. A water hole filled from the last storm emanated mosquitoes, and a dank, nose-flinching odor arose. Blood glimmered darkly on the dirt, the leaves, branches, and tree trunks. The clean-up crew had missed a small piece of intestine that dangled from the tip of a limb.

"Smell that?" Frank asked, keeping his voice low. "Someone enjoys killing. The smell of blood is tinged with…"

"Fury," Phil supplied.

"Yeah." Frank dropped down on all fours and sniffed the area around the stagnate hole, where numerous indentions and prints marred the mud. He rose and backed away, careful where he placed his feet. He smelled a couple of tree trunks that had been splattered with blood. "This was done by a werewolf, one I've never scented before."

"That doesn't help us at all," Tom stated. "We can't determine who it is when they're in human form."

That was one of the drawbacks to being a lycanthrope. When shifted, their scents were their personal signatures, but when in human form, they smelled like any other human, so finding the killer in the shape of a man or woman would be a matter of chance.

"What do we do now?" Johnny asked.

"Watch your backs and everyone else's," a scratchy female voice said. A chuckle, the sound similar to pressure applied to worn brake pads, followed.

Frank and his pack spun toward the intruder. He scrutinized the undergrowth and tree tops, but saw no one.

"It's me, Frank," the voice stated. "Scary Mary."

Chapter Eight

On the other side of the tape, facing Frank, the air wavered as if it were water, then a shape took form. A middle-aged woman appeared in a long, dark maxi dress, her feet bare, a black-and-white paisley print handkerchief wrapped around her head. A couple salt-and-pepper dreadlocks hung from either side of the do-rag.

"Fuck me!" Johnny exclaimed. "How did you do that?"

She cackled again, her laughter turning into a phlegmy cough that resulted in her hacking up a gob of goo. She spat it into a rag that she produced from one of the dress' inner pockets. "Don't want forensics finding my loogie and tying me to a murder I didn't commit." She laughed again.

"Gross," Johnny said.

"What are you doing out here, Mary?" Frank questioned. "What ties do you have to this scene?"

"None, you upstart lycanthrope!" She threw him a filthy look. "I was in the woods the day that thing killed the man and his boy. I came up on the murder after it left."

"Did you see the werewolf?" Phil asked.

She shook her head. "It was long gone by the time I got here. If I have to co-exist with things in my woods, I must know what they are, from whence they come, and what I can or can't use against various…creatures." She grasped the edges of the handkerchief and pushed the loose dreadlocks up into it again. The starlight breaking through a gap in the trees glimmered on her black skin. Mary let her gaze rove over the scene. Then she said, "I used some of the blood and a few hairs that I found to look into the future."

Frank had known Scary Mary long enough to know that whatever she did and said was true. She looked normal enough: just a middle-aged black woman with dreadlocks that hung almost to her waist, a very wide nose and the blackest damn eyes Frank had ever seen, but her eyes held a wealth of knowledge. No one knew where Scary Mary—or any of those she'd been descended from—originated, but the theory was that her family had been escaped slaves from across the Ohio River. The story went that they'd discovered excellent hiding places in the caverns of Monroe County, and the old gold mine that twined throughout the region. They'd lived off the land, and had kept to themselves, remaining virtually undetected.

Frank's family had dealt with enough witches, including a coven that had already lived here when Rebellion was settled. Also possessing a bloodline of magic, his clan had respected the coven and its successors through the decades, especially the ones who practiced the dark arts. Pissing off a practitioner of black magic was beyond stupid. Scary Mary didn't wield anything foul—at least that was her claim—but some of the things she was capable of often made Frank wonder. "What did you find out, Mary?"

"That dark times are ahead," she replied cryptically. "This lycanthrope is fueled by rage and hate. Those two traits attract dark forces, which feed on those emotions. You take good care of your clan, Frank Nightshade, but now you'll be called upon to step up more than usual." She pointed a slim finger at each member of his pack in turn. "You all need to be strong, help your leader, and give him strength, because in the days ahead your faith will be sorely tested."

"Didn't your spell give you more details than that?" Phil questioned irritably.

"Just that there's new magic in the area."

Frank studied the witch closely. "New magic?"

She nodded sagely. "It's close, too. We're merely standing on the threshold of what's to come." Turning, she started making her way into the undergrowth. She paused to pick up a basket on the ground that Frank hadn't noticed before. "Frank, should your clan need me, you know how to find me. I'm willing to help if things get out of hand."

"Thank you, Mary," he said with conviction.

"Welcome." Her voice came from deep in the undergrowth.

"Creepy," Johnny whispered, but it sounded more like a growl.

"*Bruha*," Tractor said, but the Filipino word came out strangely.

"English?" Phil asked.

"Witch," Tractor supplied. "She scares me."

"That's why she's called Scary Mary." Frank

motioned to his pack. "The next scene should be a half mile farther."

He led his pack down into one hollow, up over a plateau, and down into another hollow. He snarled at the cockleburs and beggar's lice that tangled in his fur. When he shifted back into his human form, he'd easily shuck the clingy seeds, but right now the more ground they covered, the more they collected the annoying hitchhikers.

Letting his sense of smell guide him, Frank finally came upon the second crime scene. He stopped and listened intently, his pack halting on either side of him.

"Fucking cockleburs," Phil growled as he pulled several from the fur just above one wrist.

"Itchy bastards," Tom grumbled.

"Any of you smell, see, or sense anything dangerous?" Frank snapped, annoyed with their grousing.

They all sniffed and snuffled as they waited quietly. Each pack member shook their heads.

"Okay, proceed with caution." Frank stepped out into a similar site as the last one, but this area opened into a grove of hickory trees that surrounded an old homestead, only the sandstone foundation visible. On the far side he detected the scent of fish, blood, and guts. "Someone was here fishing in that little pond. The rogue probably jumped the person while they were cleaning their catch."

They padded over to a body of water about 60 yards in circumference. After ducking under another taped-off area, Frank immediately found the kill spot.

"Same scent," Frank announced.

"The werewolf is male," Phil stated. "The testosterone and other pheromones are so strong it makes my nose clench."

"Scary Mary's right," Tom added. "Lots of rage in this one."

Something clicked in the cattails growing at the water's edge. Frank froze and so did his pack.

"That sounded like a camera," Tractor said, glancing around uneasily.

Johnny moved up to stand next to Frank. "I bet it's a trail cam."

"Shit," Frank said. "The law probably put it here because killers often come back to relive the murder."

Creeping forward on all fours, Phil nosed through the cattails. "Found it," he snarled. "Someone had it on a stake pushed into the mud."

"Now what?" Tractor asked.

"We take it with us," said Frank. "Throw the stake out into the middle of the pond. When someone comes back for the cam, they'll assume the killer either took it, someone else grabbed it out of curiosity, or it fell into the water and sank."

"I think we learned more from Scary Mary than anything else," Phil mused. He looked at the camera. "This thing says there are six photos on it, but those could be the leaves around it bobbing in the breeze."

Pulling more burs from his fur, Frank replied, "We'll head home and see if the camera reveals anything." He growled low in his throat. "Besides, I need to shift out of these fucking burs. Let's go."

* * *

Bernadette jumped into the pond, thinking it would be warm due to the horrible heat, but it shocked her, ripping the breath from her lungs. She rose to the surface, spluttering and gasping for breath.

The mother of the family lingering at the pond laughed. "The water stays ice-cold because it's fed by a deep spring that bubbles up from the bottom." She laughed again, waved, then ushered her kids up the slope.

Once Bernadette adjusted to the temperature, she found the water soothing. She swam to the other side a couple times, then lay floating on her back. Every now and then bluegills would nibble at her toes, but she didn't mind the gentle nips.

The light faded until only a dull smudge of pale orange remained then that too vanished. The tiki torches' flames wavered, their fluttering sound reaching Bernadette if the wind blew just right. She could get used to this—the quiet, the sedate pace, the close-knit relationships. She'd had that with her brothers, but now they'd gone on with their own lives, and even Alexander would be leaving soon. It was just Bernadette and her mother. She wondered if her mom would like it here, too.

"You know," a deep voice rumbled above her, "you're going to turn whiter than you already are and look like a redheaded prune if you stay in there any longer."

She gasped, thrashing upright and splashing water everywhere. Droplets somehow got up her nose, stinging her sinuses and forcing her to cough and sneeze.

Once she'd recovered, she snapped, "You scared

the hell out of me!" His dark gaze urged a thrill through her. He watched her with an appreciative light in his eyes.

Staring up at him as she treaded water, she asked, "Are you coming in for a swim?"

"I wasn't planning to, but..." He rose from his kneeling position on the edge of the pier. "Hell, might as well. I'm sweaty, dirty, and itchy, so a swim sounds great."

As he began to strip, Bernadette admired the tattoo that covered his arms and shoulders, but the light didn't allow her to see the details or their bright colors. Once he'd dropped his jeans, she realized her blunder—he wasn't stopping at his briefs. He yanked those down too. Quickly, she averted her eyes, heat rushing into her face, until he jumped into the water. He came up a few feet away from her and hooted, startling her.

"I'll never get used to that first plunge," he said, swimming over to her. "Damn spring feeds this pond, so it keeps it really cold. Feels even worse when the weather is so ungodly hot and miserable."

"It is odd weather, isn't it?" she said.

"Everyone says it's global warming. Do you believe that?"

She began to shiver, but it wasn't from the cold water. "I've always figured earth goes through cycles, and this is one of them."

He tipped his head, studying her. "Good point. Although I imagine mankind doesn't help much."

"I'm sure you didn't come down here to discuss global warming," she said. "It has to be past 10:00, yet you've sought me out, so that tells me you want to talk to me about something."

He treaded water a couple feet from her. Every once in a while, she'd catch a rush of water across her shins from where he kicked his feet to stay afloat. In the light cast by the torches his expression remained neutral, but his eyes were a different matter. There was indecision in them that warred with...was that need? For her?

Well, if the night before was an indication, he seemed attracted to her. Who was she kidding? She'd jump his bones right now and probably drown in the process. If wasn't for the fact that a sexual relationship would complicate her stay here, she'd sure as hell give it a try.

Frank turned away and swam to the other side of the pond. She couldn't see him in the darkness, but the splashing in that direction told her he was swimming back. Upon his return, he floated a little farther away than before.

"Well?" she prompted. Somehow she knew what he was about to say wasn't good. "I'm not going to like it, am I?"

His eyes widened.

Shit, she'd nailed it.

"A matter has come up," he began.

"What *kind* of matter?"

He scowled. "Something that I'm not at liberty to share with you. Rest assured, it puts everyone, including you, in danger."

"And?"

He moved his arms back and forth as he kicked to stay on the surface, his muscles flexing so enticingly that Bernadette longed to caress them, feel them flex under her fingertips and examine the artwork scrawled

101

over his skin. The torchlight cast harsh lines across his face, shoulders, and arms, but as he flipped onto his back and floated for a few moments, the firelight revealed only his profile—and what a profile it was. Bernadette imagined him in bed flat on his back with her straddling his hips, riding him until she exploded.

Startled by her thoughts, she decided to leave the pond, dress, and then head back to the house. She knew she didn't want to hear what he had to say. Yet she didn't want to leave him either. Conflicted, she swam over to the dock's ladder.

"Where are you going?" he called out behind her.

"It's late. I'm going to my room."

"No, wait."

Against her better judgment, she paused, both hands gripping a rung. He swam leisurely toward her, until he was only a foot away. That close, the torch flames almost allowed her to make out the darker pupil in the black depths of his eyes. The thickness of his five o'clock shadow complemented his wet, ebony hair. Beads of water trickled out of his curling locks and over his forehead, bumping across faint worry lines and into his black eyebrows to drip down into his eyes. He shook his head, water pelting her. Then he grinned. "Sorry."

Bernadette couldn't help but smile back. He looked like such a mischievous boy when he relaxed and let his stern, dangerous façade slip.

"Frank, what did you want to talk to me about?" she pressed.

"That you should…"

Bernadette could only label what she saw in his eyes as turmoil. But from what?

"I think you should…" He stared past her, as if something toward the house had captured his attention.

"*Frank*?" she said. "What is it?" The suspense was both killing her and scaring her. "Is everything all right? Did something happen again with the Wraithkillers?"

He shook his head. "No, it's not that. There's been some deaths in the area."

"Oh, no!"

"And I think you should stay close to the house or with someone at all times."

His words came out in a rush. To Bernadette, that meant he was avoiding the real issue. She'd grown up with four older brothers, so she knew the signs.

"Don't even go for a stroll in the hayfields or the orchard," he said quickly. "And next time you come down for a swim, make sure someone is with you, or wait and swim when the families are here in the evenings." He pushed closer to her, and she inhaled sharply, her heart rate going from first into overdrive. "The women have been told to stay out of the woods. That goes for you, too."

"Is it a bear?" she asked.

He blinked. "Wait, what?"

"A bear," she said. "Is there a rogue bear?"

"A rogue…yeah."

"Duly noted." She wanted him to kiss her. No, she didn't. If he did, it would complicate things. "Is there anything else?"

"No." He backed away slightly.

"Oh. Okay." She grasped the ladder rung again and faced it, preparing to climb. "Goodnight, Frank."

"Wait. There is one other thing," he said.

103

She let go with one hand and held on with the other so she could face him slightly. "What is it?"

"This." Frank took her by the hand and jerked her into his arms.

Before she could even gasp, he claimed her mouth, crushing her lips beneath his. Frank placed a foot on one of the submersed rungs, bracing her hips against his thigh, then grabbed the rung by her head with one hand, and slipped his free hand around her to palm her ass cheek. He slanted his mouth across hers, tasting her, tickling the seam of her lips with the tip of his tongue. It wasn't a good idea to let him kiss her, but surely one good, bone-melting lip lock wouldn't hurt? She'd enjoy this moment, then she'd tell him not to do it again, and say that she had to keep her head clear for her book, that she didn't need distractions.

When he began kneading her butt cheek, his fingers creeping steadily closer to her sex, her willpower sank like the Titanic. Bernadette pressed herself to him and opened her mouth, allowing him access. He groaned deep in his throat, a growling sound that inflamed her senses and prompted her to grind against him. A wildness descended upon her—a sexual need unlike anything she'd felt before. He tugged her closer, and she inhaled fiercely, then moaned as his cock snuggled into the apex of her thighs.

Another growl rumbled out of him. He devoured her mouth, pummeling her tongue with his. They sucked in air each chance they could, their excitement exhaling on each breath. Bernadette couldn't get enough of Frank—couldn't touch enough of his skin or feel enough of his body.

Something sharp slid along her hip. Before she could react, the elastic of her bottoms released, followed by the band that encircled her leg. Surprised, she drew back to see what had caused it to fall apart. Her gaze flew to Frank's. He stared back at her, his eyes glowing amber, looking...wild, animalistic. She froze, but he blinked and the glow vanished. She dismissed it as the reflection of the yellow tiki flames in his eyes. Frank switched hands, which distracted her, and supported her ass with his opposite one, even moving his left leg off the rung to use his right in its place—the position exactly the opposite of the one before. He smoothed his free hand over her hip. What felt like a small blade flicked at her elastic, then the band around the other leg and her bikini bottoms fell away from her body. Bernadette knew she should protest, but right now the throbbing in her pussy had become so intense that only one thing could make it go away. Defeated by her hormones, she cried out with desire as he rounded his hand over her hip and over her thigh to her crotch. Rationale evaporated from her head. All she could do was feel, and right now, she wanted to feel him inside her, whether it was his fingers or his cock.

She stiffened when he pushed his steel-hard cock through her folds, expecting to feel him penetrate her at any instant, but when he drew back and raked her pussy with his dick a second time, that action alone sent her over the edge and she shattered in his arms. Wave after wave of fierce, piercing sensation pulsed through her channel and into her lower abdomen. Hot tingles radiated into her folds. Bernadette shouted her release, going weak in his arms. Somehow Frank held them both up in the water. He captured her lips again and drank every cry she offered up as she trembled and ground herself against his cock.

Finally, she had nothing left in her to shout to the night. He released her lips, and she tucked her head into the crook of his neck, trying to gather her wits, panting against his wet skin. As she came down from her sexual high, shame hit her. She'd climaxed without penetration. What Frank must think of her? Heat flowed over her body, and, with a soft sound of distress, she pulled away and clung to the ladder.

"I…I better go to the house, go to bed."

"Wait, what's wrong?" Frank asked, his tone a combination of confusion and surprise. "I shouldn't have kissed you, but once I did, I thought you wanted me."

"I did, but… Look, I have to keep a clear head. I don't need my job complicated by anything." She started to climb out, but realized her swim bottoms were gone. "What did you do to my briefs?"

"I…uh…" He offered her a sheepish look. "You know, there's not much elastic in those skimpy things, so they're easy to break. I'll buy you a new suit."

"Don't bother." She stepped up one rung then stopped again. "Could you…you know."

"What?" He quirked one corner of his mouth.

"Not stare at my ass as I climb out," she snapped. Dammit, if her embarrassment grew any worse, she'd burst into flames and burn the dock down. As he continued to stare at her in amusement, she added, "From your angle, it's not the most flattering view."

"That's a matter of opinion," he replied. "You have a gorgeous, biteable ass."

"I have a…?" She gaped at him. "I can't believe you just said that."

"It was a compliment, Bernadette."

"I know it was a compliment, it's just that…" She sighed. "Will you please turn your head or close your eyes so I can get out of the water?"

Laughing, he shut his eyes.

"And no peeking!"

"I won't peek," he said.

She started up the ladder and reached the deck.

"Well, maybe a little peek."

"Frank!" She dropped into a squat, snatched up the towel, and wound it around her hips. As she stood, she grabbed the coffee cup she'd brought with her. "Goodnight."

She hurried up the path, but his deep, rumbling laughter followed her every step of the way.

Chapter Nine

Frank sat on the screened porch with a cup of coffee between his hands. He'd slept little. Every time he'd doze off, another image of Bernadette rose unbidden in his mind's eye. He relived every part of their encounter in the pond, from the taste of her sweet lips to the soft feel of her curves under his palms. Her response to him had taken him by surprise, and when she'd shattered in his arms, her throaty cries so damn sexy, he'd been amazed at how responsive she was. Then he'd gone to bed with the worst hard-on he'd had since becoming sexually active at the age of sixteen.

So much for his plans of sending her back to Columbus. She'd only been with them for a couple of days, but he couldn't do it, didn't want to do it, even knowing it was for her safety. Now all he wanted to do was hunt her down, bend her over something and claim her as his, as he sank balls-deep into her body.

"Shit," he whispered, sipping from his mug. Frank had to keep his head clear. Bernadette was a distraction, albeit a very sexy one. So much for his preference for blonds. Now that he had this tempting ginger underfoot, had tasted her and seen her fly apart just by gently sliding his cock along the outside of her pussy… Fuck, he *had* to have her. Maybe if he bedded her, he would get her out of his system.

"What to do, what to do …" He sipped again, burning his tongue this time. With a snarl, he thumped the mug down on the end table by his porch recliner.

"I know you're not talking about the rogue," Luella's voice came from the kitchen.

Frank looked up just as she stepped down onto the porch, carrying an oversized black mug that her old man had bought for her when he'd come back from a charity run in Charleston, West Virginia. She held it by the handle revealing the words, "A Giant Cup of Stop Your Fucking Bitching." Frank smiled. Only Beastman would buy his old lady something like that.

"So," Luella said as she sat in a nearby chair. "I'm guessing a very tempting ginger has you tied in knots."

"Funny," he said, "that's exactly what I call her in my head—tempting ginger."

"She's gorgeous, Frank. And, just so you know, she has an amazing personality to go with the wrapper. I really like Bernadette."

"You don't have to sell her to me, but right now I don't have time for anything other than a quick fuck."

"You've been doing the quick-fuck thing for the past two or three years now." Taking a moment to enjoy her coffee, Luella studied him over the rim of her cup. "You need an old lady."

"I'm happy as I am," he replied and reached for his mug again. "Relationships are a pain in the ass, and besides, she's"—he glanced toward the kitchen to make sure they were alone—"a human. You know what happens when humans find out what we are. It never ends well."

"Deputy Williamscot and his wife know what you are—what most of us are here at the community."

"That's different." Frank tested his coffee again, finally finding it at the perfect temperature, and took a big gulp. Wiping the back of his mouth with his free hand, he mumbled, "I saved his life, proving that I wouldn't hurt him and showing him that our clan, our MC, was full of good people, regardless of what we are." He shrugged. "Plus it gave Miranda a new world of healing that she enjoys dabbling in, and she made some new friends."

"Excuses, excuses," Luella singsonged and waved her free hand in the air. "The human thing is an excuse. You know full well that we have human MC members and human mates in our clan."

"But they're few." He glowered at Luella. "I'm sure there's more to you having coffee with me this morning than my love life—"

"Or lack of one," Luella quipped.

He held up one hand. "Let it go, honey."

"All right, but there is something I need to discuss with you."

"Such as?"

"You're not going to like it," Luella said.

He put his mug down again, sat back, and mentally braced himself. "Hit me with it."

"If folks don't start paying their dues soon, the community fund will be in the red."

"Shit, when did this happen?" Frank had suspected her statement, but had thought it would be a while yet before the matter arose. Financial hardship within the MC was no one's fault. It was just the way life often dealt its cards to folks, but it meant tougher times were ahead.

"It's been going on for a few weeks now," Luella explained. "For the last month, it's gotten worse. It's not that members are refusing to pay their dues. It's the fact that there's nothing to pay them with. So many worked at the mines, or at the aluminum plant, which have either been shut down, or are in the process of doing so, and others have been laid off from other jobs, too. Some of our members have gone to over-the-road trucking, but the promises those companies make don't pay people's bills. By the time a trucker's family takes care of utilities and necessities, there's nothing left of a paycheck. The companies affiliated with the energy industry have all the men they need right now, so there's a freeze on hiring."

Surprised by how much Luella knew about their members, he asked, "How do you know all this?"

"Like you, I take care of our MC, but in a different way. People come to me for advice, and just to talk, because they're scared. Not making ends meet causes folks to feel inadequate, like they're failures." Luella sighed and stared through the screen at Tractor mowing hay behind the workshop. "The community fund has enough in it for one more shopping trip. Then it will be in the red because so many members still owe for their groceries this last trip." She glanced over at him and then back at the John Deere making its rounds. "That translates to no funds to run the main house, Frank. No food, no laundry detergent, no toilet paper, no way to pay the electric bill... It takes a large chunk of money to run a household of 30 people."

"What's the total owed?"

"Right now? A little over $600, but after next month's trip folks will add more credit to their tabs. It'll be more—a lot more."

Frustrated, Frank asked, "Why didn't you say something sooner, Luella?"

"Because I thought that the money for the two motorcycles in the workshop would be paid to the MC by now." She scowled at him. "When I questioned Beastman he said that the one customer has run into financial troubles to pay for his bike, and the other bike is only into the first stages of its creation, so much of the down payment has gone to the parts and supplies."

"He's right," Frank said.

She groaned and shut her eyes for a moment. "It's not like it's the first time members have gotten behind on dues or paying off their tabs," she said, opening her eyes to look directly at him. "It's the fact that the economy is getting worse, and now folks are feeling it, and suffering because of it. There's no bounce-back money, no new hires, no new jobs...."

"I'm sorry, honey. I didn't mean for it to sound like I was accusing you of misleading me."

She relaxed and sat back in her chair, returning her attention to Tractor as he made another pass on his John Deere. "The community fund has always given leeway to folks to catch up if they don't have enough for groceries and various supplies. When I went around to talk to each family—and there's currently three who owe money—to find out why they've not paid, I realized how hard everyone is struggling. I mean, I knew that everyone was having tight times, but this time it's the worst it's been since I've handled the community's needs, which means the MC as a whole is going to struggle, too."

Frank leaned his head back as a cool morning breeze drifted through the screen. The gentle zephyr wavered over his heated face and neck, helping him focus. "Well, business is good at the tattoo and piercing parlor right now, so I'll advise Tom and Judilocks to raise prices some, which will help generate more revenue, but it won't be enough to solve this problem."

"I think it's time for some dealing, Frank."

He raised his head and stared at her, hard. "We're supposed to stay out of that shit."

"What else can we do?" she asked. "All our farming is to supplement our community. If the weather doesn't break and give us rain, the gardens will turn to shit. Everyone who can hold down a job already is—but it's not enough."

"I refuse to put our MC in jeopardy by entering the drug trade." The words came out as a growl. He shut his eyes and willed his inner beast to calm itself. "I won't even consider it, Luella."

"Dammit, Frank, cool your jets!" She huffed at him, her baby blues turning flinty. "I'm talking about a few trips transporting guns. Your daddy used to do it when things got tight."

He squeezed the arms of the recliner, his fingers biting into the soft leather until his knuckles ached. Granted, members' dues only took care of groceries, necessities, helping out a family short on money for their children's school clothes, or something like buying prescriptions if someone's insurance wouldn't cover them, but there hadn't been a need for additional funding until now. The MC and farm always made ends meet each month. After the '70s recession their community had been self-sufficient, with everyone pulling together if they got in a pinch. They'd seldom seen a profit, but they'd always rolled along just fine. They were simple people, needing little to be happy. Frank frowned and let another growl rumble out of him. The world was changing, and it appeared the MC might have to make some changes too, or the world was going to stamp over them, leaving wreckage in its wake.

"I'm *a lot* older than you, Frank. I saw how your daddy managed the MC with your mama handling the main house, and they were good people, but when things turned sour and folks were hungry or cold, they did what they had to, to take care of the MC. Something might be illegal, but doing it is called survival."

Frank shook his head. "No."

"It's either make some gun runs or sell the MC's gas and oil rights."

"I don't want to do that either, Luella."

"I know that, but—"

Frank held up one hand to her and raked his other through his hair, accidentally ripping the bandanna free from around his head. "We've had several club meetings about selling our rights, and we've all agreed unanimously that we don't want to disturb the earth on our property, and that this farm has been exceptionally good to us." With the head wrap in his hands he stared at it as if would provide him with an answer to their dilemma. "Selling our rights is a last resort."

"Be that as it may," Luella said, standing, "at the rate we're going, it won't be long before it becomes a last resort. We're the only ones in the area who haven't sold our mineral rights. And if you don't want to run guns, selling our rights is a *legal* alternative."

"Some of my father's contacts are still around, but the younger ones know more about who's in the biz."

"Such as Crow?"

He looked up. Luella wore her motherly you-never-listen-to-me expression.

"If I have to go through him, yes."

"Why do you have to go through that bastard?" Her mouth flattened into a thin line as she stared down at him in the recliner. "He's trouble. He'll double-cross you—or worse."

"He knows who has the guns, who needs only short transport trips—and you saw his clubhouse, Luella. One word for that place—damn."

A pissed-off sound burst from her. "Why do men have to be so stubborn *and* stupid?" She stomped into the kitchen. "Want more coffee, dumbass?" she shouted.

"Yes, please." He rose to join her in the kitchen. "And maybe a couple of those apple-cinnamon muffins that I smell baking."

Something clanged angrily in the sink. Deciding against going into the kitchen, he sat again and waited for Luella to bring the pot out to him. "Maybe she should be president of the MC," he mumbled.

* * *

After calling her mother and checking in with her, Bernadette decided to forgo working on her manuscript, unsure how to proceed with the next couple of pages. She'd let it bubble in her head a little longer and go in search of breakfast instead.

Downstairs she found Luella washing a few dishes by hand, dumping soapy utensils into the rinse water with a loud, angry clatter.

"Uhm, is it okay to come in?" Bernadette took one step back.

"Sure is," Luella commented. "Come in and get something to eat. I'm just venting my frustration because of that dumbass on the porch."

Bernadette didn't want to intrude on an argument, but her belly gurgled in protest, so she took a huge muffin from the bowl on the table, and then poured herself a cup of coffee from the carafe next to it.

"There's a nice breeze on the porch this morning," Luella said. "Enjoy it before the heat starts." She winked and returned to washing dishes.

Wondering what the wink was about, she took the first step down into the porch and froze. Frank sat with a mug next to him and a plate with a half-eaten muffin on his lap.

"Don't worry about Luella. She's pissed off at me," he said with his mouth full, "but she'll get over it. Sit and eat."

Her face heated, the warmth spreading down into her neck and even to her chest. Without looking at him, she chose a chair right next to a window, where several pots of violets in different hues bloomed on the sill. The voices of Phil, Tom, Beastman, and a couple others Bernadette didn't recognize clamored loudly in the kitchen, followed by Luella scolding her old man for spilling creamer all over the counter.

"Luella bakes the best muffins in the county," Frank stated. "The apple-cinnamon ones are my favorite."

Bernadette couldn't look at him. Silently, she cursed herself and him. Muzzy-headed, she cradled her coffee cup and sipped several times. Sleep had eluded her. After she'd returned to her room she'd jumped into a cold shower to shake herself out of her sex-crazed stupor. She couldn't believe she'd achieved an orgasm just by being kissed and touched by him. He hadn't even penetrated her with his fingers, his cock only grazing her folds, but she'd come apart as a crumbling iceberg upon entering tropical waters.

Staring out the window, Bernadette focused on the carport's concrete slabs, a cluster of blooming dandelions, the violets on the sill—anything to avoid looking at Frank. She nibbled on the muffin, not even tasting it. Dimly she heard the others quarreling and joking in the kitchen, someone yelling at a guy named Ass Crack. All she could center on was the feeling of Frank watching her, his gaze burning right through her clothes, probably seeing her skin covered in water droplets and the heated flush of arousal.

She gulped and a piece of muffin flew down her throat. Choking, she tried to swallow, but the morsel had a tidbit of apple in it and wedged so that she could barely breathe. Cinnamon burned her throat. Involuntarily, she sucked in a harder breath, the bite wedging tighter. She started seesawing between gasping and choking.

In an instant, Frank leaped to his feet and rushed to her side. "Bernadette? Honey, keep coughing. Get it out of there!" He pounded her on the back between her shoulder blades. "Come on, baby. Don't scare me like this!"

"What's going on out—?" Luella kneeled on the floor in front of Bernadette. "Look at me, sweetie."

"What's wrong with her?" Tom asked.

"She's choking, fuckwad," Phil snapped.

Beastman hollered, "Hold her up by her feet!"

"That's for babies, you moron."

"Well, do something," Beastman bellowed.

Still struggling for air, Bernadette tried to focus on the woman.

"When Frank hits you on the back again, cough really, really hard, okay?"

Bernadette blinked that she understood. Another strike connected between her shoulder blades, and she coughed extra hard. The piece of apple, wearing a wet, glistening coat of breading, flew out and landed on Luella's bare knee with a *splat*. Bernadette sucked in and let out several lungfuls of air until she'd regained her composure, tears of relief and fright spilling down her cheeks.

"You okay now, honey?" Luella used the kitchen towel in her hand to wipe up the coughed-up morsel.

"I am now. Thank you both."

"Double fuck," Beastman rumbled. "First time I've ever seen bikers rooting for someone to puke. Usually they wager on who will upchuck last."

Straightening, Luella demanded, "Will you please go outside? All of you, go on! Fill your cups and travel mugs, get your fucking muffins and get out." She threw her hands up in the air. "It's like an episode of Bikers Gone Stupid in here!"

"Fuck me sideways," Frank said on a big exhalation. "I've had enough chaos for one morning."

He rubbed Bernadette's shoulders, then pulled her back so that her head rested on his side. The action comforted her, and she smiled through the tears of relief and embarrassment.

Luella burst into a fit of giggles, looking at Frank. "And you think being in the main house is the easy part of the MC!" She picked up Bernadette's cup. "I'll warm this up for you, and I'll make you some scrambled eggs instead of another muffin."

Offering her a watery smile, Bernadette nodded. "Works for me."

The others collected their breakfasts and coffees then shuffled out to do chores, work in the garage, or drive off to their day jobs.

"You sure you're okay now?" Beastman asked as he brought up the rear.

"Yeah." She accepted her refilled mug from Luella who leaned around Beastman to hand it to her.

Beastman patted Bernadette awkwardly on her shoulder, surprising her with his show of kindness. Then he faced his old lady. "See you at lunchtime, babe. I'm in the office today, if you should need me." He kissed Luella and walked straight out to his Harley.

Soon the sound of him startling up his bike rattled the screens.

* * *

Frank sympathized with Bernadette. He'd been babbling about Luella's baking abilities to make small talk. What they'd shared last evening had been intense:

119

a combustible chemistry that should've evaporated the pond water, but Bernadette seemed ashamed by it—why?

He sat quietly finishing his breakfast, allowing Bernadette to recover herself, and, hopefully, realize that there was nothing about their steamy encounter that should embarrass her.

Luella appeared in the doorway. "Your plate is on the table with a cup of fresh coffee."

Nodding, Bernadette rose, swaying slightly so that Frank had to suppress the urge to jump to her side. She steadied herself and joined Luella in the kitchen. What the hell? What was he? The Plague? He'd be damned if she was going to live here for a few weeks or months and avoid him the entire time.

Wait. What was he thinking? He was going to send her back to Columbus where it was safe...right?

He groaned and ate the last two bites of his second muffin. He'd let her eat, calm herself by talking with Luella. Then he'd take Bernadette aside and tell her she needed to pack. Once she was gone, he would be able to think clearly again. With the rogue loose, and some possible arms transport deals brewing on the club's agenda, it was better that Bernadette was gone. If the deals, providing he secured one or two, went sour, he didn't want Bernadette involved in club business.

So why did it feel like someone had just hammered a stake through his heart?

Chapter Ten

With Frank on the porch, Bernadette could breathe easier. Every time she thought about their encounter in the pond, heat and prickles swept over her skin. She had to put the memory of how he'd made her come so easily to the back of her mind and padlock it.

"You seem really tense this morning," she said to Luella. "Is everything okay?"

"Not really." Luella poured herself a cup of coffee and across from her sat at the table "Mmm, it's nice to get off my feet. I hit the floor running at 6:00 a.m."

When she met Bernadette's gaze, Bernadette quirked her eyebrows and said, "So, if I'm not being nosey, what's up?"

"You're here to get dirt for your new book, so I don't see why I can't explain some things about our MC without giving out names or too many details," Luella said as she stirred sugar into her coffee.

A few minutes later, Luella finished her story.

"I can help," said Bernadette. "I don't expect the MC to provide free room and board and I just had a nice royalty payment go into my account, so I'll transfer a sum to the MC for…say a thousand dollars?" When Luella blinked at her, seemingly flabbergasted, Bernadette laughed. "Well, it's only fair, right? I think a grand will take care of my rent and food for the summer—unless you feel it should be more."

Blinking rapidly, Luella came back to herself. "No, not at all. I think a grand is fair for the summer. You've already shown you have no problem helping out with chores around here, so this is great—thank you."

"Wonderful," Bernadette stated. "Send my phone the info, and when I go upstairs, I'll transfer the money."

"You're something else, you know that?" Luella said.

"Nah, I'm just me, that's all." She stood and was about to put her dirty dishes in the sink, but they glided out of her hands and settled in the water on their own. Fear wedged in her gut. Cautiously, she glanced over her shoulder at Luella, who sat staring at her with wide, shocked eyes.

"Shit." Bernadette prayed the woman dismissed what she'd seen. Quickly Bernadette washed and rinsed everything, then set the items in the drainer.

"It's been a very long time since I've known a white witch," Luella said quietly. "Now I know why Frank's grandmother, Galina, was so interested in you. She must've sensed your power." She rose and placed her empty mug in the dishwater. "I knew something was different about you, but I never guessed it was magic."

"I'm not a witch," Bernadette said. "I don't practice magic. Things just...happen."

"You're Irish."

"So?"

"Oh, come on. You have to know about magic and things that normal people can't see."

Bernadette shook her head. "I don't. And I don't want to talk about it, okay?" When Luella said nothing, Bernadette deliberately changed the subject. "Thank you for the eggs. Anything you need help with?"

Luella favored her with a disapproving look but didn't push the issue. "Well, there's a mountain of dirty clothes in the laundry room," her friend said. "If you don't mind managing that today, I'll sort everything to go to the correct people later."

"I'll get busy."

* * *

Bernadette started another load of laundry and dropped the lid down with a *clang*. There was already a dryer full of finished clothes, so she pulled them out into a basket, then set it on a utility table pushed against a window where sunshine streamed across it. As she folded work-worn jeans and stained T-shirts, something popped into her mind. Luella had said it had been a long time since she'd known a white witch and that Frank's mom and grandmother must've sensed her power. How could they have sensed something like that? Did Luella know many witches?

Magic ran in the Kelly family, but her mother had told her it often skipped several generations. It had been so long since the Kellys had exhibited anything more than knowing things before they happened that when

Bernadette began moving objects without touching them, and occasionally shattering items with a glance, her mother had instructed her to keep the gift to herself, to hide it from others. Her mom had insisted that having such powers today would either make her the butt of jokes, ruining her life, or she'd end up in a laboratory somewhere and never see the light of day again.

Uncertainty danced at the back of Bernadette's mind, but she dismissed her anxiety that her ability always caused. Instead, she let her mind wander back over what had happened with her and Frank at the pond.

She barely knew the man and had come apart at the seams. He must think she was a floozy. *Oh hell, does he consider me a sweet butt?* Mortified, she tried to focus on the sound of the washer kicking over to the rinse cycle. The water trickled into the tank, the sound oddly soothing.

"Can I speak with you?"

She gasped and performed a little jig where she stood. Turning, she glared at Frank. "Why do you insist on scaring the hell out of me?"

"I'm the Big Bad Wolf." The huge, rakish smile he offered Bernadette took her breath away. "So it's my job to scare you."

She huffed at him and faced the mountain of laundry she'd been folding.

"Hey, I'm only teasing you."

Wilting, she said, "I know. I guess I'm just uptight."

"About?"

She sensed more than heard him move closer. Instantly, her pulse kicked into warp drive.

"Bernadette."

The way he said her name rumbled right through her and stoked an ember in her pussy.

"Just leave me alone, Frank, please."

His hands settled on her shoulders, the heat from his palms stoking that glowing ember within her to an even brighter coal. He turned her around, landing his hands on the tops of her hips. She couldn't meet his eyes. Instead, she stared at the cotton T-shirt peeking from behind his cut, a cut with numerous patches from how many charity runs he'd ridden in to ones that commemorated someone's death, another denoting how many miles he'd accumulated on his Harley, to the patch that stated he was the president of his MC, which was a smaller, slightly different version of the MC's emblem, a howling wolfman on the back of his cut. She'd have to remember to take some pictures for her book.

"Hey, you're here in my MC. I'm the president and I own this house, this property. I'm allowing you to stay here, so talk to me." He hooked two fingers under her chin and forced her to look up at him. Heat flashed into her cheeks and along her throat, then down into the swell of her breasts. "My, my, you sure do look pretty in pink," he mused, his eyes bright with amusement. "Don't be ashamed about last night. I'm not."

She couldn't look at him, so she closed her eyes. "I've..." She swallowed. Heaven help her, this was difficult. "I've never done anything like that before."

"What? Kiss a man in a pond?" More humor tinged his voice.

"No, not that."

"Shatter in someone's arms like you did?"

Oh, there it was. The ugly, embarrassing truth. Why did it have to sound so crude when he vocalized the words? Unable to even glance up at him, she nodded, once.

"Aw, baby, don't be embarrassed," he murmured and placed a delicate kiss on her forehead. "You were a beautiful sight to behold."

Her eyes popped open. That was the last thing she'd expected to hear.

At her reaction, he chuckled. "Seriously, I've seen some pretty women, but you're…"

Before she could react, he kissed her again, this time on the mouth, tickling the seam of her lips with his tongue. Unable to help herself, she moaned and eagerly sought more bodily contact with him, slipping her hands under his cut and palming his sides. The chugging of the John Deere in the back field, the trickle of water in the washer and the *tings* and *clicks* of zippers and snaps in the dryer all faded. Only Frank's touches and low groans of enjoyment mattered to Bernadette.

He embraced her, fully pulling her against his body, cupping her ass cheek with one hand and the other under her arm and splayed across her back. The closeness inflamed her senses. She drew in his scent, a wild mix of pure testosterone, skin warmed by the sun, and a light, crisp cologne. If aromas could inebriate her, Frank's did. Her senses spun and she gave herself over to him.

With a growl that roused her from her sex-hazed stupor, he palmed her ass harder and hefted her, swinging to the right and planting her on top of the washer. The cold metal on the backs of her bare thighs jolted her senses. She shouldn't be doing this. It wasn't right to let a man she barely knew kiss and touch her, was it? Would he think she was going to be one of the MC's sweet butts?

He stepped between her knees and wrapped his arms around her. When she stiffened, he frowned. "What's wrong?"

"Nothing. I…"

"Talk to me."

"I'm not a…" Every word she settled on seemed so crude. Finally, she said, "I don't want you to think I'm a sweet butt."

He blinked. "Is that what's bothering you? You're afraid that I think you're easy or that if you're here, you'll be expected to fuck whoever wants you?"

Humiliated, she stared at the snap on his jeans and barely nodded.

Again, he used to fingers to draw her head up. "Oh, baby, don't worry."

Lord, why did he have to have to call her "baby" in such a deep, sexy voice? Already she sensed her willpower, what little she'd managed to gather, faltering.

"I'm sorry," she whispered.

He kissed her words away, once again leaving her breathless. "None of the women here are expected to be sheep. They have sex with the men because they want to—not to keep a roof over their heads or clothes on their backs. You already know that the Werewolves of Rebellion isn't a one-percenter MC. Everyone here has free will and we take care of each other. No one is expected to put out, and any man who may think otherwise will be dealt with harshly. Women are to be respected, not used."

She gaped at him, and he chuckled, the action deepening the laugh lines around his mouth and eyes.

"You have a lot to learn about the Werewolves of Rebellion," he added. "As for last night with you, I don't regret it one bit. But if I offended you, I apologize."

"No, it wasn't that. It was…" How did she explain it without sounding sappy?

"It was the fact that you've never felt that way before?"

Again, she stared at him, awestruck. How did he know what she was thinking?

"Yeah," she said. "It shocked me."

"Then let me shock you some more," he murmured against her lips.

He wedged himself tighter between her knees, simultaneously pulling her to the edge of the washer so his pelvis hugged her pussy. He held her tightly by her hips, his fingers biting painfully into the muscles, but at the same time the pain further aroused her.

As he slanted his mouth over hers, deepening the kiss, the washer switched over to the spin cycle. The drum began spinning, jiggling the machine, the vibrations penetrating Bernadette's folds. She whimpered at the sensory overload.

Frank delved his tongue into her mouth, moving it in a rhythm that imitated sex. Between the washer's vibrations, the hard rise of his cock through his jeans rubbing her slit, and the way he kept her firmly rooted to his pelvis pushed her ever closer to another orgasm. How was it possible that this man could make her climax without actual penetration? The few relationships she'd had had been all about getting her to that point only for her to experience a firecracker orgasm without the entire firework display. What would Frank do to her if they actually made love?

She moaned, then moaned again until she dimly noticed she sounded just like the soundtrack on a skin flick. Each time she made a sound, Frank's arousal seemed to climb higher. Soon, he was moving his hips in time to the gyrating drum in the washer. If he built the friction any more against her pussy, she'd—

A long, high-pitched whistle startled Bernadette, followed by, "Holy fuck, Frank! At least close the door!"

A cry of dismay ripped from her. Frank froze. The washer kept spinning. Sitting on top of it with the vibration buzzing her ass and jiggling her boobs, Bernadette wished a hole would open in the floor and swallow her, never to be seen again. Not knowing how to react, she hid her face against Frank's chest.

"Fuck, Phil!" Frank bellowed. "Don't you know how to look the other way?"

"Fucking hard to do when I was just on my way in here with some dirty laundry."

The sound of a basket hitting the linoleum startled Bernadette again and she flinched in Frank's arms.

"Get lost!" Frank growled. The sound rolled through him and sounded like thunder in her ear where she had it pressed to his skin.

"Damn, Frank," Phil protested. "How was I to know the laundry room had become the house fuck room?"

"*Out!*"

Phil's footsteps retreated to the kitchen.

Pushing at his chest, Bernadette managed to get Frank to step back reluctantly. With her crotch tingling, pulse pounding, and her knees feeling as though they'd been replaced with gelatin, she moved away from him and leaned against the folding table for support.

"Sorry about Phil," Frank said. "Hell, I'm sorry I never thought to shut the door. I got so wrapped up in kissing you that it never crossed my mind."

"You…you said you wanted to talk to me." She turned her back to him and reached for a towel from another stack in the center of the table, her hand trembling.

He stood quietly, her sudden avoidance of what had happened between them becoming the elephant in the laundry room.

His silence was excruciating. How could she discuss their physical attraction when she didn't understand it?

"Fine." He shuffled his feet.

Bernadette placed another folded towel on the growing stack. "And?" she urged.

"I want you to go back to Columbus."

Stunned, she spun to face him. "What? Why? I mean, no!"

"You're not safe here," he said, face stoic. "I've already explained this to you."

"So now you want me to leave?" A barrage of emotions—anger, hurt, disbelief, humiliation—bowled her over. "Is your kissing and touching me all about manipulation? A way to get me to do what you want

130

me to? If so, you're an ass!" She whirled and folded towels through a blur of tears, but they only pissed her off more. Blinking them back, she decided she'd be damned if she let Frank see her cry.

He sighed. "No, that's not why I've kissed you. I don't want you to go, but—"

"Then why send me away?" The slight crack in her voice silenced any more questions or retorts. If she opened her mouth again, she'd burst into tears despite her resolve not to. Crying in front of Frank would make her weak.

"If you're here at my MC," he explained, "you're my responsibility. Another matter aside from the one I told you about has come up. You're not safe here."

She barely managed to gulp down another round of tears. If she couldn't stay here to do her research, then she'd go back... Elation suddenly swept through her. "Fine. Send me away. I'll just go back to Crow. I'm sure he can use my thousand dollars for *his* club."

"You're not going to stay with—wait. What thousand dollars?"

Suddenly triumphant, she kept her voice neutral. "I transferred a grand over to your MC's household account. I didn't want to stay here for free, eating the club's food, using its supplies..." She shrugged. "I'll tell Luella to send it back to me."

"Fuck!"

She cringed at the forcefulness of his curse.

"Luella!" He walked to the kitchen doorway. "Luella!"

"What the hell, Frank?" Luella's voice came from the living room. "The toddlers are upstairs napping, and you're rattling the rafters with your big mouth."

131

He lowered his voice to a normal decibel and ground out, "Will you please come in here?"

Slowly, Bernadette turned, a towel clenched tightly in her hands. Frank strode back to her, pausing in the threshold of the utility room. Behind him, Luella appeared and stood in the center of the short hall connecting the kitchen to the laundry.

"What has your panties in a knot?" The woman fixed Frank with a disapproving look.

"Did you accept money from Bernadette for rent and food?" he demanded.

She met Bernadette's gaze briefly. Bernadette could only imagine what she looked like to Luella. Her heart tapped out a dance that had spots flitting in front of her eyes, and ringing began in her ears too.

The woman flicked her attention back to Frank. "Yes, I did. Why? She offered, we needed the funds, and it seemed to make her feel better to pay the MC rent and money for groceries. After all, she *will* be here for the next three months or so, right?"

"Did you not hear me when I said that…?" He swung his gaze from Luella to Bernadette, then back to Luella. "I told you it wasn't safe here for her, that I…" He raked one hand through the top of his hair, dislodging his bandanna. It fell to the floor unnoticed by him. "Aw, fuck it."

He brushed past Luella, then through the kitchen and out onto the porch. The screen door slapped shut, echoing his anger.

"What was that all about?" Luella asked.

"He was sending me back to Columbus. I said I'd go back to Crow for my research, that he'd take my money."

"But you haven't transferred any money to us—oh, I get it now." She laughed, the sound light and warming. As Luella went into the kitchen, she said, "It appears that Frank has *finally* met his match."

Bernadette followed her. "You knew Frank was going to send me home?"

At the sink, Luella began washing a few odds and ends of dishes that had been dropped into the wash water. "Yeah, he mentioned it this morning, but I didn't really think he'd do it."

"What do you mean he's met his match? We're not a couple."

"You are, you both just don't realize it yet."

"I'm here to write my book, that's all. I believe it will be a best seller, and I want to convey through my words and pictures what bikers have been saying for years about being normal, everyday people like anyone else."

"Chill, girl." Luella turned and confronted her, water dripping off her hands. "All I'm saying is there's major chemistry between you two and I think it scares him. That's the reason he wants to send you home, whether he wants to admit it or not."

Bernadette read the sincerity in her friend's eyes. "If Frank wants me to stay close to the house," she told Luella, "that's fine, but there's no reason to send me home. I'll go back to Crow if I have to."

"You're not going anywhere, honey," Luella replied. "You scare Frank."

"I what?"

"You're different, a type of woman Frank has never encountered before, and you challenge his intellect. A smart woman scares the hell out of all men, let alone Frank." She rinsed the dishes and put them in the drainer. Finished, she faced Bernadette. "He doesn't know how to handle you, honey. You're not the giggling, willing pieces of ass he's used to, and if you have abilities like I witnessed earlier, some part of Frank must sense the power in you too."

"He doesn't know anything about me," Bernadette stated. How could she not have noticed they hadn't shut the door? What they must have looked like to Phil. Inwardly, she grimaced. "Now Frank is telling me that another matter for the MC has come up and that it puts me in further danger."

"It's the money matter," Luella stated. "He may have to line up some…distasteful work. Something that makes fast, easy money but it's dangerous too."

"Oh?"

"The less you know, the better, but it's not drugs—I promise. The Werewolves of Rebellion never make, sell or transport drugs." The way Luella said it with such conviction left no doubt in Bernadette's mind that she spoke the truth. "Once this job is handled," Luella continued, "the club should be right as rain for a while."

Bernadette nodded. It wouldn't be right to push for more information. For now, she was still with the Werewolves of Rebellion, and that's all that mattered.

Chapter Eleven

Phil found Frank in the garage putting a belt back on one of the rider mowers. In the back, Hudson sat on an old milk crate hand-sanding rust off another mower.

"Hey, Frank," Phil said as he walked in.

"Hey."

"I'm sorry about today."

Frank snorted. "Not your fault. I just never even thought to shut the door, so it surprised me when you were suddenly there."

"You got a hard-on for that ginger?"

"Seems that way. Pisses me off too."

Phil chuckled and patted him on the shoulder. "So bed her, then forget her."

"You know I can't do that, Phil. Fuck 'em and truck 'em isn't my style."

"Yeah, that's probably why I've never settled down," Phil admitted. "I just don't see myself attached to only one woman."

"One day it'll happen," Frank told him. "A woman will walk past you and you'll be floating three feet off the ground behind her with your tongue *and* your dick hanging out."

"Well, from what Galina said, you've found the flame to your fire."

"Fuck you," Frank growled.

Laughing harder, Phil shook his head.

Frank glanced over at Hudson, who had finished the sanding. The guy began prying the lid off a small can of paint with a screwdriver. "Do you have news, Phil?" Frank asked.

"Yeah." He helped Frank put the mowing deck into position to attach it to the rider. He dropped his voice. "I rode over to the Wraithkillers' MC. Asked to speak with Crow, got an audience and explained that we want him to line something up for us. It'll cost us 20 percent of what we make, though."

"Damn!" Frank fastened the deck then stood. "Why so much?"

"He said it was ten percent for helping and ten percent for the first-time hookup."

"More like for the first-time fucking."

"Pretty much," Phil agreed as he straightened and stepped back. "But we're getting a high four figures." He passed a slip of paper to Frank with the pickup destination, the date and time, and amount for transporting the weapons. As Frank studied it, Phil said, "That will help, won't it?"

"Yes," Frank answered, pocketing the note. "But I think we'll have to do a couple runs, maybe three, to keep our heads above water for a while."

"Crow said if we wanted more work and there were no probs with our run, he could probably line up a couple more jobs for us."

"The paper didn't say who we're running guns for?"

"Actually, I have some new information," Phil stated.

Frank eyed him skeptically, an uneasy feeling winding through him.

Behind him, a thud, followed by cussing, forced him to turn around.

"Sorry, Boss," Hudson said as he rushed to set the paint can upright again. Red paint pooled on the floor at his feet, and splatters of the liquid covered his pants and boots.

Frank pulled a big box out from under the work counter. "Here are rags. There's paint thinner and turpentine under there too. Do the best you can to get the paint off the floor."

"Will do," the young prospect-to-be said and began wiping paint up with rags.

"A new MC has moved into the area," Phil began. "I think you need to call a meeting with your top men, and I'll explain everything then. They're the ones we're working for."

Frank nodded. "All right. Let everyone know we'll meet an hour after dinner."

"I'm on it," his second-in-command said as he left the workshop.

"Phil?"

"Yeah?"

"What was on the trail cam?" Frank questioned.

"Not a damn thing except a bird and cattails. We disposed of the cam too."

"Good."

Once Phil was gone, the bad feeling that had suddenly descended on Frank grew worse, darker. Part of him wished the cam had had something on it that would give them a clue who was responsible for the murders, but the other part of him was relieved.

However, something wasn't right about the gun run, which pushed thoughts of the rogue from his mind for now. Maybe he should find another way to make some money. Hell, the only other thing they could do would be to have a fundraiser, and that would make his MC look greedy and lazy. They could resort to making and selling drugs, but that went against everything the Werewolves of Rebellion stood for, and he refused to enter into the drug trade. Too many people's lives were ruined by drugs whether someone made them, transported them or sold them.

Uneasy, Frank got on the mower. "When you get that mess cleaned up and a coat of paint on the mower, get back to work on mucking stalls."

"I will, Boss," Hudson replied from where he had mopped up the last of the paint.

Frank started up the rider and puttered out of the garage and onto the grass. He lowered the blades and focused on mowing the lawns around the house. Maybe if he was in the sun long enough, it would burn all the worries out of his brain.

* * *

After Bernadette finished with the laundry, she headed up to her room to work on her notes, then her manuscript. The heat building in the upstairs eventually forced her to quit early.

She pushed up from the chair, her ass half-numb from the hard seat. She stretched, her back popping pleasantly, and strode to the bathroom to wipe herself off. Feeling better, she headed downstairs. Luella had asked her to gather eggs from the chicken coup when she was done working. She'd never gathered eggs before, but how hard could it be?

As she passed through the kitchen, she snagged the basket Luella had set out for her on the table, waved to Phil and Puppy resting on the porch and walked out into the unbearable weather. On the carport, the day's heat radiating from the concrete slabs had Bernadette feeling as though she were cooking on a hot plate.

The coop was supposed to be to the right side of the main barn. As she walked the path leading to the barns and outbuildings, she admired the neatness of the lawns. Since the sun was going down, several members were out tending to and watering the huge vegetable gardens on the flat side yard. Others watered the riot of blooms in flowerbeds, pots and anything else that served as a good place to plant flowers. She got a glimpse of Frank mowing grass behind the workshop, but when he passed behind the building, the sound of another mower drew her attention and she caught sight of the John Deere making passes back and forth in the apple orchard. She smiled. One thing was certain, the MC was a hub of activity seven days a week.

Drawing closer to the barn, she paused when chunks of manure flew over the fence of an outdoor pen to land in a growing pile. She resumed walking and stepped off the path to make sure a piece of manure didn't accidentally strike her. When she saw Hudson, as the potential prospect, she kept her gaze averted.

He noticed her and used it as an excuse to rest. "Hey!"

"Hi." She kept walking.

"Bernadette, right?"

Damn. Something about Hudson really unnerved her. She didn't want to be rude, but somehow she got the feeling that talking to him wasn't a good idea. Besides, standing in the cloying humidity was the last thing she wanted to do. Sweat had already begun to form between her breasts and at the small of her back.

"Yeah," she answered and kept walking.

"The chickens are probably going to go off their laying," he continued.

"Oh?" Bernadette paused. She didn't want to talk to him, but she knew next to nothing about farming and animals, so she was curious.

Nodding, he gave her a huge, toothy grin. "I grew up on my uncle's farm. When it gets really nasty like this or too cold, it messes with the chicken's laying habits. They prefer steady temperatures. People with poultry farms have to use air-conditioning and heaters in the big chicken barns to maintain constant temperatures."

"Didn't know that," she said. "Don't get overheated out here." She waved politely and hurried on her way, praying he didn't say anything else to deter her.

At the coop, she entered through a back door just big enough for a person to step inside. Someone had hooked up a fan on one end to blow air through to the other. The racket of the small generator powering it overwhelmed the space. Twenty or so chickens surrounded the outside of the coop or sat on box nests. She didn't know the breed of the birds, their vibrant, deep red color reminding her of the water barrel full of red geraniums she'd passed on the way there, but their feathers were quite pretty. She approached the first hen and slid her hand under the bird's body like Luella had instructed her. The bird stiffened, but nothing was in the nest. Bernadette progressed from box to box, some with eggs, some without. When she reached the last nest, the hen pecked her hand.

"Ow!"

She looked at her skin to find a bit of blood. Trying again, Bernadette jerked her hand away when the hen pecked her a second time.

"You nasty little shit!"

She snatched her hand back and decided to move on to the last bird, but just as she reached toward the hen, it lunged, flapping it red wings in a blur, sending dust and bits of straw into the air. The chicken battered Bernadette about the head and shoulders. She screamed, stumbling backward and dropping the basket of eggs to guard her head and face with her forearms. The chicken wouldn't back off, repeatedly pecking her on the head and gouging her with its feet. Bernadette screamed again.

As she finally managed to reach the door, another chicken flew out of its nest in alarm and joined the first hen in flogging her. More screams burst from Bernadette, her heart flailing hard against her ribs.

The door opened behind her and someone grabbed her by the waist. He yanked her outside, then, once she was out of the way and pressed against the hot wooden wall, he slammed the door shut. She looked up into Hudson's sweaty face.

"Are you okay?" he asked.

"I don't know." Shaking, she tried to keep her tears at bay. "I was collecting all the eggs, then the last chicken just went crazy and came at me." She held out her arms and turned them from side to side. Bloody scratches covered her skin. "I didn't do anything to that hen," she said, touching the stinging places in her hair. "Honest."

"Stay here." Hudson stepped inside, then returned with the basket of eggs. "Looks like only two are broken, so you still have a good haul this evening." Smiling, he set the basket on the grass, then straightened and examined her arms and even bent forward to check the places she indicated on her head. "None of the pecks on your scalp broke the skin. Just red marks. And your arms are scratches."

"Thanks for the help," she said. "It's a miracle you even heard me with the generator and the mower going."

"I kept hearing something, but only when the mower passed behind the garage." Hudson brushed a thick lock of hair out of her eyes and tucked it behind her ear. "I quickly realized what direction it was coming from and figured you'd found a mean-tempered hen."

Her pulse slowed and the adrenaline rushing through her system began to abate. "Thank you, Hudson."

Before she could stop them, tears leaked from each eye.

"Aw, honey." Hudson used the pads of his thumbs to brush the drops away. "You're not a farmer's daughter, are you?"

Lower lip trembling, Bernadette shook her head. She met his gaze, intent on thanking him again, but as she started to speak, he lowered his head and claimed her mouth. Shocked, she stood ramrod stiff as her brain processed what was happening. The rough-hewn planks of the coop met her backside again as Hudson pushed her against the wall, his entire length pressed firmly to her front.

He tasted of mint gum and his own personal flavor, and the scent of perspiring male body invaded her senses. Bernadette finally came to herself and shoved at his shoulders, but he didn't even budge. As she refused to kiss him back, he kissed her harder, made it more demanding.

"Mmph!" She shoved at him again. When he didn't move, she raised one knee, but he must have been expecting the move and slid one thick thigh between her legs, wedging his hip tightly to her pubic bone.

She uttered another indignant sound, but he swallowed it as he persisted in kissing her, a hand on either of her arms, pinning them to her sides.

The sound of the rider grew louder and drowned out the noise of the humming generator and fans. The mower's engine suddenly stopped, followed by the halt of whirring blades. Out of the corner of her eye, Bernadette caught movement. Hudson was fully in her personal space, his mouth locked to hers, then he was suddenly gone, his body airborne. He landed on his back several feet away. The young prospect-to-be leaped to his feet with such speed and ease that Bernadette gaped at him, unable to believe what she'd just seen. Although his face registered surprise, it soon flashed to anger.

Bernadette swiped the back of one hand over her mouth, trying to remove the taste of Hudson. She met Frank's gaze, a murderous light in his eyes.

"Did he hurt you?"

"No," she answered.

"Dude, what the fuck's your problem?" Hudson snapped.

Judging by his stance, Bernadette figured he was about to attack Frank.

"Why the fuck did you have her pinned against the wall, taking liberties that aren't yours to take?" Frank countered.

He drew himself up to his full height, shoulders back, chest out. Bernadette knew Frank was tall, but standing straight, the lines of his body rigid with hostility, drove home just how large of a man he was, one whom she wouldn't want to piss off.

Hudson studied him for a long moment, then said, "I rescued Bernadette from a flogging. I was checking her over for injuries, then one thing led to another."

Frank looked at Bernadette. There, deep in his eyes, doubt resided.

"I didn't invite him to kiss me," she said forcefully. She turned her attention to Hudson. "I never gave you any sign that you could kiss me. I was scared. You helped me out of a jam, but that's all it was."

Several emotions twisted across Hudson's face—anger, surprise, realization, and 'oh shit, I just screwed up.' "Damn, Bernadette. I'm sorry. I just... I thought..." His shoulders slumped. He met Frank's gaze. "Are you two...?"

"No," Frank bit out. He bent and retrieved the egg basket and handed it to Bernadette. "Go up to the house and let one of the women take a look at your wounds. Next time, Luella needs to send someone down here to show you how to gather eggs." He pointed at Hudson. "Take your ass back to the barn and finish mucking stalls or get out and don't come back. You get one strike and this was it."

Hudson threw a last, lingering look at Bernadette, but she glanced away, hating the guilt she felt, despite the fact she was the one who had been wronged.

"Am I going to have to worry about him now?" she asked Frank.

"I'll keep an eye on him," he said. "Can't blame him for being smitten with a beautiful woman, but if he tries anything with you again, I'll thrash his ass seven ways from Sunday." He smoothed a finger along the longest scratch on her left arm. "Go up to the house, baby. Get some ointment on these."

Confused, legs trembling, Bernadette gripped the basket and trekked up the trail to the house. She couldn't seem to wrap her mind around what had just happened. She was grateful for Hudson's aid, but marveled at how she'd been offended by his kiss when she'd let Frank feel her up and kiss her as though she belonged to him. Hudson was a great-looking guy, well built. But she felt no attraction to him whatsoever.

And there was an element about Hudson that put Bernadette off. It wasn't overtly strong, but still there nonetheless. She couldn't lay her finger on what it was. From now on, she'd make sure she avoided the guy.

When she reached the house and walked inside, Puppy jumped up from where she sat mending jeans.

"Holy shit, Bernadette!" She rushed over to her. "What happened?" Her gaze landed on the basket full of eggs. "Luella, you forgot to tell Bernadette about Boxer Betty!"

"What are you talking about?" Luella appeared in the doorway. "Oh Lord. I just assumed you know how to…" Red crept up the woman's neck and settled in her cheeks. "I am so *very* sorry, Bernadette! Come into the utility room. I'll get you cleaned up and put some antibacterial ointment on your scratches. I feel so stupid. I never thought about the fact that you wouldn't know anything about farm animals."

As Bernadette followed Luella into the kitchen, Puppy carried the eggs behind them.

In the laundry room, she sat on a stool while Luella took out a first aid kit from a cabinet. The dryer still tossed laundry, the aroma of Downy thick in the air. On the tabletop, tall piles of folded clothes still remained, but the neat stacks of towels, baby blankets and sheets had all been removed. At a loss on how to process what had happened with Hudson, she began telling Luella about it.

"He's lucky Frank didn't break him in half," Luella said as she fished through the box for bandages. "Our MC treats women with respect. We're not here as sheep."

"I don't want to have to worry about Hudson trying anything else with me," Bernadette replied. She held her arms out for her friend to examine, the longest scratch beginning to burn. "And I'm conflicted about…"

Luella didn't even look at her, merely focused on swabbing ointment on her scratches. "About Frank?"

"Yeah."

"I heard about what happened this morning. Poor Phil felt really bad about walking in on you two."

"Oh hell." Fire rushed to Bernadette's face.

A giggle escaped Luella. "Me and Beastman got caught in the actual act when we were first together. Sweet Butt night isn't like it is at other MCs. Here, nights are designated for those who want to scratch an itch, so everyone vacates the house during those hours or goes to non-sex rooms like the kitchen. One night— a normal night—we thought we had the house to ourselves because everyone was down in the community for a big barbecue Tractor was hosting. Beastman bent me over the side of the sofa, pounding into me like there was no tomorrow, then Puppy and Shirley walked in on us."

"What happened?"

"Oh, they were embarrassed and bowed gracefully out of the room—although it sent Puppy into a fit of laughter. I was mortified, but Beastman bragged about it to anyone who would listen." She laughed again and peeled the paper off a Band-Aid. "Do you like Frank?"

The question caught her off guard. She waited as Luella checked the places on her scalp that still smarted, then replied, "I'm attracted to him—a lot. But I don't know him. I mean, he's gone or off somewhere doing whatever it is that he does, so I've not been able to learn much about him. But I've only been here a couple days. He did tell me about his last name, how his family are known as healers."

"Chemistry," Luella said. "It's dangerous, so be careful. Don't lead him on. If you're not sure whether or not you really want to get to know him—even if it's purely physical—tell him up front. There's no sense in letting him develop feelings for you if you don't think you'll come to care for him or be here long enough to build something with him." She kissed the top of Bernadette's head. "No broken skin here."

"Thank you for the first aid," Bernadette said, grabbing one of Luella's hands and squeezing. "And what you said about me and Frank makes a lot of sense, so thanks for the advice too. *Really*."

"I'm a pretty good judge of character." Turning, Luella threw the bandage papers away. "And I know you're a good person with firm ethics. However, you come in an incredible package, honey, so that's bound to create problems. You send out signals of raw sex, even though you don't mean to."

"Good grief." Bernadette covered her face with her hands. "Sometimes having a great body and a pretty face is a nightmare."

Warm hands touched hers. She looked up into Luella's eyes as she pulled Bernadette's hands away and smiled at her. "I imagine it's very frustrating. If Hudson tries anything else, kick or punch him in the nuts and scream your head off. Someone is always around to help. If he persists with you, it'll ruin his chances of becoming one of the MC's prospects. Okay?"

Finally relaxing, Bernadette nodded. "Okay."

Chapter Twelve

That evening, after the dining room had been ridded of supper dishes and everything wiped down, Frank called the men together while the women settled on the porch with the children and relaxed. He'd made sure Bernadette sat to his side again during the meal, but every time he'd tried to meet her gaze, she'd turned so red it nearly matched her hair color. It had taken all his energy not to beat Hudson into a bloody pile that afternoon, and even more strength not to launch himself over the dinner table at him.

Tractor ushered the prospects-to-be, including Hudson, out of the dining room, then shut the double doors.

"This meeting starts now," Phil announced as the men settled in chairs or stood around the room. "We're here to discuss the new prospects-to-be and a business matter." He nodded to Frank. "Boss."

Quickly Frank filled everyone in on what had transpired with Hudson and Bernadette. "Keep an eye on this guy," he said. "I put him in his place and he swears he didn't mean any harm, but..." He looked at Tom. "I'm sorry, Tom. I know you've vouched for Hudson, but there's something not quite right about this guy."

"Hey, no problem, Boss," Tom said. "This is your MC, your farm."

"Make sure he straightens up and flies right or he's out of here," Frank said.

"Will do."

"The next matter at hand," Frank said, "is a business opportunity for the MC." He explained the situation of the three families in the worst financial trouble, the work that was no longer available, and the financial hardship they were all facing if they didn't make some money soon. He paused, allowing the information to sink in with everyone.

"Business is slow with Nightshade Wolves. As you all know, the first half of the money paid to us for a custom-made wolf goes to supplies and anything we can't make here in the shop. The other order for a wolf is on hold because the customer is having some of his own money matters he wasn't expecting." He sighed and let his gaze wander over everyone in the room. "So it all leads us to why I've called this meeting. The Wraithkillers have agreed to set us up with someone to run guns and make some fast dough." He launched into the explanation with all the run details. "I don't want to do this, but I'm at a loss on what else we can do to make some money. Also, I'm not going to force anyone to participate in the runs, so I'll ask for volunteers."

Later, with volunteers in place for two separate runs, Frank sat back as Phil adjourned the meeting. Running guns didn't sit well with Frank at all, but what else could they do? Ginseng hunting wouldn't provide enough money fast enough, and it digging ginseng wouldn't be legal for several weeks. Neither would women's yard or bake sales yield helpful funds. And no one wanted aid from the state—too many questions were asked that were none of the government's business.

Once only Phil and Beastman were left in the dining room, Frank leaned forward and rested his forehead on his folded arms and groaned.

"You okay, Boss?" Beastman asked.

"Yeah, it's just that this gunrunning thing makes me want to sprout fur. My wolf is telling me this is a bad, bad idea."

"It's either guns or drugs," Phil interjected. "Besides, if we don't do something soon, families will go hungry."

"Prison time doesn't feed mouths either," Frank replied, straightening.

"Well on that happy fucking note"—Beastman rose, then pushed his chair in—"I'm going to see if there's any dessert left.

"I'll go with you," Phil said. "Don't know what that stuff is called the gals made, but it's awesome."

Once they'd left, Frank sat quietly, listening to their bantering as they dished out more of the cobbler. Something about the meeting left him unsettled, as if there were more going on with the gun delivery than he knew. Perhaps it was the new gang in the area. Maybe it was the fact they could get caught and serve time. Whatever it was, it raised the hair on his nape.

That meant only one thing—trouble. If Bernadette insisted on remaining with his MC, then he needed to have a long talk with her and lay down some ground rules.

* * *

Bernadette finished a scene in her manuscript, then read over it. She'd have to change the names of the MCs and the people, unless they gave her written permission to use their names, and the same applied to any photographs she might take. She'd discuss it with Frank when she had the chance.

Bernadette saved her file on the hard drive, backed it up on a flash drive, and shut her laptop. She sat watching the flare from the pad the next ridge over, it's color white-yellow, and pondered whether to shower and go to bed early or to wander downstairs for a snack.

A soft knock on the door brought her up off her seat. She hurried to the door, expecting Luella or one of the other women. As the door swung back, Bernadette froze.

"Oh. What do you want?" she asked.

"Wow. Close the door and I'll knock again," Frank replied.

"I'm sorry," she said. "I wasn't expecting you." She stepped back and motioned for him to come inside. "You just startled me, that's all."

He entered the room and stood so that she couldn't close the door. "I thought I'd ask you out to a movie."

"Really? I didn't see a theater in Rebellion. Well, I did, but it looks like it's an auction house now."

He smirked. "It is, but I wasn't talking about an actual theater."

She quirked an eyebrow. What was he getting at?

His smirk slid into a wide grin. "Trust me, you'll like it."

"Sure, why not?" She looked down at herself, then let her gaze rove over him in fresh jeans and a clean, pocket T-shirt. "Should I change?"

"Nah, you're fine. Meet me at my bedroom in five."

"Where *are* we going?"

"Like I said, trust me." He turned and walked down the hall.

Now thoroughly curious, she hurried to freshen up. She pulled her hair out of its ponytail, brushed it quickly, then swept it up into a messy, curly bun and secured it with a hair tie. She checked her face in the mirror over the dresser, put on a coat of deodorant under each arm, and slipped her feet into her flip-flops. Flicking off the lights, she shut her door and met Frank at his bedroom door just as he stepped out. In one arm, he held a folded, fuzzy blanket. In the other two fat throw pillows were wedged under his armpit.

"Would you get the door, please?" he asked.

She reached past him and drew it shut.

"Follow me." He smiled and started down the stairs.

Intrigued, she followed him downstairs, through the house and out onto the carport. She'd noticed the house was truly quiet for the first time since she'd arrived. What was going on?

He walked around the house to the back lawn. Below them at the pond, someone had set up a framework with a white sheet stretched across it with the opening credits of a movie just starting to scroll across the fabric. People lay sprawled on blankets or sat in lawn chairs and loungers. Some held toddlers, others cuddled or held hands with their significant other.

"How cool," Bernadette exclaimed.

Frank chuckled and jostled her shoulder with his, startling a soft laugh out of her. "When you live in the sticks, you figure out alternative methods of entertainment."

"I've seen this done on TV, but this is the first time I've actually attended an outdoor movie like this." Delighted, she grinned up at him. "I think it's wonderful."

Her heart skipped a beat. He smiled so wide she wished she could make him smile like that all the time. When the sternness around his eyes and mouth melted, a dashing man looked back at her. To have him favor her like that as he undressed her and…. She shook herself. Those were dangerous thoughts better left locked in the back of her mind.

"Are you cold?" he asked, glancing pointedly at the blanket. "I have a lighter one folded up inside this one. Once the temperature drops like it is, the damp air is uncomfortable."

She played along with his assumption. "The light blanket sounds nice."

He favored her with another one of his soft, prize-winning smiles. She jostled him back like he had her, earning a sexy chuckle from him that sent tingles racing into her panties.

They reached the flat lawn under the tree nearest the pond just as the title of the movie flashed across the homemade screen.

Bernadette anticipated lying next to him to watch the flick. He shook the lighter blanket from the heavier one, then spread the larger of the two on a vacant area under the tree. He sprawled on his side, then patted the spot in front of him. Once Bernadette lay next to him, he tossed the light cover over her bare legs.

"How's that?" he whispered.

"Perfect, thank you."

The beginning of *Starman* drew Bernadette into the movie, but as it progressed, she became more and more aware of Frank's warm length along her backside. Soon, she lay spooned tightly against him, the blanket hiding how snugly they fit together. About halfway through the film, several families with very small children left. Bernadette assumed they were heading home to tuck their kids into bed for the night.

Gradually others yawned and left too until there were only a Luella and Beastman, Tractor and his wife, and a three young men whom Bernadette assumed were older teenagers. Bernadette snuggled closer to Frank. She just couldn't help herself. His hard, warm body steadily raised her temperature until she found herself pressing her ass into his lap.

He gasped softly and stiffened.

Bernadette pushed her ass back against him again. A low rumble told her he was just as aroused as she, but when he shoved his pelvis tighter against her bottom, the hard ridge of his cock left no doubts how much he desired her. The chemistry between them grew almost palpable.

He slid the hand he'd been resting on her hip over her lower abdomen, then under the waistband of her lightweight shorts, his palm rough on her skin. She sucked in a breath, fiery heat racing to her pussy.

He leaned into her, his mouth at her ear, breath hot on her neck. "You are such a tempting ginger, but let's see if I can heat you up."

At his words, her pulse jolted, and adrenaline zinged through her body. Frank removed his hand, passed it over her hip, then slipped his fingers into the leg opening, where he also found the edge of her panties.

"Ah, feels like lace," he whispered, further stimulating her pulse. "I wonder what the lace is hiding?"

She bit her lip to prevent a whimper from escaping. Her clit pulsed, warmth thrummed in her folds, and her juices were quickly dampening the crotch of her panties. She gulped and tried to rein in her hormones, but failed miserably. Already she felt as if she would orgasm. How was it possible that a man she barely knew could affect her so deeply?

"I'm going to touch you," he said, his deep timbre sending quivers through her body. "If you don't want this, tell me. I'll stop."

His breath fluttered over her nape, stirring the fine hairs there and urging goose flesh to rise up her scalp, run down her neck, and along her shoulders.

"Mmm…." She leaned her head back so it rested in the crook of his neck, as if they were two swans in an embrace. "I don't know what it is about you…."

He let her shoulders fall gently to the blanket, turning her hips as he did so and laying her on her back next to him. Capturing her lips, he kissed her gently at first, then gradually deepened the kiss until all Bernadette knew was his taste, his scent, the way his tongue dueled with hers. He wiggled his fingers beneath the elastic of her underwear and palmed her mound. She stiffened and arched her hips.

The thought of others noticing them doused her ardor, and she pushed at his shoulders. "Someone will notice," she whispered.

"So what if they do?" He grinned down at her, the light of the film backwashing his face in white and blue. "I've caught others in the act from time to time. It's a natural part of life."

"I barely know you, Frank." Even so, she felt safe with him. It didn't make any sense, but it was there just the same.

"Then let me show you more about me."

He kissed her again, rubbing the heel of his hand lightly over the hair covering her pussy. If he didn't stop, he would rip her underwear, but she didn't care. All she wanted was Frank, to be one with him, to know what it felt like to be filled by his cock as he pumped into her. He curled his fingers and began stroking them through her folds. She tensed, her eyes flying open.

"Frank, I—"

"Shh. If you want me to stop, tell me."

Before she truly realized what she was doing, she raised her hips, pushing his fingers along her pussy.

He growled low in his throat. For an instant, she thought his eyes glowed, but dismissed it as the film reflecting in them.

"I want you, Bernadette. I've fought it all week and just can't take it anymore." He lowered his head and licked the tendon that lined the side of her neck. It sent an electrical-like jolt through her. "I should send you home, but I can't. You're like moonshine. Once you've had a taste, you have to have more."

She started to say something, but he claimed her lips again and simultaneously pushed two fingers into her, wedging them far into her passage, then flicking his fingertips gently. The wave of pleasure hit her

157

without warning. She bucked and cried out. Frank swallowed her sounds, drank from her lips and coaxed the orgasm out of her until she lay spent and gasping. She raised her head, fearful Luella and the others had witnessed how easily he'd pulled another climax from her, but the movie had ended and everyone was gone.

"Don't worry," Frank murmured as he kissed down her neck. "No one paid us any attention. Beastman took the projector to the house, and Luella and the guys followed him. We've been alone for several minutes."

"We shouldn't...." She struggled to string words together, but her body still tingled from the orgasm. Her brain wrestled to reboot, and her body desired more of the amazing sensations Frank evoked in her.

"Shouldn't what?" He stroked his fingers inside her until the coil that had snapped within her began to wind tightly again.

"Oh my...." She began pumping her hips in time to his strokes. "It's not fair."

"What's not?" he whispered, then flicked his tongue over the shell of her ear.

"It's not fair"—Hell, she was going to come again!—"that you can make me feel like this."

He chuckled, the sound shooting more energy to her pussy. "You have the same effect on me, Bernadette. I can't wait to sink my cock into your hot, pliant body."

"Frank...." She grabbed his head and pulled him down for a kiss.

He rolled on top of her, his weight delicious as he pressed her into the blanket-covered earth, the hardness of his cock against her lower belly and pubic bone both painful and delightful. She couldn't move. He pinned every part of her from her breasts to her thighs. Bernadette tried to wriggle, anything to feel more of him, but he had complete control over her—and she relished it.

He rose slightly and tugged her shirt up, then unfastened the front clasp of her bra. The instant it released her breasts, he sucked in a breath. "Holy hell, you're gorgeous." He cupped her boobs, pressing them together, and rubbed his face into her cleavage, laving the skin. "I've dreamed about doing this since I first saw you," he mumbled.

"Oh...." She couldn't touch enough of him. The ache in her cunt grew unbearable.

When he seized one of her nipples with his mouth, she cried out and threaded her fingers into his thick, soft hair.

"Fuck, Bernadette," he groaned as he paused to gain control. "Tell me to make love to you."

"Please, make love to me, Frank." She might regret it later, but right now, all she wanted was to feel him straining between her legs, filling her and thrusting until she couldn't walk tomorrow morning.

Chapter Thirteen

Anticipation rocketed through Frank. Although he wouldn't have believed it possible, his cock hardened even more at her words. He couldn't wait to push into her, feel her body accept him, feel her passage wrap around him and milk him until he surged into her and filled her with his seed. Just the thought forced his balls to draw back tightly. He desired her so badly it actually hurt.

"We're getting wet," he said. "The humidity is pure fog now, so let's go up to the house. We'll go to my room, which has a small bathroom that we can use later…" He nuzzled her breasts again. "I plan to fuck you into the mattress, baby, so be sure you want this."

"Stop talking and take me to your room."

He raised his head to look at her. Her beautiful emerald eyes were dark, but enough light cascaded down from the house that he could see her enlarged pupils. Her arousal washed over Frank, inebriating him with her pheromones, her femininity, her gorgeous face and body. He was humbled to have such a beautiful woman, both inside and out, who wanted him. And oh how he planned to worship her. If he had his way, she'd sleep all through tomorrow just to regain her energy.

"Come on, sweetheart. I can't wait to have you in my bed." He rolled off her and adjusted his clothes as Bernadette clumsily refastened her bra, hiding her glorious breasts. He couldn't wait to have her totally naked in his arms as she shattered and cried out his name. That was if he could even walk up the hill. If he didn't get release soon, his damn cock was going to burst through his zipper.

"Ready?" he asked once she'd fixed her clothes.

"Yeah." She stooped and picked up the light blanket, and quickly folded it.

He did the same with the heavier throw. She offered him a small, nervous smile that pulled at his heartstrings. Although she'd shown that she wanted him, she was also hesitant, unsure of him. It would be his privilege to show her that she had nothing to be ashamed of, nothing to fear or doubt. Nervousness suddenly spiraled into his gut—what if he didn't live up to her expectations?

He'd never doubted his abilities as a lover before, so why was he having misgivings now?

Once he held out his crooked arm, Bernadette wound hers through his and allowed him to lead her up the path to the house. The *scree-scree* of tree frogs serenaded them as they climbed the trail, and big puffs of silvery fog blew over the gentle slope in the form of ghostly dancers. From the barn, a screech startled Bernadette so that she jumped and pressed to his side.

"Just a barn owl," he soothed.

"Those pretty, white-faced owls?"

He nodded.

"Funny how a lovely bird makes such an ungodly sound."

He smirked. He liked how her writer's mind worked.

At the porch, Frank held the door open for her. Beastman sat watching the late night news with Luella asleep against his side. The big man grinned like an idiot as they walked through to the kitchen, but as Bernadette climbed the two steps to the doorway, he held up his thumb to Frank.

Frank glowered at him and shook his head, hoping like hell Bernadette didn't glance back and see their exchange.

Thankfully, no one was watching television in the family or living rooms. The house was quiet save for the sound of the weather report following upstairs.

When they reached the top of the stairs, Frank opened his bedroom door and nodded. She walked inside and waited for him. He shut the door, momentarily plunging them into total darkness, then tossed the blankets toward the straight-back chair sitting under the light switch.

"Let me turn on one of the lamps," he told Bernadette.

She said nothing as he gently touched her on his way toward the highboy that sat directly across from the bed. There he switched on a small electric hurricane lamp. Golden light from the top and bottom globes provided just enough mood to be romantic.

Frank faced her and smiled. "It's nothing fancy, but I like it."

"The room suits you," she said, gazing around.

He pointed to a door. "That's the bathroom, should you need it."

She nodded, her nervousness showing in the way she held herself.

"Hey," he said and crossed the room to her. He placed his hands on her shoulders and met her eyes. He wanted her so much, but it wasn't worth it if she didn't want him the same way. "You can change your mind. If you have, I completely understand. It's important to me that you want this."

Bernadette stared up at him with such wonder and desire that his breath hitched. By the total innocence and trust in her eyes, he knew with certainty that she was a woman who didn't sleep around, one who didn't offer her affections easily. Hell, he doubted she'd slept with more than one or two men.

"Wh-why don't we talk for a bit?" she suggested. "Get to know each other more."

He grinned and walked over to a cabinet that sat under one of the two windows in the room. "I think that's a great idea," he said as he opened the double doors and swung them out in opposite directions. "How about a drink?"

"Whiskey, neat." She moved over to the bed and sat on the end of it.

"I've wanted to discuss a couple things with you anyway," he stated as he poured whiskey into two heavy tumblers.

"About?"

"Well, how much time have you spent in these mountains? What do you know about this part of the Appalachians?"

"Never been this far east before," she said. "Until my first book came out, I'd never had the means to travel. My mother says we have family in these hills, but after my father died, she stayed in Columbus where there was some extended family, but most of them have moved away now. It was difficult for her to make ends meet raising the five of us."

So Bernadette came from a big family. No wonder she'd assimilated into the MC so easily. All the people, the arguing, the laughter...she probably found it soothing.

He turned and handed her a glass, then sat next to her. After taking a sip of his drink, he said, "From here down into Virginia, the mountains are...different. I know I've told you before, but don't wander into the woods alone." His desire to keep her safe rose so strong in him that he wanted to pull her into his arms. "There are dangers you would be hard-pressed to comprehend."

She sipped from her tumbler, her eyes catching the amber lighting as she studied him over the rim of the glass. Lowering it, she asked, "Like what?"

"Well, for one, abandoned houses in the woods are magnets for those who cook drugs, and there are still people who make moonshine."

She sobered at that. "Ah, those kind of dangers."

Shaking his head, he added, "No, not just *those* sorts of hazards. There are others."

"Like?"

He sat quietly as he gathered his thoughts. He could tell her the stuff of nightmares walked the forests and hollows, but she'd just laugh at him. After she'd taken a couple more sips of whiskey, he said, "You wouldn't believe me."

"Ghosts?" She chuckled.

Her laughter told him what he'd already

suspected. He rose and set his glass on the top of the liquor cabinet.

"I'm sorry," she said behind him. "Somehow I've offended you."

"Not at all." He stared down at the lawn lying in complete darkness, the only light stemming from the burn-off on the next ridge. "It's just that if I tell you what dwells in the forests around Rebellion, let alone farther south, you'll laugh just as you have."

"I'm sorry, Frank. Really."

He faced her again and smiled wanly. "Please trust me, Bernadette, when I say there are things around here you're not prepared to deal with, okay?"

She nodded vigorously. "I'm not sure what you mean, but I believe you."

Relief swept through him. "There are firm rules for the women of my MC when they go into the fields or woods." Frank wanted her to take him seriously, but at Bernadette's rapt attention, he fought to keep from smiling. She looked like a redheaded angel, her eyes wide and filled with sweetness. His cock twitched, but he forced himself to focus on their discussion. "One, always take someone with you. Two, if the person who accompanies you is another woman, one of you *must* carry a weapon."

She blinked, her mouth forming a small O. "A weapon? Seriously?"

"Yes."

"I understand having a gun if you'd run into a drug den, but what other dangers could possibly be in these hills? Snakes? Bears?" Bernadette gulped down the last swallow of her whiskey and stood. "I do know enough about the wildlife in Ohio to know that unless cornered, an animal will avoid humans, so what are you getting at, Frank?"

"There are…things that go bump in the night." He didn't look at her, couldn't. If he did, he knew he'd see her skepticism, or worse. If she began to doubt him, he wouldn't be able to handle it. Why her belief in him mattered, he didn't know. Now that she was determined to stay and he'd accepted it, he didn't want to do or say anything that might shake her faith in him. Frank frowned and sought out the flame dancing over the treetops. Why should it matter what the woman thought of him?

"Frank?"

He snapped back to himself and turned.

"If your MC is involved in illegal matters, I'm not here to bust you." She placed her glass on the cabinet top next to his, then laid a hand on his forearm. The simple touch ignited a need within him that zipped straight to his cock. "I have forms for you and others to fill out, allowing me to use the MC's name, their names, and to publish any photos I may take," she said softly, "but if no one is comfortable with doing that, the faces can be blurred in the pictures and I'll change all names, including the MC's."

What had he done by taking her into his MC? How did he tell her there were real monsters in the world? No one save for the few who encountered these monsters believed they existed. How did he tell her that he was one of the things that prowled the darkness and worshipped a full moon? If he did, he was certain she'd abandon her book and run like hell as far away from him as possible. He couldn't bear the thought of her leaving.

But he couldn't have Bernadette, couldn't keep her. He'd enjoy her company—and her body if she was still willing—but anything more with the woman wasn't possible. He highly doubted there was any room in her life for one werewolf, let alone an MC full of them.

"Frank?"

"We'll discuss the book later." He settled his hands on her waist. "Right now I only want to know one thing—have you changed your mind about tonight?"

She shook her head and offered him a shy smile. "No, I haven't."

* * *

Bernadette was unsure what was bothering Frank. He seemed fixated on protecting her, but why? Sure, she understood the dangers of the drug world, having lived around it with Candy Apple and the others, but Frank talked as though there was more in the woods than moonshiners and meth labs.

Now, as she stared up into his dark, soul-searching eyes, she realized the draw to this man had grown into an obsession, one that had her thirsting for his touch. Frank might be domineering, stubborn and often aloof, but Bernadette couldn't seem to get him out of her mind. The chemistry crackling between them was almost combustible, so maybe if they enjoyed a night together, she could get him out of her system and focus strictly on her book.

Lord knew she needed some stress relief.

"Are *you* having second thoughts?" she asked.

"Hell, no," he replied, drawing her closer. "I just don't want you regretting it in the morning."

"Just so you know," she said, "no strings. I'm not here for a relationship."

A somber expression passed through Frank's eyes.

"My book is important and I do have a deadline, so I need to concentrate on it. I also have a chapter for you—"

"Shut up, Bernadette," Frank said an instant before he brought his mouth down on hers.

Everything she was going to tell him evaporated. Frank slanted his lips across hers, tugging her to him so her breasts were flattened to his chest. He kissed her so deeply that her lungs strained for air, then suddenly raised his head, breaking their contact.

"I'm going to snap in two if I have to stand bent over to kiss you," he said.

"I can't help it you're so tall," she said, her head reeling.

"I can't help it you're so little," he countered with a low chuckle.

He grasped her by her waist and lifted her. Instinctively she wrapped her legs around his waist, hooking her ankles at his back, her flip-flops falling to the carpet with soft thumps. He nuzzled her neck, flicking his tongue out to taste her skin in one spot, then another. His taut belly pressed tightly to her crotch ignited a need in Bernadette that she'd never experienced before. All she could think about was feeling him inside her.

"How about a shower first?" he suggested against her throat. "Wash away the grime of the day—" He dipped his tongue into the little hollow of her neck, sending tendrils of fire straight to her pussy. "—"and any inhibitions you might have."

"Okay," she gasped.

He turned to the left and bent toward the liquor cabinet. "Glass and bottle."

Heart thumping crazily and her pussy throbbing in time to it, Bernadette hooked her fingers over the rim of a glass, passed it to her other hand, then grabbed the neck of the whiskey bottle. With a wicked smile, Frank headed to the bathroom.

He stepped through the doorway with her, hit the light switch with his elbow, then set Bernadette on her feet again. He opened the glass shower door and turned on the water. Bernadette waited as he adjusted the temperature. He took the bottle and glass from her and set them on a high shelf inside the stall. Finished, he shut the door.

"Clothes." He grinned, and her heart stuttered in response. "Off with them now," he said, pulling his up shirt over his head. He let it drop to the floor. "Or do I get to unwrap you?"

Unable to form words, Bernadette could only gape at him. She'd known he was a large, tall man— but then so were most of the Werewolves of Rebellion—but with Frank's shirt off, she had full view of how wide his shoulders and chest were, the size of his biceps, the way the muscles rippled and shifted as he made even the smallest movements. The tattoos that had been teasing her for days were now at her fingertips. Bernadette traced her fingers over the barbed wire that encircled his left wrist and wound midway up his forearm among leaves and thorns so artistically done they looked real. From there, what Bernadette had first thought was a mottle of blues

169

turned out to be diamonds and sapphires, then above his elbow, the start of fur that became the leg of a wolf until its shoulder became Frank's shoulder, the wolf's head inked down his front with its muzzle ending just above his left nipple. Around the animal's neck, expertly drawn so the eye had to be keen to pick it out, Frank's name had been blended with the fur.

Bernadette drew her fingers across Frank's chest, through the smattering of dark, silky hair and over to his other shoulder where a variety of tattoos blended into one another, each one apparently something meaningful in Frank's life. Incredible artwork composed both his tat sleeves, but the wolf drew Bernadette's eye the most.

"This is beautiful," she said just loudly enough to be heard over the water.

Quickly Frank tugged her tank top over her breasts, prompting her to raise her arms, then he took it off and let it drop to the floor too. "You're beautiful," he said, popping the front snap on her bra.

When her breasts spilled from the garment, he caught them in his warm, rough palms. His touch stoked the fire in her loins. All she could think about was being skin to skin with him, feeling him inside her as the shower pelted down on them. She shimmied out of her shorts and panties, shyness hitting her as she did, but it quickly vanished as he jerked her against him and her bare tits met with his hard, hot body.

Frank encircled her in his arms, hugging her tightly and rubbing his face against the top of her head. He inhaled, which tightened his embrace, then suddenly released her. "This has to go," he said and unfastened her messy bun.

170

He smiled down at her as he shook her locks free and ran his fingers through them. She winced when he caught a snag.

"Sorry, baby." Frank unhooked his fingers, then carefully untangled the knot. He kissed the spot on her head where he'd pulled her hair.

She couldn't help smiling at his thoughtfulness and marveled at how such a huge man could be so gentle. He cupped her breasts again, then bent and licked each of her nipples. The warm roughness of his tongue shot spears of heat to her core. She moaned and her knees threatened to buckle, but somehow he sensed what she needed and pulled her to his body again. Supporting her with one arm, he opened the shower stall with his other and swung her inside.

Stepping back, he grinned, his eyes devilish. He stooped and untied his boots, pulled each one off with its sock, then kicked them over to the toilet. Frank quickly unfastened the button and zipper to his jeans and shucked them with his briefs.

Bernadette could only stand agape as she took in his nude form. She'd never seen a man so beautifully made before. No one in magazines or movies came to mind to even use as a comparison. His long, stout legs were muscled and corded, but not overly so. His lean hips led to his defined abs, then up to his wide, sculpted chest and shoulders, where his beautiful skin art flowed down his arms again. However, his cock, erect and proud, gave her pause. He was perfectly proportioned in all areas. Saliva actually pooled in her mouth, and Bernadette quickly swallowed, fearing she would embarrass herself by drooling.

He smirked at her and closed the distance

between them. "I'm glad you approve."

Heat rushed to her face, and she was thankful for the tepid water. "I didn't mean to stare."

"It's okay. That means I can ogle you all I want, too." He stepped into the shower stall, invading her personal space. "You're gorgeous, Bernadette. I mean it. I'm sure you're aware of how men stare at you. I'm blessed to have you in my arms tonight."

She met his eyes, saw pure sincerity in them, and her heart melted.

Frank grasped the door and pulled it shut. Standing toe-to-toe with her, he drew her into his arms. "Come here, Beautiful."

Chapter Fourteen

Bernadette moaned when their bodies connected. He kissed her long and hard, running his hands up and down her body as he devoured her mouth. Palming her ass, he snuggled her hips against him, his cock rigid against her belly. Finally, he released her, chest heaving, eyes so black with desire that she couldn't tell the difference between his pupils and irises.

"Turn around," he commanded, his voice gruff.

She did as he instructed, the water cascading over her head, plastering her hair to her scalp and over her face. The click of a bottle being opened sounded loud in the small cubicle. He placed one hand on her shoulder and ran something soft yet firm down her back.

He washed her from her neck down, turned her around and scrubbed her from her face to her feet, then drew her under the water to rinse her thoroughly.

"Stay still," he said.

Another click followed, then he placed his hands on her head and began massaging her scalp. He washed, then conditioned her hair.

"Your turn," she said. Following his example, she used the scrubby to wash him as he had her, although he had to lean over so she could scrub his hair. He grinned at her through the bubbles that flowed over his face.

"I can't help it that you're so little," he burbled through the water.

"I can't help it that you're so tall."

Their continued bantering about their heights made her laugh, and he joined her. His deep chuckles seemed to vibrate the walls.

He rinsed his hair, then shook the water from his eyes and looked down at her with such intense desire, it took her breath away. Something clenched in her core, and throbbing resumed in her pussy. She wanted him so badly, needed him to make her his property for the night.

Leaning back with his wolf-tatted shoulder in the corner beneath the showerhead, Frank put his foot on the little molded seat behind Bernadette. He held out his arms, and she stepped into them. Without any effort, he lifted her and set her bare ass on his thigh.

"What are you do—?"

"Shush. Relax." He nipped her earlobe, sending a thrill through her and stirring gooseflesh over her body. "Let me love you."

He held her as if she were no more than a light sack of groceries. He let his gaze wander over her body as he smoothed his hand over her shoulder and down to her breast. He cupped the mound, testing its weight in his palm, stroking the pad of his thumb over the nipple. Bernadette closed her eyes and gave herself over to the pleasure he provoked. Blood thundered in her ears, almost drowning out the patter of the water. She relaxed slightly as he passed his hand along her side to swipe it along the curve of her waist, then over the fleshy part of her hip. The roughness of his palm and fingertips heightened her pleasure and shot spear after spear of excitement into her cunt. Tingles began there, spreading into her folds and out farther to the junctures of her thighs and into the tender inner muscles of her legs.

A whimper escaped her, followed by another and another. She found herself wriggling on her perch, the hairs of his thighs tickling her skin, the tiny brushes serving to add to her pleasure that steadily soared skyward. Keeping her eyes closed, she waited for him to move farther down one leg or the other, but he stopped. Suddenly his mouth was on hers, and she sighed into his kiss.

Without warning, he palmed her cunt. A wail, part surprise, part delight, burst from her, but he swallowed it as he pushed first one finger, then two into her pussy.

"Mmph!" She wanted more, needed more, but sitting on his thigh braced against the wall, she feared moving too much and unseating herself. She thrust her hips into his hand so slightly she didn't think she'd moved at all. He pumped his fingers in and out, winding the coil inside her so tightly, she thought she'd go insane. She tore her mouth away from his and sucked in air. "Frank…please…."

"In time, Beautiful," he murmured, his lips against her forehead now. "I plan to make you come so many times you'll beg me to stop."

His words were gasoline to the flames licking through her body. She wiggled her hips again. Sensing her need, he pushed his fingers in farther, harder. She groaned. Then a slight pain followed, and she realized he'd added a third digit.

"Oh, my...." She let her head loll back, and it bumped the wall.

Weak with desire, unable to obtain the friction she wanted, she simply let him finger-fuck her as the shower grew colder and continued pattering down on them. He worked his fingers, curling and uncurling them, somehow stroking places inside her that she never knew existed. The ache inside her continued to mount. If she didn't get release soon, she feared she might burst into a million pieces. Frank continued driving into her. Soon the pleasure grew so great that her hot juices spilled from her, mingling where the cool water trickled over her belly and into her crotch.

"Come for me, baby," he whispered into her ear. "Shatter in my arms as you did in the pond. Show me how fucking beautiful you are as pleasure streaks through you."

As if he'd pushed a special button, the tightening coil snapped. She bucked, unable to control herself, fearing he might drop her, but somehow she stayed on her seat as wave after wave of intense sensation pulsed from the point his fingers stroked, farther into her channel, up into her lower abdomen, forcing her to clench and shudder and cry out over and over until he kissed her and drank in every noise she uttered. As the pleasure began to diminish, he flicked his fingers in her, then shoved them into her harder. To her surprise, a second tremor flashed through her.

"Oh, my...fuck!" she screamed. "Frank...." The orgasm struck her so hard, it rendered her immobile. All she could do was fall lax against the wall as he finger-fucked her until she thought she'd go mad. "I can't…." A third tremor passed through her. "I…fuck, fuck…." She tossed her head from side to side as the final vestiges of the third mini orgasm trembled through her pussy and out to her extremities.

She sat there, panting, weak, utterly sated.

"As I said," Frank rumbled in the confines of the shower. "Absolutely beautiful."

* * *

Frank dried her off, taking his time and admiring every part of Bernadette's body, every flat plane, the way her breasts were so large yet so firm, her round, pert ass cheeks, her short yet curvy legs. The flaming-red patch at the apex of her thighs that hid a special kind of heaven. He even liked her little feet and tiny toes. She was perfection in a compact form.

He threw the towel over her head and ruffled her hair. After a moment, he stopped and removed the towel. "Red spaghetti."

She blinked at him. "What?" Realization dawned on her face. "Oh!" She swatted at her hair, and he let loose with a deep, long belly laugh.

"Come here." He tossed the towel on the floor and picked her up. In four big strides, he took her into the bedroom and set her on her feet by the bedside. He kissed the tip of her nose, her forehead, then each cheek, followed by her chin. Next he kissed along her neck to one shoulder. Reaching the curve of her right shoulder, he switched to her other side and proceeded to do the same down the left side of her neck.

"You're like this new, amazing candy I can't get

enough of," he mumbled against her skin. "I can't wait to eat the prize."

He drew her firmly against him, cupping her ass cheeks so his hard-on pushed into her belly, the throbbing of his cock growing more persistent, but he knew the wait to take her would be worth it. Bernadette had made it clear that she didn't want a relationship, so he planned to draw out and relish every minute of their time together. He thrust his hips against her, and she groaned long and low, stirring his libido even more. Frank wanted her more than he'd ever wanted a woman. Out of all his flings, one-night stands and short relationships, no one had lit his blood on fire like Bernadette.

He pushed her back until her knees gave against the bed. When she started to sit up straight, he placed a hand between her breasts and nudged her backward so she lay flat, her thighs splayed, the lips of her sex still damp from the shower and glistening through the thin patch of hair she obviously kept neatly trimmed. She was a woman who paid attention to detail, he mused. He liked that she cared for her body so well.

He dropped to his knees between hers.

"What are you doing?" she asked, raising her head.

"Shush. Let me pleasure you."

"But I've never…." She stiffened and shut her legs as much as she could with him between them. "No one has ever…."

As he met her gaze, he realized what she was trying to tell him. Incredulous, he asked, "Never?"

She shook her head vigorously.

"Then let me be the first."

When she stared at him aghast, her eyes full of

worry and shame, he decided to just show her the feelings he could create for her. He placed a hand on either of her knees, pushed them apart and plunged his face into her cunt.

"Frank!"

Her clean, musky odor penetrated his nose, and he groaned and lapped at her folds.

A low keen came from Bernadette, followed by "Holy hell…oh…oh…."

She began moving her hips, but he pulled back so he could part her folds to access her better. Her disgruntled protest made him chuckle. He smoothed his thumbs over her plump outer lips, then pulled them aside, revealing the inner, bright pink lining. He swiped his tongue up one satiny furrow, then over the other. Bernadette whimpered, her hips seemingly having a mind of their own as she writhed beneath his ministrations. With his throbbing cock pinned painfully against the mattress, Frank held the hood of her pussy up and fluttered his tongue over her clit.

Arching off the bed, Bernadette let out a deep, guttural groan that fired more need directly to his cock. He wanted to take her now, thrust until he was balls-deep in her, but he made himself wait. The objective was to make her come again, have her so relaxed that he could thrust for a long time before making her orgasm one final, explosive time.

He continued to draw his tongue up, then down over her clit. The little bud grew redder each time, so engorged with blood that it stuck out at him, inviting him to nip it—and he did.

"Mmph!" Bucking her hips, Bernadette threaded her fingers into his hair. "Frank, that's…. Oh, hell."

He sucked her clit into his mouth, pulling on it rhythmically until she shattered. Pumping her hips into his face, she convulsed so hard he felt the throbbing in her folds against his face. Frank still didn't relinquish the tiny nub, sucking voraciously until she screamed and her juices wetted his face, her aroma growing heavier, more pungent, heady. She kept bumping her pelvis upward, her fingers so tightly laced in his hair he figured she'd come away with strands stuck between them, but he didn't care. He'd made her shatter yet again, and his dick was so fucking hard that if he didn't sink into her soon, he might lose his cum all over the blanket.

Without releasing her clit, he continued sucking, but not as hard as before. Gradually Bernadette came down from her orgasm, her breathing rapid. Frank glanced up her body. Her breasts, so damn big and firm, heaved up and down. For an instant, he had an image of their pillowy softness cradling his cock as he came between them.

"I've never had anyone do that to me before," she gasped.

Finally he let her clit slip free, then rose slightly to lay his head on her belly. Panting, she caressed his hair, her fingers deft yet gentle. He could get used to her touch, her breathy sounds, the way she whimpered so softly, one of the sexiest noises he'd ever heard.

"I don't think I have another orgasm in me, Frank," she said, half laughing. "Holy hell, you've worn me out."

"Honey," he answered, "I'm only getting started."

* * *

She raised her head and looked own at him, his impossibly wide shoulders covering her hips and legs, the lamplight picking out blue highlights in his inky hair.

"You can't be serious," she said. "You made me come on the blanket, in the shower—three times!—and again here on the bed. There's no way I have another one in me."

"You'll be surprised at how your body will betray you," he said, chuckling again.

The vibration of his laughter penetrated her belly and sent tingles to her over-sensitized pussy. She raised both eyebrows as she studied his shiny, wavy hair. Was it possible to have that many orgasms? She'd sat quietly as her friends had discussed their sex lives and talked about multiple orgasms, one even claiming she'd had twelve in one night—something Bernadette had always thought was an outright lie until now. But after five with Frank, she was wonderfully drained, lethargic.

Smiling, he palmed each of her breasts and began squeezing them rhythmically. "Want to bet me?"

"Bet you?" Did she dare? After all, she'd never had anyone go down on her until now, an act she'd always thought was too dirty, but she'd exploded in a way she'd never thought possible, making it the orgasm of all orgasms for the night—so far.

"Mmm-hmm." That wicked grin, the one that always caused her panties to moisten, crossed his face. "If I don't make you come again, I'll buy you a leather bike outfit. If I do make you come at least one more time—"

"At least?" She gaped at him, but she was still

intrigued. "You're terribly sure of yourself, aren't you?"

"Yes," he said, "I am. If I do make you come again, you owe me a blowjob, a legitimate one."

"What does that mean?"

"You swallow."

She frowned at him, then she.realized what he meant. "Oh."

He laughed. "'Oh' is right."

She'd never been fond of giving blowjobs, especially when one of her boyfriends had held her head, insisting she swallow, but with Frank, she was curious and wanted to make him feel good, too. She shrugged slightly. "Okay, you're on."

"We forgot to have our drink in the shower," he said. "Let me go get the bottle and glass and we'll have one."

She nodded.

As he stood and walked into the bathroom, she gaped. Heaven have mercy, the man had one fine, fine ass! She couldn't wait until she could dig her fingers into those butt cheeks and squeeze as he thrust into her. Too bad she was so damn tired. But what a fantastic way to feel. Five orgasms. She smiled to herself and rolled farther up on the bed, enjoying the crisp, smooth cover against her heated flesh.

He returned to the bedroom, whiskey bottle in one hand, two tumblers in the other, and strode over to the liquor cabinet, his still-hard cock bobbing against his belly, the head flush with the bottom of his belly button.

She eyed his cock, really studying it this time. *Oh, hell. I don't know if I can accommodate that.*

As if he'd heard her thoughts, he said, "Don't worry, sweetheart. It'll fit."

She gaped at him an instant before an indignant sound fled her lips. Laughter burst out of Frank as he filled both glasses with about two fingers each of amber liquid.

He handed a glass to her, then stretched out alongside her with is drink. "I'm guessing you haven't had many lovers?"

"No." She sipped, then let the firewater slide down her throat. "Not what you'd call lovers. More like guys who just wanted to get their rocks off, not caring what I wanted or needed."

"Fucktards."

"Well, you've made up for them and then some," she said.

He stroked the hair out of her eyes, and the action sent a wave of warmth through her. "I'm glad you feel that way," he replied. "Anyone who's with you should strive to make you happy."

Unnerved by the intensity in his eyes, Bernadette took another sip. They lay quietly together as they finished their whiskeys. Frank set the tumblers on the cabinet, then indicated she should flip over on her belly.

She frowned. "What are you going to do?"

"I'm going to give you a massage."

Eagerly she rolled over.

"Damn," he said. "That's the finest ass I've ever seen."

She giggled into a pillow.

"I'm serious." He straddled her thighs, his weight comforting and erotic. "It's perfectly round and so firm."

He swatted her ass. She jumped, squealing then giggling.

"And it even turns a beautiful shade of red," he said. "Matches your hair."

She started to respond, but he began rubbing up and down her back. Kneading the muscles gently at first, Frank gradually grew more forceful, eliciting pleasured groans from Bernadette. The man had hands of magic. He worked on her neck for a few minutes, moved to her shoulders and upper arms, then down her back on both sides of her spine.

When his cock nestled into the crack of her ass, Bernadette let out a hiss of desire. He shifted so his cock slid into the little space between her thighs and flush against her pussy. Working his fingers into the muscles at her waist, Frank leaned forward, the action pushing his dick into the space so it twitched against her cunt. She bit her lip, nearly puncturing it when he shifted again, dragging his cock back through her folds. Unable to restrain herself, she raised her hips, offering her ass, and was rewarded with a deep-throated, animalistic growl.

Frank moved to one side, then drove a knee between her thighs, forcing her legs apart. When she widened them, he settled between them, grasped her by the hips and hefted her onto all fours.

"I can't take it any longer, Bernadette," he rumbled behind her. "Tell me you want me."

Oh, how she wanted him. Already her cunt pulsed with need and her breasts were growing heavier, the nipples perking with desire. "Yes, I want you."

He placed the head of his cock at her entrance and thrust into her.

"Ungh!" The sudden entrance, the girth of him, was sensory overload. She breathed through the pain, but it was a pleasurable pain, something she'd never before experienced with any of her lovers.

"Fuck," Frank moaned. "You're so wet and hot. You're gripping me like a hand...." Another growl burst from him.

He pulled out until the head of his cock was barely in her entrance. Bernadette mewled at the loss of fullness. But just as she was about to push back, Frank lunged forward and buried himself balls-deep into her. The sudden intrusion, the girth and length of him, the slight burn and the feel of his pelvis flush against her ass was almost enough to send Bernadette over the edge again. She couldn't believe how good he felt inside her, how much he stretched her. Even the burn amped up her desire. That place deep within her core began aching impossibly hard. Her breasts were so heavy, hanging so the nipples brushed the coverlet just enough to send frissons of need straight to her cunt.

Frank kneeled behind her, his hands on her hips, fingers biting into her flesh. Unmoving, she maintained the doggy-style position, wondering why he wasn't thrusting. Although she'd never had sex this way before, she suddenly understood why her girlfriends had raved about it. The position was primal, vulnerable and gave power over to the dominant partner—and she loved it. With his cock buried to the hilt, Bernadette pushed back slightly.

"Hold on, baby," he panted. "You're hot and tight. And this position gives me a delicious view of your ass...." He gulped. "I'm trying to keep control so

I don't fuck you through the headboard, so give me a moment.

Something about the way he spoke only turned the heat up in her pussy. "Frank...." She couldn't help wiggling slightly in enticement. Here she had this huge cock inside her and he refused to move. "Dammit, fuck me!"

The sound that came out of him startled Bernadette. It sounded like a furious animal bent on ripping something to shreds, but before she could react, he drew back and slammed into her, nearly buckling her arms. He withdrew and did it again and again.

"Fuck," he snarled. "Your pussy is so damn tight. Got to make you scream, Bernadette."

At that, she lost herself to him. She leaned forward on her forearms, her ass in the air and let him have her. He thrust like a madman, their flesh slapping together so loudly she dimly wondered if someone would hear it. Soon she realized he was driving her across the mattress, the bedspread wadding up around her knees and elbows, yet he continued plunging his big cock into her. The coil inside her grew painful, and he pummeled her so hard the head of his cock butted her cervix—and she welcomed it. This time the ache inside her climbed until all she could focus on was the way Frank shoved his cock into her over and over, his fingers biting into her hips painfully.

Something bumped the top of her head. She looked up to find herself against the headboard. Gripping one of the bars, she held on for dear life. Frank fucked her harder, the headboard rattling against the wall. The picture of a valley with a sprawling farm in it fell and landed behind the headboard, and still Frank thrust into her.

Suddenly, he withdrew. Bernadette cried out in protest, but the moment she made the sound, she found herself flipped onto her back. Frank penetrated her again, filling her to his root. He kneeled between her thighs again and hefted her ass slightly so her butt rested against the tops of his thighs. It changed the angle of his cock, and she took more of him into her, if that were possible. She held on to his thighs, her calves on his shoulders as he fucked her harder and harder, his groans and grunts filling her ears. Pride filled her that she was making him feel so good.

As he pumped into her, she felt him grow just a little harder, signaling his impending orgasm. This pushed her closer to the edge, the ache in her core so damn intense she whined in pain an instant before leaping off the precipice. The force of the orgasm hit her so hard it stunned her. She pushed her head back into the pillow, arching into him, his cock hitting again and again against her cervix.

"Oh, my God, Frank!"

He stiffened, his head falling back. His snarl shocked and thrilled her. He pumped one, twice, then his cock throbbed inside her as warmth followed the sensation. She screamed, locking her legs behind him and raising her hips so her pussy pressed tighter against the base of his cock. She instinctively thrust against him, drawing every bit of pleasure through her body, her limbs tingling, toes curling, and bright spots dancing behind her eyelids. Another burst of pleasure shot through her, zipping sensation into her breasts until her nips stung. Frank thrust again, this time

187

easier, then again and again as he milked the last of his essence into her. He shuddered, then collapsed on top of her, breathing heavily.

"I…won…," he gasped.

"Yes"—She gulped noisily.—"you did."

Chapter Fifteen

Something warmed the side of Bernadette's face. She frowned and rubbed at it, but it didn't go away. Brightness seared one of her eyes. She opened them to find a slender shaft of early morning sunlight cutting through one of the windows to land on her face. Rolling away from it, she sighed and tried to settle back into sleep. She reached out for Frank, and her hand connected with cool sheets. Raising her head, she blinked away sleepiness to find herself in bed alone.

Bernadette lay there for a few minutes, thinking Frank might be in the bathroom, but when she finally realized the door stood open, she sighed again and sat up.

After taking a quick shower, her muscles and crotch sore and tender, Bernadette wrapped a towel around herself, made the bed, gathered her clothes and flip-flops, then quietly returned to her room. Her pride smarted. Although she'd made it clear to Frank that she didn't have time for a relationship, the fact he'd left her without so much as a note bothered her. She supposed he had things to do, but it would've been nice if he'd at least told her good-bye. Soreness in muscles she hadn't known existed told her just how incredible their night together had been. She'd have to be careful not to show any discomfort around Luella or Puppy. If they suspected she'd been with Frank last night, they'd tease her all day.

Her time with Frank last night had shown her there was more to sex than she'd ever imagined. Now she knew what her friends had been talking about during their lunches. Bernadette grinned to herself as she pulled her spare tank top over her head. Sex with the right person was mind-blowing.

Finished dressing, she pulled her hair up into a curly ponytail. It would be nice to let it hang down, but until the god-awful heat wave passed, there was no way she could stand her thick tresses on her neck and shoulders. And makeup was pointless in the high humidity. Satisfied with her appearance, Bernadette stepped into her sneakers, picked up her dirty laundry and headed downstairs.

The house seemed quieter than normal. No voices chatting over breakfast reached her. No sounds of a tractor or mower came from outside. She entered the kitchen to find it void of people. In the laundry room, Bernadette tossed her clothes into the washer and dropped other dirty items in with them to make a full load. She set the washer cycle, then returned to the kitchen in search of a cup of coffee.

Soft voices drifted in from the porch. She poured herself a cup of joe and headed out to the sunporch.

Puppy, Luella, Beastman and Carol sat with coffee cups in their hands. Their sober, worried expressions alarmed Bernadette.

"What's wrong?" she asked,

Beastman let out a big lungful of air. "Another

body was found. Happened about halfway through the night."

"Where this time?" She met Luella's pensive gaze.

"At the pad on the next ridge over," Beastman answered. "One of the drivers got out to use the shitter and was attacked on his way back to the truck." He leaned to the side and retrieved the carafe on a stand. "Until further notice, the MC has a mandatory curfew of 9:00 p.m. Everyone is to lock all doors and windows. Turn fans up and use window air units to beat the heat. Should you need to leave the grounds for any reason, Bernadette, you must clear it with Frank. If you're given permission to leave after nine, at least two escorts will accompany you."

She paused with her mug halfway to her mouth.

"That goes for all the women, teenagers and children," Luella added, casting a pointed look at her old man.

"With the latest attack so close to us," Beastman continued, "we're on high alert until the killer is caught."

"It's like this animal is headed straight for us for some reason," Bernadette said.

"I'm scared," Puppy told them. "I think someone has it out for the MC."

"Puppy!" Luella shot her a harsh look.

The young woman straightened. "What? If Bernadette is going to stay with us for a while, she needs to be clued in a little."

Luella slumped back in her seat again and turned her attention to her old man. "Puppy's right."

"It's not like I don't know some of what goes on

in motorcycle clubs," Bernadette stated, trying to defuse the tension. "I saw a lot I never dreamed of when I wrote my book about prostitution. I even got into a near scrape with the authorities."

Beastman offered her a smile that said he was only humoring her. "I'm afraid what we're dealing with isn't anything like you're thinking." He rose, then placed his cup on the side table. "Luella, I'm going to work, but on my way out, I'll alert everyone of the situation. If you see Frank before I get back, have him call me with what he finds out."

She rose and kissed her husband. "I will."

He cupped her ass and drew her in for another, deeper kiss. "Love you."

Once he'd left, the rumble of his Harley echoing up the hill, Bernadette looked at the women and asked, "What's really going on?"

"It's up to Frank whether or not to bring you in on the matter," Luella replied, as if the weight of the world rested on her shoulders. "There are things that need doing but I don't want to do the outdoor chores in the heat of the day, so if you ladies would help me in the garden, I'd appreciate it."

"I'll help," Bernadette offered. "My mother always kept a garden. I've always found it calming to work in the dirt, pull weeds…." She shrugged.

"I'll help, too," Puppy said.

Carol rose and headed to the kitchen. "I'm going to prep stuff for dinner. If someone brings me things for a salad, I'll make a big one, then set it in the fridge to chill."

"Thanks, Carol." Luella looked at Bernadette and Puppy. "Ladies, grab a basket." She pointed to the handbaskets stacked in the corner nearest the door. "And remember, we watch each other's backs while we're outside."

* * *

Bernadette spent the morning with Luella and Puppy in the garden. She pulled weeds, hoed the dirt higher over the potato plants, and picked leaf lettuce until her basket was full. In the next row, Puppy picked wax beans. On the other side of the garden, Luella spread grass clippings on the ground to smother the return of weeds and keep moisture in the soil.

"Pick some peppers and a few tomatoes," Puppy said. "I'll get some green onions, cucumbers, and pull a few radishes."

Nodding, Bernadette selected four fat green peppers, then moved over to the tomatoes. She still hadn't heard the roar of any motorcycles coming up the drive. Frank had been gone all morning, and it still rankled that he hadn't even told her good-bye. What they'd enjoyed last night was merely stress release and hopefully a way to extinguish the sexual tension that had developed between them since the day Crow had sent her away with Frank.

As she knelt next to a bushy tomato plant, something moved in her peripheral vision. She paused and looked over at the tree line.

Nothing.

Frowning, she picked another tomato, then straightened. She glanced toward the house, then scanned the surrounding lawn and garden. Both her friends worked silently. In one corner of the vegetable plot, blooming zinnias, cosmos and black-eyed Susans swayed in the hot breeze. The knee-high corn waved its leaves at Bernadette.

Shrugging, she leaned over to pick up the heavy handbasket, but again, movement in the trees caught her attention. She turned toward the woods, searching for the source of distraction. There, off to the right of a tall maple with a thick trunk, stood…someone.

She set the basket down and walked out of the garden.

"Bernadette?" Puppy called.

She strode faster, desperate to reach the person before he or she vanished into the forest. From what she could see as she drew closer, it appeared to be a woman. She peered at the tree where the figure was leaning.

"Hey!" she yelled. "What are you doing there?"

"Bernadette?" Luella hollered behind her. "Who are you talking to?"

"Don't you see her?" Bernadette threw over her shoulder.

She stopped at the edge of the lawn. An African American woman with salt-and-pepper dreadlocks hanging to her waist stood staring back at her with an amused expression.

Footsteps behind Bernadette told her that her friends had joined her.

"What are you looking at?" Puppy asked.

"That woman." Bernadette pointed.

Luella moved to stand next to Bernadette. "What woman?"

"Right *there*." She took a few more steps until only six feet or so separated her from the newcomer. "She's leaning against that big maple."

"Shit, you really *can* see me?"

Luella and Puppy gasped.

The air around the woman wavered and rippled like disturbed water, and she moved away from the tree.

"Holy fuck!" Luella jumped. "Scary Mary, what are you doing here?"

Bernadette struggled to understand what was happening. "Wait," she said. "You two couldn't see her until just now? Why?"

"She's a *bruja*," Puppy said.

"What?" Bernadette looked back and forth between her friends, then met the black woman's inky eyes.

"Witch," the woman supplied. "But if you can see me, that means you have magic in your blood." She turned to Luella. "Were you aware of this?"

"Yes." She shot Bernadette an I-told-you-so look. "But she refuses to even discuss it."

Bernadette scowled at her.

"I came to keep an eye on things," Mary said. "I told Frank if he needs my help to ask, but I found myself drawn here today." She passed her gaze up and down Bernadette a couple times. "Now I think I may know why."

"She doesn't know about...the way of our people." The pointed look Luella shot Mary wasn't lost on Bernadette.

"What's you're lineage, child?"

Bernadette faced the black woman. "Irish."

"Ah, born with the sight, and possibly other gifts, it seems." She rummaged in the voluminous pockets of her long, brown skirt and withdrew a baggie of hand-rolled cigarettes. After lighting one with a stick match, also from the little bag, she puffed several times, shook out the match, then spewed a cloud of smoke into the air. The wind caught it and bore the aroma of cloves to Bernadette. "It seems your MC has an ally and potential weapon to defeat the evil coming your way." Mary turned and walked deeper into the trees. "You might want to consider bringing her into the light...."

Stunned, Bernadette searched the trees and undergrowth but saw no signs the woman had ever been there.

"What the hell is going on around here?" she demanded. Unease slithered through her. Had she accidentally gotten herself into something she would regret? "Will one of you please answer me?"

Puppy stared silently at her naked toes and wiggled them, the bright pink polish stark against the green grass.

A sigh drew Bernadette's attention to Luella, who met her gaze boldly. "It's up to Frank to tell you what's going on, but if he decides not to bring you into the light, as Scary Mary put it, then you'll have to accept that." She dipped her head toward the garden. "Let's get back to work. We still have things to do, and the heat is getting worse."

The women started across the lawn. Still edgy, her head spinning with denial of what she'd just witnessed, Bernadette followed them back to the garden. She helped Luella finish spreading the grass clippings, but as she did so, she reflected on the attacks and the uncanny way Scary Mary had appeared. Was the woman really a witch?

Am I really a witch?

One way or another, Bernadette would find out the truth.

* * *

Frank knew he wouldn't be permitted to see the crime scene, so he'd parked his Harley out of sight on tractor trail leading to a hayfield. The next road over was the pad's access road, and Frank knew without even riding past it that cops would be stationed there.

His cell vibrated in his jeans pocket. He took it out and read Deputy Williamscot's text.

If you're determined to investigate, do it after *dark. This place is crawling with heat and white hats.*

Damn. He'd have to come back later. Dealing with authorities was bad enough, but if the place was rife with the big shots too, getting close to the scene would be doubly difficult.

His phone vibrated again. Swearing softly, he dug it out of his pocket a second time.

Delivery date moved up. Today. Meet me at the entrance to the community center.

He texted Phil back stating he'd be there in about 20 minutes. It bothered him to have to drop everything to escort the shipment today when they should have had another week to plan for it, especially since the rogue had killed again.

However, there would be plenty of men at the MC to keep an eye on things, and everyone knew better than to ignore a mandatory curfew when they had loved ones to protect.

He mounted his motorcycle and rode out

197

Plainview to SR 800, then headed south to meet Phil. As he coasted down the long slope to the first bend by the community center, Frank spotted Phil resting on his bike in the shade of a tree.

He pulled in and stopped, placing his feet on the ground and letting the engine idle.

"Boss," Phil said. "You ready for this?"

"As ready as I'm going to be." He frowned. "Why has the delivery date been moved up?"

His second-in-command shrugged. "No idea. Bloodbath contacted me and said the River Rebels needed to move the shipment up a week, so they decided to do it today. When I asked Bloodbath about it, he said that's all the information he'd been given."

"I don't like this." Frank stared up the winding drive leading to the building that had once been a grade school. "Dealing in illegal arms is something that's prepped and carefully thought through, so this sudden change…." He looked back at Phil again. "Something's up."

"Like?"

"That's what we have to figure out."

"So what do you want to do?" Phil tugged a pack of cigarettes from beneath his cut, then shook one out. "If we back out of this deal with the River Rebels, we could start a war."

"If we follow through with this, we could get a bum rap and lifetime butt buddies."

At that, Phil grimaced, a shudder racing through his body.

Frank hid his smirk.

"What if we just don't show up?" Phil asked.

"Then the River Rebels will know we're on to them."

"I don't know about this, Frank." Fill produced a lighter from the same hidden pocket, flicked it and lit his cigarette "Our MC needs funding, our people are faced with whether or not to buy food or pay a bill. If we don't follow through with this deal, it won't solve anything for our clan—and this new MC we're dealing with will bc pissed off."

"And what if Crow has set us up?" Frustration gripped Frank. He threaded his fingers through his hair, catching his do-rag and ripping it from his head. "Things are touchy between the Wraithkillers and us as it is. What if Crow has decided he wants us out of the picture and is doing it through the River Rebels?"

Phil blew out a cloud of gray-white smoke. "If that's the case, what's his objective? He'd be pissing in the River Rebels' Wheaties too."

His question took the wind out of Frank's sails. He slumped his shoulders and stared at the wolf muzzle and bared fangs that covered his Harley's gas tank. After they'd returned the guns they'd discovered, Crow had been true to his word and had let Luella go, even offering him the best 9 mm, then allowing him take Bernadette with him instead.

Worry snaked down Frank's spine.

"You have that look on your face you always get when something's about to go down," Phil said.

"There's been three murders by a rogue werewolf, and the one last night was less than half a mile from our MC," Frank began, his thoughts racing. "Then the River Rebels change the shipment arrangements immediately after last night's murder."

He waited as Phil puffed out another cloud of

smoke. The hot breeze twirled it around his head and shoulders before whisking it away.

"We need the money, Boss."

Frank sat quietly as his second-in-command mulled over all the facts.

Phil pitched the cigarette butt on the pavement and crushed it out under his boot heel. "We still have a couple hours before we have to meet the transport in Fly. Maybe we should pay Crow a visit first."

"Good idea." Frank revved the Harley, then duck-walked it around so he could pull out of the drive. "Let's get over there now."

Phil started his motorcycle. "Lead the way."

Chapter Sixteen

Frank thought it strange that the gate to Crow's compound was closed and guarded. Normally someone simply met him in the lot in front of the clubhouse.

"Are they worried someone will trespass or attack?" Phil asked.

"I have no idea, but something's definitely odd."

A biker walked out of the house. The butt of a rifle rested in his right hand, the weapon leaning on his shoulder. "What do you want?" he shouted as he drew closer.

"Need to talk to Crow," Frank called. "Check us for weapons. We're carry knives but no firearms."

"Plan on it," the guy said.

Once the man reached them, another Wraithkiller descended the stairs from a guard post on the upper level of the clubhouse and quickly joined his comrade. One frisked Phil while the other did the same to Frank. They collected Frank and Phil's weapons, then nodded for them to ride on over to the clubhouse.

Once there, Frank waited for the men to lock the gate, then meet them at the front door. The Wraithkillers escorted them into the clubhouse. Inside, most of the members lay asleep on furniture or lay asleep across tabletops.

As Frank passed a sectional, he recognized the sheep with the big tropical scene tattooed across her back. She bobbed her head up and down as she gave a young prospect a blowjob. The guy sat with his thighs splayed, chest bare, hands in the blonde's hair guiding her movements. His head rested on a sofa cushion, his eyes squeezed shut as he concentrated on the sensations the blonde was giving him.

Judging by the beer bottles, empty beer cans and Mason jars as well as numerous whiskey bottles and ashtrays full of cigarette and joint butts, Frank surmised the MC had had one hell of a wild party. Naked sheep slept on pool tables, their limbs entwined. Men lay everywhere, including several sprawled on the hardwood floor. They snored so loudly Frank wondered how anyone could sleep through the racket.

Crow emerged from a room at the back of the bar. His face registered surprise as he saw them, but he waved them over. "I wasn't expecting anyone today," he said. "To what do I owe this honor?"

Frank sat on one of the stools, removed his wallet and pushed a ten across the countertop.

Shaking his head in refusal, Crow retrieved a couple beers from a cooler, twisted the tops off and set a bottle in front of Frank, then Phil.

After putting the money back in his wallet, Frank said, "Thanks, Crow." He sighed. "I'm sorry for barging in on your club, but I need to ask you a couple questions."

"Sure." The man removed a bottle of high-end

whiskey from a shelf and poured himself a shot. He met Frank's gaze, his eyes so dark Frank wondered if the guy had a soul. "What's eating you?" Crow questioned.

"It's this arms deal." He shared a quick look with Phil, then took the plunge. "Moving the date up makes me uneasy. I don't want to test our tentative truce, but—"

"Wait, what do you mean the date has been moved up?"

Frank stared into Crow's black-as-tar eyes. Confusion shone brightly in them.

"You didn't know about the change of plans?"

"No." Crow placed his forearms on the bar top and leaned forward so he could speak in a lower voice. "What's going on?"

Quickly Phil filled him in on the details, then Frank told Crow about the latest murder.

The sudden way Crow straightened and took a step back nearly sent Frank off the stool. He wanted to reach for a knife, but Crow's men had confiscated them. Behind them, someone farted in their sleep, the sound loud and startling, as if someone were strangling a goose.

Phil snorted and reached for his beer, and the action calmed Frank's frayed nerves.

Pouring another shot of whiskey, Crow said nothing until he was finished and had capped the bottle. "Frank, I know we've had our issues over the years, but I'd like to keep the peace between our clubs. In doing so, we can help each other. When I say I have no knowledge of what you're talking about, I mean it. I never set up an arms transportation deal." He knocked back the firewater and slammed the shot glass down on the bar top. "Things might be done differently with the Werewolves of Rebellion, but I'd never allow anyone outside of myself or my second-in-command to set up any sort of deal, not even something as simple as transporting weed, let alone guns."

The expression in Crow's eyes told Frank all he needed to know. Someone was using the Wraithkillers to manipulate the Werewolves of Rebellion. An ice-cold lump of dread wedged in his gut. He chugged the rest of his beer in the hope it would settle his stomach.

"Who was it?" Crow turned his unholy gaze on Phil. "Who have you been talking to?"

"Bloodbath," Phil said.

"Fuck." For the third time, Crow uncapped the whiskey and poured a shot. "Fuck, fuck, fuck!"

"What aren't you telling us?" Frank questioned.

"I took Bloodbath as a prospect because the River Rebels vouched for him," Crow began. "Bloodbath didn't want to be in the River Rebels because they've had so much trouble with heat in Steubenville, which is why they moved their MC downriver and settled near Clarington." He threw back the shot, grimaced, then set the glass down. "Somehow, Bloodbath always avoids having a murder rap pinned on him, but the law gets him for other offenses, so he's been in out of prison so many times they installed a revolving door."

"So Bloodbath wanted in the Wraithkillers because…?" Phil asked.

"The River Rebels didn't want any more attention than they already had," Crow explained. "Their new location keeps them out of the spotlight and allows them to dodge the law more easily when it comes to their drugs and weapons. If they took Bloodbath on as a prospect, their president, Garsell, said it would just keep leading the pigs to them, so he suggested Bloodbath pledge to us since he's chummy with a couple of my Wraithkillers."

Garsell? Frank perked up. *Why does that name sound so familiar?*

"That way," Crow continued, "we could help each other out once in a while and the law wouldn't watch him as closely since Bloodbath would be up here in bum-fuck Egypt with the Wraithkillers. I wasn't worried about the guy bringing us grief. Figured he'd be the perfect set of fists to handle probs in my club." He shrugged. "Not to mention the fucker's an ace bartender."

Frank nudged Phil. "Why does that MC president's name sound so familiar?"

Phil shook his head, then his eyes widened. "Fuck! Garsell—Hudson Garsell!"

"Our newest prospect," Frank said, feeling as though he'd been kicked in the gut by a horse. "The same son of a bitch who was kissing Bernadette against her will. The same fucker who's been learning all about the Werewolves of Rebellion, our people, our ways, the same bastard who has been conveniently nearby whenever business is discussed...." He squeezed his eyes shut and fought his rising panic. Was Hudson Garsell the rogue werewolf? Where was the guy now? And why was he infiltrating Frank's MC?

"I don't understand," Crow stated. "Garsell, the president of the River Rebels Motorcycle Club, is one of your prospects?"

"Yes—well, posing as such," Frank answered. He raked his hands over his hair. "Garsell and Bloodbath have fucked us both over, Crow." He jumped to his feet. "Watch yourself and keep an eye on your club. When we find out more, I'll contact you."

Crow studied him for a moment, one eye scrunching slightly, a deep furrow appearing between his black eyebrows. Finally he nodded and held out his hand. "Good luck."

"Thanks." Frank shook his hand, then turned and nodded to Phil. "Let's fly."

Outside, Crow's men returned Frank and Phil's knives. Within minutes, they'd straddled their bikes and were racing through the barely opened gate and down the dirt lane. At the end of it, Frank stopped his Harley.

"Send a group text out to the men, but make sure they know not to tell Hudson."

Phil nodded, withdrew his cell phone from his front pants pocket and rapidly tapped out a text, addressing it to everyone except Hudson.

Frank took his phone out too. "I'll text Luella so she can gather all the women into the main house."

"Good idea," Phil said, replacing his phone in his pocket. He revved his Harley impatiently.

Finished, Frank put his cell away too. "If I find Hudson and Bloodbath"—he swept one hand through his sweat-drenched hair, a nervous habit he could never seem to break—"I'll kill them."

"Once everyone reads my text," Phil said, "you might have to wait in line for your turn."

"Like hell I will," Frank replied and shoved off and onto the main road.

* * *

The heat of cooking the evening meal had all the women, including Bernadette, exhausted and a bit on the woozy side. Bernadette poured herself a glass of iced tea from the third pitcher Puppy had made for them. Tonight the supper was a simple one—spaghetti, garlic bread and salad. Right now, however, she was too hot to even think about eating.

"I'm going outside," Bernadette told Luella. "It has to be a few degrees cooler than this kitchen is right now."

Luella nodded and swiped a dishtowel over her face. "Yeah, I think we may wait until dark and sit outside to eat. What I wouldn't give to have central air in this house." She smoothed the towel around her neck, then down over her cleavage. "I know it's not even close to getting dark, but don't go far."

"Is the pier okay?"

"Yeah," Luella said, "you'll be within sight of the house."

On the sunporch, Bernadette waggled her fingers at everyone. Puppy and the women who had replaced Carolyn, Shirley and the others for house duty all sipped from their sweating glasses as they watched the evening news.

Puppy raised her eyebrows at her, her deep brown eyes questioning.

"I'm stepping outside," she explained. "It's too damn hot in here."

"I'd join you," Puppy said, her voice tired, "but I don't have the energy to move right now."

Laughing, Bernadette shoved the door open. "I'll

be back in a few minutes to help with the final supper chores."

She crossed the carport, her glass of tea in hand, and followed the path across the back lawn and down the slope to the pond. The humidity hung over the treetops in heavy curtains of silver. Leaves and flowers drooped. Tall grass stood limply. Off in the pasture, some of the cattle and a half dozen horses stood chest-deep in the livestock pond in an attempt to fight off the heat and the biting insects.

Even the breeze wafting up the hill felt like it was coming out of an oven. Bernadette grimaced and sipped her tea. She loved summertime but hated the humid days. At least she wasn't in the city where the concrete absorbed the heat, then radiated it all night when everywhere else it was cooling off, but as she reached the pier and crossed it at the end, the treated wood exuded an unbelievable amount of heat too.

Sitting wasn't an option; the planks were too hot to endure. Instead, she turned and headed over to the shade tree where Frank had kissed her during the movie. She missed him, wished he was with her now, kissing her, caressing her...thrusting into her. The heat was unbearable, even under the tree's leafy branches, so she wandered back up the hill, almost finishing her glass of tea as she walked and berating herself for thinking of Frank and how he made her feel. She couldn't let herself fall for him.

She swallowed the last of her tea, then paused and ran the cool, perspiring glass over her forehead, then along the back of her neck. If it wasn't for suppertime preparations that needed finishing, she'd go for a swim. The pond was the only way to escape the unbearable weather, but she'd promised to set the tables. Maybe she could take a quick shower afterward, then sit next to her bedroom window or a fan.

Movement over by the barns caught her attention. Unsure what it was, she stopped. Something cracked in the woods behind her. She spun toward the noise, only to come face-to-face with Hudson.

Holy shit, where did he come from?

More movement drew her gaze to the woods behind him. Men she didn't recognize emerged naked from the trees. As they approached the main house, they fell to all fours, their bodies twisting and reshaping. Fur sprouted across skin of different hues. Their feet turned into part paw, part foot as their calves and shins shifted into the legs of canines. Disbelieving her eyes, Bernadette blinked several times, only to see they'd become a strange combination of half-man half.... No, it wasn't possible. She glanced over her shoulder again toward the barns where more men, who looked similar to the first group, were heading toward the house. Her pulse raced and blood boomed in her ears. Fear slammed into her until she thought she might faint from the adrenaline alone.

"I'm glad I found you," Hudson said. "I'm here to protect you."

"Protect me?" She fought to focus on him as spots flitted in front of her eyes. The things she was seeing looked like werewolves, but they were make-believe, creatures of myth, stories told to scare children.

"What you're seeing *is* real," Hudson stated. "Come with me. Frank would want me to keep you safe."

"No." She shook her head. "I have to warn Luella and the others."

She dropped her glass and sprinted toward the house only to have Hudson catch her before she'd gone half a dozen paces. He encircled her waist, then jerked her against his hard, overheated body. She looked up into Hudson's handsome face.

"I'm taking you somewhere safe."

"No, Hudson. Let go!" She struggled but couldn't budge. "Luella! *Luella*!" She screamed so loudly her throat hurt.

Hudson clamped one hand over her mouth and pinned her to his torso with his other arm. "Be quiet and cooperate, Bernadette. If you do, it'll be an easier transition."

Transition to what? She tried to move, but the man possessed unnatural strength.

The gangs on either side of the house continued to transform into frightening wolfmen in various colors of fur, each one with wicked fangs and muzzle-like faces. Many swarmed the house as others bypassed it and headed down the lane toward the community in the valley. Screams erupted from the house.

There was no way Bernadette was seeing werewolves, but there they were in broad daylight, loping, snarling, and speaking in guttural English, their intent to overtake the MC clear. But why? And how was it possible these creatures existed?

The roar of motorcycles coming up the lane gave her hope, but it was quickly dashed when the riders turned out to be from another MC. Twenty choppers stopped on or next to the carport. The bikers shut off the engines, put the kickstands down, dismounted, then to Bernadette's surprise, they promptly disrobed. Naked, they morphed into more man-beasts. They groaned and snarled as they completed their transformations.

Bernadette tried again to break free of Hudson to no avail, even with all the adrenaline zinging through her system. She had to warn Luella and Puppy, help them send out an alarm. If possible, help protect the children and the elderly of Frank's MC, too.

"You're mine, baby," Hudson said, his hot breath flowing over her ear. "Don't fight me and I'll treat you like a queen."

Her eyes widened. He was taking her as his woman? The man was crazy.

More shrieks came from the house. Then, from farther away, shouts and cries drifted up from the community.

Before she could move or protest, Hudson changed their positions and flung her over his shoulder, pinning her thighs firmly against him. She beat on his back and ass with her fists. Tears flowed down her heated cheeks.

"Don't worry, baby," Hudson soothed. "As long as no one tries anything stupid, we're not here to kill or maim."

"Then why *are* you here, and who are you, really?" she snarled. Outrage for Frank's MC overwhelmed her fear. "These people haven't done anything to you!"

"You're right, they haven't, but just like one tribe or country conquering another, we do what we must to expand our territory."

"Territory? What the hell are you talking about?" Hanging upside down, staring at his heels as he walked with her over his shoulder had blood rushing to her head. The heat of the day at its highest only added to her discomfort. "Put me down before I puke, Hudson!"

He reached the carport and set her on her feet. The sudden change to upright sent a wave of dizziness over her. She swayed sharply. Grabbing her, Hudson steadied her on her feet.

"Whoa, honey. Easy now."

More screams burst out to the driveway. Bernadette started toward the porch, but Hudson stopped her.

"Do anything stupid like calling 9-1-1 will get you hurt and put everyone in jeopardy." He drew her close and kissed her quickly on the lips. "Humans won't be able to accept the truth of what we are, including the Werewolves of Rebellion. Funny how Frank's MC hides what it is in plain sight, isn't it? Besides, by the time the others get home from work and Frank realizes we've infiltrated his MC with a Claiming and Maiming—minus the maiming, if possible—it'll be too late. He either accepts my demands or…." He shrugged.

Panicked, her voice abandoning her, she could only stare at him. He smiled, brushed his lips over hers again, then held her tightly by the wrist as he led her to the door. Someone shrieked as though dying, and another woman cried softly just inside the door. Bernadette's heart went out to the frightened women, but her own upset was steadily fading the more pissed off she became. She looked down at Hudson as he pushed her up the steps and through the entryway.

"You're going to regret this."

He blinked. "You say that like it's a fact."

"It is." She didn't know how she knew it, but without a doubt, there would be hell to pay once Frank and the rest of his men returned.

He pushed her inside. There, on the floor within a couple feet of the threshold, two of the women sat huddled together with a tall, shaggy werewolf standing over them. One cried while the second woman hid her face against the first one's shoulder, her trembling so fierce it shook both of them.

Bernadette let her gaze travel from the sunporch to the doorway to the kitchen. Puppy and Luella sat at the table, their arms outstretched, palms flat on the tabletop. Beyond them, constant shrieks and cries emanated from the living and dining rooms.

"Sit at the table with your friends," Hudson instructed. "Keep your hands on the tabletop."

The huge bartender from Crow's MC entered the kitchen. Bernadette gaped up at him. Confused, she looked at Luella for answers.

"Apparently," Luella began, her expression disgusted as she stared at the hulking man, "Bloodbath was a plant in Crow's MC so the Wraithkillers would be blamed for what's happening now."

"A plant from what MC?" she asked.

"Mine, babe," Hudson stated. "I'm the president of the River Rebels."

She looked at Bloodbath, who grinned at her with a perverted gleam in his eyes, then back to Hudson.

"We moved into the area to escape the heat's constant interference in our business," Hudson explained. "Now I'm exercising our right for a

Claiming and Maiming." He shifted his attention to Bloodbath. "You're in charge, but do not—I repeat—do *not* kill anyone unless it's absolutely necessary. None of your lame excuses just so you can murder someone, understand?"

"Yeah," Bloodbath rumbled.

The sinister tone of his voice sent ripples of fear through Bernadette. Although she didn't know how, she sensed the man would kill without remorse, kill because he enjoyed it.

"What about the females on the porch?" the brute asked.

"Someone is watching over them," Hudson answered irritably. "You've probably already claimed more than your share, Bloodbath, so don't push your luck."

"I want that one." Bloodbath pointed at Bernadette.

"No, she's mine." Hudson stepped in front of her. "I'm president. If you have a problem with my claim, you can leave the MC—but if you do, I'm cutting off the tats and taking your patches back."

Bloodbath's face grew calm, serene. His expression stabbed Bernadette with fresh fear. She knew everything was about to go to hell.

Chapter Seventeen

Bloodbath launched himself at Hudson. Bernadette ducked under the table as Luella and Puppy shouted in surprise. Bloodbath flipped the table out of his way, leaving Bernadette huddling on the floor. It flew into the air and hit the porch entrance. The strength and weight of Bloodbath's body knocked Bernadette backward into the wall. The chair absorbed most of the impact, but the sudden crash against the plaster brought a shelf of decorative plates down on top of her. Glass shattered, porcelain cracked and tinkled.

Pinpoints of pain flared on her head, shoulders and chest. She flopped to one side on top of the debris, then scrambled to her feet. Warm trickles of blood meandered down the side of her face and over one shoulder to settle in her cleavage. The brute swung a meaty fist at Hudson, who ducked it. Bloodbath drove his hand through the wall as if it were a battering ram.

Werewolves rushed into the kitchen. Some carried women under their arms or over their shoulders. The sound of motorcycles cut through the din.

Thank God, the men are here!

Someone yelled from the carport. More shouts followed, then growls and howls joined the racket in the kitchen as Hudson continued fighting Bloodbath. A snarl brought Bernadette's attention over to Luella. Her mouth dropped open as fur sprouted across Luella's face, neck and arms, her hands transforming into paw-hands, face morphing into a muzzle of sorts. Golden fur thickened and spread over Luella's body. The she-wolf vibrated with snarls and growls as she shifted.

Bloodbath slammed Hudson through the wall. Plaster imploded into the dining room; more dishes, pictures and decorative items flew helter-skelter, and glass and porcelain bounced and tinkled across the hardwood.

"Luella?" Bernadette whispered.

"Beastman must be home," her friend said, her words garbled.

"The women can't change unless their mate, father, or sometimes a brother, commands their shift," Puppy explained from where she still sat.

Luella leaped at the werewolves who had entered the kitchen. The strength of her attack surprised them. They dropped the women they held, who ran for the table and righted it so they could escape the house.

"Come on, Bernadette." Standing, Puppy held out a hand to her.

Another crash brought Hudson and Bloodbath through the same jagged hole-in-the-wall. Hudson carried Bloodbath to the floor, both now in werewolf form. Hudson, chocolate-brown with black accents on his ears, muzzle and paws, wasn't as large as Bloodbath, but he still held his own with the bigger werewolf. Bloodbath presented a frightening image, silver from head to toe, but his size made Bernadette wonder how long Hudson could fight him off.

"We have to run—now." Puppy quickly ducked an earthen jug Hudson flung at Bloodbath and missed. The crockery shattered against the edge of the sink, firing shards of clay in every direction. Puppy hissed and pulled a sliver from her cheek. She looked at Bernadette. "We'll help as many escape as possible, but we can't stay here. A Claiming and Maiming is old-world, but if used, it stills stands firm as our law. If you love Frank, you need to run, too. Otherwise, you'll become Hudson's mate."

The vicious sounds coming out of Luella as she fought the two male werewolves spurred Bernadette into action. One of the males slammed Luella into the pantry door, buckling it inward. Gasping, Bernadette started toward her friend.

"No, don't!" Luella said, her blue gaze fierce.

Indecisive, worried about her friend, she met Luella's eyes, the same bright blue ones that always held a smile for her. Reluctantly Bernadette grasped Puppy's hand. After Luella nodded her approval, she focused on the males again, bared her fangs and launched herself at them a second time.

Bernadette hurried along behind Puppy, who yanked on her hand. The screens encasing the porch hung in ruins. Werewolf battled werewolf as the women huddled against the wall behind the recliner. Puppy motioned to them, and they skulked over to her and Bernadette.

They ran out onto the carport where Beastman had transformed into a great golden beast, his size even bigger in his transformed state. Bernadette halted, her eyes refusing to cooperate with her brain and vice versa. He howled, hefting a black werewolf over his head. With grace and startling speed, he spun and threw the wolfman toward the workshop. Its body hit one of the windows, the glass imploding.

"Where's Luella?" Beastman garbled at Puppy.

"She's fighting two in the kitchen," Puppy called back as she led Bernadette and the others toward the barns.

"I'll kill them!" Beastman surged across the concrete, his fur glistening in the sunshine, the remnants of his shirt and jeans barely hanging on his body. "Run, Puppy. Hide the women and any others you might find."

As she ran alongside Puppy and the rest, Bernadette glanced over her shoulder just in time to see Beastman rip the door off its hinges and toss it onto the carport. His roar as he entered the house spurred her to run faster.

* * *

By the time he let off the throttle, Frank had nearly missed the end of the lane. He turned onto the grassy area they kept mowed at the mouth of the drive and rode over it to the gravel. He gave the Harley more gas as he sped toward the MC with Phil on his right.

Chaos ensued in the community. It took only a moment for Frank to realize what the River Rebels had begun. Terror seized him. He hadn't heard of a Claiming and Maiming I decades. So many good people could be lost to injuries, or worse. Women could be taken as mates—especially if Hudson was following the old-world law, which was unshakeable.

I could lose Bernadette.

The terror coursing through him concentrated on his heart until he thought it would cease to beat. He struggled with the fear and managed to tamp it down into his gut where he could use it to fuel his anger.

Glass from doors and windows lay on porches and steps. A huge dent smeared with blood in the hood of a pickup revealed the battle that had been fought there. Potted plants lay pell-mell, their contents spilling onto walkways and across lawns. A few men sprawled over the grass or in the lane, but whether they were dead or just knocked out, Frank couldn't tell. Lycanthropes Frank had never seen before fought it out with some of his men, also in werewolf form, between two of the bungalows. Shouts and roars from within some homes trailed them up the hill to the clubhouse.

The sun beat down on them as they raced up the gently curving slope. Humidity hung thick over the trees, as if the universe had thrown a mourning shroud over the property.

Upon reaching the carport, Frank barely got the kickstand down before leaping off the Harley. Phil matched him move for move. When they were halfway to the porch, a werewolf rushed out and stopped, his eyes meeting Frank's.

Hudson.

He didn't know how he knew the lycanthrope was Hudson, but there was no doubt in his mind.

Inside, Beastman's enraged howl rattled the house. More roars followed, but Frank didn't recognize any of them. The cries and screams of women punctuated the pandemonium.

Hurriedly Frank shrugged out of his cut and

removed his boots, keeping his attention on Hudson the entire time, but Hudson darted away, loping on all fours toward the barns.

A body burst through a screen and landed in the flowerbed below the window. Luella's golden wolf form looked out at him. "Puppy took Bernadette and a few of the women," she said slowly. "I'm not sure where they've gone"—She flicked her long tongue out to wipe blood from her muzzle.—"but Hudson plans to claim her as his mate."

He looked at Phil, who was just shrugged out of his cut. "I'm going after him," Frank said. "Bernadette is mine, and I'll be damned if I let anyone touch her."

"I'm right behind you," Phil replied, pulling off his boots.

As Frank ran, he called upon his lykoi side. Tingling swept over his body. The sting of emerging hair and the slicing pain of fangs poking through his gums kept him focused on his task of finding Bernadette. Normally his people lay still as the change overtook them, as simultaneously running and transforming created more pain. Still, he focused on finding Bernadette.

Behind him, a sharp bark of pain then a thud stopped him in his tracks. He looked back to find Phil half-shifted as he stumbled back onto his paw-feet, only a handful of denim threads holding his jeans on his body.

"Go!" Phil said. "I'm coming."

Still in the midst of his transformation, his jeans ripping apart along the seams, his shirt shredding against his morphing muscles, Frank managed to lope down the path to the barns. His only thought was to stop Hudson, even if it meant killing him.

* * *

Puppy led Bernadette and the others into the woods. She waved for them to follow her across a shallow ravine and up the other side. At the top of the slope, she paused so they could catch up with her.

"I don't know about this," Bernadette said. "Won't they catch us in the woods?"

"The other clan is concentrated on the MC and the community," Puppy explained. "We have hiding places in the clubhouse and beneath the barns"—She glanced around, her black eyes sharp for any movement.—"but we have to come here so the other clan doesn't find our refuge points. There's one a few yards that way."

"Werewolves," Bernadette said. "Never in a million years would I have dreamed that your motorcycle club's name was the real thing." She stepped back and studied Puppy and the other women. "Are you all...?"

"All of us except Callie May." Puppy pointed to the tiny woman nearest Bernadette.

She turned to the woman with ash-brown hair and pale green eyes. She was so delicate-looking that Bernadette wouldn't have been surprised if a summer breeze could knock her over.

"My mate is a lycanthrope," Callie May said, "but I'm 100 percent human. Even if I allowed my husband to turn me, I wouldn't be able to shape-shift unless he was nearby." She shrugged. "I'm not sure yet if I want to be turned."

"You too?" Bernadette asked Puppy.

"Yes, through lineage," she answered. "Both my parents are lykoi."

Bernadette frowned. "Lykoi?"

"Greek for *wolf*," Puppy said. "I'm Filipino, but the wolf gene was given to my family several generations back." She offered her an apologetic smile. "It's a long story."

"Puppy, we should keep moving," the chunky, older woman of their group urged.

"Right, let's go." Puppy led them along a faint trail.

They walked as quickly and as quietly as they could through the forest. Dodging trees and pushing through undergrowth full of briars, they finally stepped out into an area where a hole in the canopy allowed sunlight to bake a small glen. The meadow was big enough for about three middle-sized tents and a fire ring in the center, but all that resided in the clearing was field grass, nodding daisies, clumps of purple-headed clover, and sticks that had fallen from the surrounding trees.

Puppy crossed to the center of the tiny meadow and paused. "You must never say anything about this place, Bernadette. Its secrecy is why we're able to use it for protection now."

With a curt nod, Bernadette replied, "I understand."

As Puppy and one of the others searched for something in the tall, thick grass, movement caught Bernadette's attention. She gasped and faced where she'd seen the shift of light and shadows.

"What is it?" a raven-haired woman asked.

"I don't know," Bernadette whispered, keeping her eyes on the spot. "I saw something move."

"Oh, hell," the woman said. "Where?"

Her arm shaking, fingers trembling, Bernadette pointed toward a tree with large sheets of peeling bark. "By that tree with the strange bark."

"Puppy!" the woman called.

Puppy and the others stopped what they were doing to join them.

Again, something moved in the shadows by the same tree.

"There." Bernadette pointed again. "Do you see it?"

"I don't see anything," Puppy answered. "Anyone else?"

A chorus of "no" with the shake of heads followed.

The air rippled like a stone had been tossed into water. Immediately Bernadette knew who it was. "The black lady. She's here."

"The *bruja*?" Puppy stiffened.

Suddenly she saw Scary Mary. "I see you."

The air rippled again, then the woman strode out of the shadows and into the sunshine. The women gasped and stumbled back, but Bernadette held her ground. "That is the coolest trick I've ever seen."

Scary Mary grinned from ear to ear, her teeth bright against her light brown skin. "That, my child, is the first time anyone has ever said that. I quite like it." She laughed, the sound that of an ancient motor trying to turn over, then sobered. "A Claiming and Maiming is in progress. Frank may be too late to stop it."

Puppy said, "We were going to hide in—"

Everyone except Mary jumped at the snap of a branch.

"Quickly," Mary whispered, "surround me—now."

Bernadette grabbed Callie May's and the black-haired lady's hands and drew them over next to Mary. Puppy and the others did the same, encircling the witch. From one of the many pockets of her skirt, Mary pulled out a handful of something and tossed it up into the air. As the gray-green powder fell over them, landing in their hair and upon their clothes, Mary muttered in some language Bernadette couldn't identify. The air shimmered around them, then brightened in clarity as though she were staring through a brand new sheet of glass.

More snaps echoed through the woods. Rustling came from different directions.

"They can't see or hear us," Mary said, "but this glamour spell won't last long, so pray they're just passing through the glen."

Two men wearing River Rebels cuts, and three werewolves strode into the clearing. The werewolves tipped their noses up in the air and sniffed loudly several times.

"There are women nearby," one said, his words guttural.

Callie May slapped both hands over her mouth, her whimpers muffled against her palms.

"I hope they don't find the ropes to the hidden door," Puppy whispered.

"Well, they're not here," a tall, skinny biker said. "Hudson said for us to keep looking until we found them. They have to be in the woods near their MC, or they've backtracked to help their clan."

They headed straight across the clearing. A sharp inhale drew Bernadette's attention to Puppy. Her eyes were huge, round and full of fear.

"What?" Bernadette asked.

"They stepped right over the ropes and the hidden door," Puppy replied. "I can't believe they missed it."

In moments, the River Rebels vanished into the woods.

One woman started to walk away, but Mary put a hand on her shoulder. "Wait," Mary told her. "Give them time to get out of range and allow my spell to fade."

Minutes ticked by. The high adrenaline racing through Bernadette slowly began to ebb, leaving her tired and shaky. Callie May offered her a sympathetic smile. The raven-haired woman drew her hair back into one hand and produced a hair tie from around her wrist and fastened her tresses into a high ponytail. She fanned herself in the oppressing heat, perspiration glistening on the back of her neck.

Puppy turned first one way, then the other, sweeping her gaze along the edge of the tree line.

About to ask when the spell would stop working, Bernadette kept quiet when the air around them shimmered, the clear-glass atmosphere disappeared, and what sounded like electricity sizzled in the air. Abruptly tiny embers rained down on the circle, then it, too, vanished.

"So cool," Bernadette whispered, winning another big smile from Scary Mary.

"You ladies get into your hiding place," Mary instructed. "I'll go find Frank and tell him where you are. Those men could come back through here, so be as quiet as you can."

Together, they walked over to the center of the glen. With the help of the women, Puppy raised a big square by the ropes. It turned out to be a large door constructed of planks and metal supports. Steps carved out of the earth descended into total darkness. Staring into the black hole, Bernadette shivered.

"I'll bring Frank back as soon as I can," Mary promised.

"Now why would we want you to do that?" a male voice said.

The others gasped or cried out. The same bikers and werewolves had returned. They'd all left in the same direction, but now they were emerging from the tree line in different spots, completely surrounding the clearing.

"Oh, for the love of God," Mary grumbled. "They backtracked on us."

Fear rose in Bernadette, but it was short-lived as anger replaced the sensation. She turned to the tall, skinny biker closest to her. She eyed him up and down, taking in his buzzed, sandy-brown hair, his scraggly mustache, his dirty, stained cut covered in a menagerie of patches, and jeans ripped at both knees with cottony fibers fluttering in the breeze.

"What do you possibly have to gain from attacking the Werewolves of Rebellion?" she asked him.

He strode over to her.

"They're a quiet, peaceful clan," she added, refusing to back down. "You River Rebels sure as hell don't look like the farming kind."

Behind her, Mary snorted.

Somehow she sensed the strike before she saw it coming, and ducked.

"Why you smart-assed ginger," the man snarled. "I'm going to—"

A black-and-white wolfman with a patch of fur missing from his head grabbed him by the shoulders and jerked him back. "Touch her, Stickman, and answer to Hudson," he garbled out.

"Hudson can kiss my fucking ass!"

"We've got the women," the wolfman added. "All we have to do is return to their MC with them, so don't make this harder than it is."

"He's right, Stickman," the other guy, burly with a small paunch, said. "There's no point in hurting the women. Let's just do the job Hudson gave us, okay?"

Stickman gave Bernadette the once-over, his eyes full of rage. Inwardly Bernadette shivered, but she met his eyes with a cool confidence she did not feel. Behind her, she sensed Mary moving closer. She soon stood next to her, then reached into one of her many pockets. Bringing her hand up to her face, Mary blew across her palm. Red dust bloomed into the air, the breeze bearing it directly into the River Rebels' eyes.

"Go around the red powder!" Mary shouted. "Run, girls. Run!"

The men and werewolves howled in pain. The wolfmen dropped onto all fours, their eyes pouring tears, their black, moist noses running with snot. The men rubbed at their eyes, cussing at the top of their lungs.

* * *

"They had to go this way," Frank told Phil as they entered the forest. "Puppy knows the dug shelter is the closest place to hide."

"Why the hell did the River Rebels attack our

MC, Boss?" Phil loped along beside him. "It doesn't make sense. We haven't been in a real war with another MC for years, and our issues with the Wraithkillers was more bullshit than anything."

"I don't know, but whatever the reason, it's obvious we have something Hudson wants, including Bernadette."

"Yeah, but he didn't even know about Bernadette until he came in here as a prospect…did he?"

Frank paused as he caught the direction the wind was flowing. "Somehow I'm going to find out." He pointed deeper into the forest. "There. I'm catching a whiff of lycanthrope in that direction, and they're not of our clan. If they're in our woods, then they're pursuing the women."

* * *

Running through undergrowth and briars wasn't as easy as it looked in the movies. Bernadette cursed, gasped and squealed with each prick from a blackberry thorn or multiflora rose that snagged her body. Every whip and slap of a branch left red marks on her skin. The crackles of the others' progress in the woods reached her from time to time along with the hollers and roars of the bikers and wolfmen.

She halted at another wild berry patch and squatted so she wouldn't be seen. The forest had gone quiet save for the wind in the canopy and the chatter of chipmunks.

A rustle drew her attention to a small standing of pines.

She waved to Scary Mary. Cautiously the woman

ambled toward her until she crouched next to Bernadette.

"What did you blow into those men's eyes?" Bernadette asked.

Mary grinned. "Powdered ghost peppers. It's worse on the lycanthropes because their sense of smell is similar to a dog's, which is ten thousand times more powerful than a human's."

"No wonder it put them down so fast."

"I'm heading back to the farm," the woman said so low Bernadette almost didn't hear her. "Maybe I can gather enough men to come help." She glanced around, then stood on her knees. From behind her and under her blousy shirt, she withdrew a pistol. "Here. Take this. It's only a .22, but if you're face-to-face with a human, it'll drop them. If it's a lycanthrope, aim for the chest. Don't hesitate to pull the trigger. Frank and his people will take care of any bodies."

"Are you sure?" She gaped at Mary. The idea of shooting another person, even a werewolf, went against her conscience. "I don't know if I could kill someone."

"It's better than being raped." Mary squinted at her. "You're different, child. Follow your instincts."

With that, Scary Mary rose and picked her way over to the pines, then turned slightly to the right and kept walking until Bernadette could no longer see her.

She didn't know anything about guns except that they each had a safety that had to be flicked off to fire. After finding the tiny switch and sliding it to the Off position, she rose and looked in every direction for danger. Low-hanging branches swaying in the strengthening wind and all the shadowy areas gave

Bernadette pause. A werewolf or a River Rebel could be waiting to pounce from anywhere.

Her pulse grew faster, her heartbeat so loud it was a miracle the wolfmen couldn't hear it and home in on her. A shriek from down the hill frightened her so badly she performed a little jig and almost dropped the pistol.

Galvanized into action, Bernadette began moving uphill. She had a vague notion they'd descended a gentle slope to the clearing, but she hadn't been paying enough attention to notice any landmarks or trails that might trigger recognition. The heat seemed a hundred times worse in the woods, the humidity amplifying the aroma of earth, pine needles and decaying leaves.

She jumped as a deer emerged from a thick patch of ferns. Its sudden, bleating appearance frightened her so badly she nearly shot it.

Finally she stood on a faint path, so much adrenaline whizzing through her that she couldn't stop shaking. Her heart flailed so hard against her ribs that she saw spots in front of her eyes. Sweat coated her palms, forcing her to grip the weapon's handle tighter to keep it from sliding out of her grasp. Up the path, she paused once, just for a moment, to catch her breath, then continued on. She wondered if she should stay to the undergrowth but tossed the idea aside. She'd be out of sight, but the amount of noise pushing through the branches and bushes would help anyone pinpoint her whereabouts. Staying on the trail allowed her to move faster and put more distance between her and the River Rebels.

But what would she do if she encountered more of Hudson's men? Shoot them? Even if she could aim well enough to put each one down, did she even have enough shells? There could be more scouts she hadn't seen yet.

Summoning courage she didn't feel, Bernadette hurried on, keeping the pistol firmly in her right hand.

Chapter Eighteen

A familiar scent tantalized his nostrils.

Bernadette.

Elated, Frank hurried onward. He'd scented Hudson's people on the trail, following their foul essence down the path toward the hidden dugout. With as strong as Bernadette's scent was, she had to be nearby.

"I smell a female," Phil said. "A human."

"It's Bernadette. We have to be close."

They pushed through a dense area of multiflora roses, the damnable things encroaching on the trail, thorns tearing at their fur, and emerged several yards above Bernadette. She stopped cold. Her eyes widened, the whites stark in her heat-flushed face. Mouth agape in a perfect O, she raised a pistol and pointed it at him.

He started to say something to her, anything to calm her, and realized he was fully in his werewolf alter ego.

"Fuck." The word came out of his muzzle-like mouth as "fuff."

"Get back!" Bernadette commanded, the fear in her voice bordering on hysteria. The pistol wobbled in her hand. "I don't want to shoot you," she hollered up the trail, "but I will."

"It's me, Frank."

The guttural way he spoke seemed to frighten her more.

"Put the pistol down, baby," he said gently, or tried to. Nothing out of a werewolf's mouth sounded gentle. He took one step then another toward her as he tried forcing his beast side into submission so he could revert to his human form. As usual, the lycanthrope within him fought the shift.

"I don't think she can understand you," Phil said behind him.

"Baby, it's me, Frank."

He took another step, but something in her eyes hardened, and Frank dodged to the left just in time. The report of the pistol cut through the trees. Thorns tore at his nose and ripped across one eye. The mild poison in the multiflora barbs stung terribly, and his eye teared, momentarily blinding him in it. Another report rent the air, and a howl that stood his fur on end echoed throughout the treetops.

Frank forced his animal side to obey. The fiery sensation of receding fur and claws assailed him. He groaned and whimpered, writhing in the damnable briars as his legs reformed and his muzzle shifted into his human face. Still in the midst of his shape-shifting, Frank managed to extract himself from the thorns and flopped out onto the trail. A spatter of blood painted the dirt. Phil lay on his side, also shifting, but the hole in his back just under his left shoulder blade was unmistakable. Stunned, Frank gingerly rolled him onto his back.

"Phil?"

"I'm alive…for now," he wheezed. "Your stupid ginger shot me with a silver bullet." He sucked in air and pain registered on his face. "Thank God…she has…lousy aim."

"Frank?" Bernadette kept her place on the path. "You're both…both werewolves? H-how is that even possible?"

Frank looked down the trail at her. He wanted to go to her, hug her, ravage her mouth in a searing kiss as he hugged her round hips to his groin and murmur how happy he was that she was safe, but right now he had to get Phil to the clubhouse.

"Calm down," Frank told her in a soothing voice. "Werewolves exist. It's as simple as that, but so do many other beings humans believe are myth." He met her eyes and tried to convey comfort through his. "Are you all right?"

She nodded.

"Can you keep it together?"

Something passed over her face—resolve? She nodded again.

"Good girl. You're one hell of a strong woman, Bernadette. I admire that."

She offered him a soft smile as the resolve intensified on her face and brightened her eyes.

"We need to get Phil back to the house. Puppy may be tiny, but she's a cunning lycanthrope. She'll guide the women, who all know how to protect themselves, but even if they're caught, we'll have to barter for them later." He took scraps of denim from the remains of his jeans and wrapped them around Phil's shoulder to stem the blood flow. "Can you walk, Phil?"

"Maybe long enough to reach the clubhouse." He shut his eyes for a moment. "But that's gonna be pushing my limits. The silver poisoning is running through my body."

Bernadette rushed up the path to them. "Oh, hell! Phil! I'm so sorry!" She landed in a heap next to them. "Scary Mary gave me the pistol for protection, but I had no idea it was loaded with silver bullets."

"Let's get him up," Frank said. "We'll have to do the best we can and pray that Beastman has regained control of the MC."

* * *

Bernadette couldn't do much to help Phil, but she cleared the way of branches and brambles as Frank half walked, half carried him up the hill. The oppressing heat weighed so heavily that it seemed as if it were trying to push them into the ground. They finally emerged from the woods and headed up the path to the barns. Phil's breathing grew more ragged. They'd come in search of her and the others only for her to shoot Phil. Hell, if Frank hadn't dodged to the side, he'd be the one wounded. Regardless, Bernadette hated that she'd hurt anyone.

"I feel so bad about this, Phil," she said.

"Don't…apologize," he gasped out.

The chickens seemed nervous around the coop, and the horses nickered as they passed the big barn. The sounds coming from the main house revealed why the animals were jittery.

"Fuck," Frank said. "Sounds like Beastman still hasn't regained control of the MC. We can't call in

Deputy Williamscot until everyone shifts back into human form, including the River Rebels."

Bernadette glanced up at him.

"Deputy Williamscot and his wife are the only ones who know what we are," Frank explained, "but what the deputy doesn't know is that there's another lycanthrope clan in the area."

"It certainly changes....things" Phil said.

"Save your strength." Frank hefted him into a straighter standing position and pulled him firmly against his side. "I'm going to put you in Beastman's truck. You lay low there until we can get control of the situation. There's a first aid kit in the workshop. It should have antidote in it."

The battle in the house kept the River Rebels occupied as Bernadette helped Frank settle Phil across the bench seat of Beastman's old pickup.

"Stay here," Frank instructed. "Keep out of sight for a moment. I'm going to get the antidote."

He sprinted away, his naked ass glistening with sweat. Even standing there with the possibility of being discovered, Bernadette couldn't help admiring his physique. Werewolf or not, he was a fine man.

In moments, Frank returned with a vial of something that looked like motor oil. He pulled the cork free and handed it to Phil. "Drink this, then pull that rain slicker on the floor over you. It'll be god-awful hot, but you need to stay hidden. You're too weak right now to fight anyone should they find you."

Phil downed the vial's contents, then yanked the yellow slicker over himself.

"Bernadette, I want you to hide in the workshop.

There's a cabinet beneath the workbench that's big enough for you—"

"No!" She grabbed his arms, the tat sleeves bright against her pale hands. "I may not understand how werewolves are possible, but all it means is that this world has more races of people in it that society realizes." She stared up at him with her best pleading face. "Those are my friends in there, Frank. I will defend them just as you're going to—minus the fangs, fur and claws."

Worry etched lines into his forehead and around his mouth. "I don't want something to happen to you."

"That's how I feel about you, too," she replied with conviction. "Tell me what to do and I'll do it, but let me help."

"Find a different weapon," he said. "Anything to inflict pain that will keep you out of arm's reach." He straightened slightly and peered into the bed of the truck, then smiled. "Perfect." He removed a shovel. "Here, use this. Swing it like you're going for a homerun."

Grateful she could help, she nodded and smiled back. She pushed the gun into Phil's hand where she saw it peeping from the raincoat. "Use this to protect yourself," she told him.

A muffled thanks reached her as he gripped the .22.

Leaning by her ear, Frank said, "Don't get hurt, baby."

His hot breath and nearness swirled gooseflesh over her neck and shoulders.

He led her around the truck and over to the porch. "Beastman! You okay?"

"The sons of bitches just keep coming out of the woods!" Beastman hollered from somewhere in the house.

A werewolf rushed around from the front of the Victorian and launched himself through the air. He connected with Frank and knocked him flat on his back. Stunned by how fast and far the wolfman had leaped, Bernadette then realized she was holding the shovel. She raised it over her head, gulped, then swung it with all her might at the beast's head.

Clang!

The werewolf rolled off Frank, its big, clawed hands going to the back of its head. Frank jumped to his feet, transforming back into his lycanthrope form. He threw his head back and howled his anger and pain to the sky until the shift was complete.

At his howl, silence fell over the battle. Werewolves looked out at them through the shredded screens and shattered windows. Bernadette had no idea who was who, but one thing was obvious—everyone knew Frank exuded power.

The moment passed, and the shrieks, howls, roars and the racket of destruction resumed. The werewolf that had attacked Frank shook its head and jumped to its feet.

Clang!

This time the creature stayed down. Blood dripped from its forehead.

"Damn, baby," Frank said. "Babe Ruth would be proud."

He rushed inside. Lycanthropes began running out the doors, some even leaping through windows.

Bernadette hefted the shovel and was about to

follow him inside, but a crash at the backside of the clubhouse drew her attention. She kicked off her flip-flops and jogged to the corner of the house just in time to see Bloodbath carrying Luella, still in werewolf form, over his shoulder. He headed in the direction from where the first wave had appeared.

Brandishing the spade end in the air, Bernadette ran as hard as she could toward Bloodbath. He must've heard her, because he turned. With Luella lying over his torso, Bernadette couldn't strike him, and he was too tall for her to reach his head.

"What's this?" he snarled. "A tasty piece of ass? Frank's little ginger?" His tongue lolled around his mouth as he spoke.

He dropped Luella unceremoniously on the ground. The she-wolf landed with a hollow thud, and Bernadette grimaced. Upon impact, air burst from Luella's muzzle and she groaned in pain.

"What are you going to do?" At his deep-well voice and guttural way of speaking, shivers needled Bernadette's spine. "Swat me?" He peeled his lips back as best he could and leered at her. "I killed that stupid hunter and his whelp. I killed that guy who was fishing. And I killed that fat white-hat bastard who dared shine a light on me up at the fracking pad." He leaned closer and drew in a deep breath, scenting her. "I could use something to take the edge off, then I'll kill you, too."

What *could* she do? Bloodbath towered over her by at least two feet, his body pure muscle. He took a step toward Bernadette. There was only one thing that popped into her mind to defend herself. She lowered the shovel and swung upward, bashing him in the groin with all her strength.

Bloodbath dropped to his knees, paw-hands clutching his genitals, and roared in agony.

Bernadette wanted to turn tail and run, but she couldn't. There was no way she was leaving Luella at his mercy.

"Fucking bitch!" He struggled to his feet then lunged for her.

Dropping onto all fours, Bernadette scrambled between his legs and over to Luella's prone form. Slowly Luella's fur and werewolf attributes were fading back to human.

"Luella, wake up!"

The woman moaned.

"I'll claim you," Bloodbath roared, "then I'll make your death slow and painful!"

He sprang toward her.

Bernadette squeezed her eyes shut and threw herself over Luella.

Another growl reached her, this one different from Bloodbath's. A heavy thud followed. Snarls, one deep and the other lighter but still all male, overwhelmed the area. Bernadette opened her eyes.

Several yards away, Hudson and Bloodbath fought again. They kicked up sod and rolled over a small rhododendron, squashing it against the grass.

Luella moved, and Bernadette eased off her body so she could sit up. Several werewolves with their paw-hands tied behind their backs appeared, led by others onto the back lawn. When Frank saw her, he handed a lycanthrope over to Tom and rushed over to her.

"Are you all right?" he asked, peering at her with familiar dark eyes. "Did he hurt you or Luella?"

"No," Bernadette said, "but Hudson saved both our lives. Bloodbath would've killed us if Hudson hadn't attacked him."

"I'll kill Bloodbath myself!" Frank leaped to his feet.

A yip drew their attention. Hudson fell flat on his back. Bloodbath stood over him. Jagged wounds over Hudson's face and shoulder spilled bright blood.

"Time for someone to knock that big fucker down." Frank picked up the shovel and launched himself toward Bloodbath, but the brute was prepared and flung one arm out, knocking the shovel from his grasp and catching Frank on the shoulder. He flew backward and fell over a barrel arrangement boasting Luella's impatiens and geraniums. Blooms and potting soil burst into the air as Frank's weight smashed the wooden vats.

"No!" Bernadette scrambled to her feet.

"Don't!" Luella snarled. She grabbed at one of Bernadette's hands, but Bernadette shook the she-wolf off. Marching toward Bloodbath, all she wanted to do was hurt him, make him suffer for what he'd just done to Frank. Red settled over her eyes, the color seeping into everything before her just as Hudson's blood spread through the grass.

"Bernadette, stop!" Frank yelled as he wrestled himself upright in the mess he'd caused.

She heard him, but it didn't truly register. She kept walking toward Bloodbath.

A low, sinister laugh rolled out of the brute. "What are you gonna do, Little Red? Swat the end of my nose?" He took a couple steps toward her. "I'll make you red all over, bitch!"

241

Hostility overwhelmed Bernadette. She raised her arms, palms out at him and screamed her fury, screamed until her voice disappeared. A shimmering wall appeared in front of her. Bloodbath stopped in his tracks, the whites of his eyes glowing, his nostrils flaring.

"What the fu—?"

Another scream managed to rip free of Bernadette's throat. She flicked all eight fingers down then up. The clear, glistening wall shot toward Bloodbath and struck him, then flames engulfed his body as he hurtled back about 20 yards, crashing into the backside of the workshop. A dent formed upon his impact.

As she came to herself, Bernadette gasped in horror at what she'd done, her hand flying over her mouth. Bloodbath rolled and flopped on the ground until he'd smothered all the flames. He struggled to his feet, smoke puffing off his fur, a tiny flame still dancing on the tuff of hair on one pointed ear, black patches of skin sizzling audibly.

With a roar that sounded like a combination of trumpeting elephants, barking dogs, and a pride of lions, Bloodbath rushed toward her as if he had the devil on his tail.

"Run, Bernadette!" Luella shouted.

Just as the huge lycanthrope reached out to snare Bernadette around the throat, Frank appeared in front of her and swung the shovel across Bloodbath's neck. Blood sprayed in a crimson arc, splattering over her, the warmth of it intense, the odor gagging her.

Bloodbath grabbed at his throat, his eyes widening, then rolled back in shock, tongue falling out one side of his mouth. Red squirted between his paw-hands, sprinkling Frank and Hudson in crimson drops. It spread through Bloodbath's silver chest fur like a lacy, crimson vest, then the fur became a large wad of matted red. He dropped to his knees, eyes bulging. He slumped to on one side, nearly landing on Hudson. Gurgling in his own blood, he bled out on the ground.

Repulsed by what she'd just witnessed, and the surge of power she'd wielded suddenly gone, Bernadette twisted to the side and vomited on the grass. She kept retching, unable to stop herself. Gradually she became aware of someone alternating between patting her on the back, then smoothing a hand up and down it, then patting....

"You okay, honey?" Luella asked.

She gulped several times, the taste of bile thick in her mouth. "Yeah, I—" She sucked in a shuddering breath. "—think I am now."

"Told you," Luella whispered gently, "white witch."

"Is the house clear?" Frank bellowed over to his men. Several of them nodded. "What about the community? Have we regained control?"

"I sent men down there," Beastman grumbled from where he'd just forced two River Rebels to their knees. "I'm waiting to hear back, but I don't have a fucking pocket in this fur to hold a cell phone."

Luella snorted in amusement, and Bernadette laughed despite her gyrating senses and the grizzly scene.

Frank loped back over to Bernadette. As he approached, his lycanthrope side began to recede. He paused to allow it to finish, moaning in pain as he morphed. Finally Bernadette stared at the man she'd come to love.

Love. She gasped softly. Luella sent her a curious glance but said nothing. As the last bits of his wolf side vanished, Bernadette realized she did, indeed, love Frank.

I don't even care that he's a werewolf. She met Luella's pretty blue peepers. *Hell, I don't care what any of them are. They're family.*

When Frank crouched next to her, he placed a hand on either side of her face and stared directly into her eyes. "I know I asked earlier, but are you all right?"

"I'm fine."

"No, she's not," Luella protested. "She just puked her guts up. After all that power she released, it's a wonder she's not in a coma. Poor woman's scared out of her mind."

"Not because you're all werewolves," Bernadette protested. "It was…it was…because…." A coppery aroma hit her nostrils. She jerked away from Frank and vomited again, but all that came up was a bit of bile and foam. She groaned and began to shake.

"Aw, baby." Frank gathered her into his arms. "We're not violent people unless it's to protect our loved ones or what is ours. I don't like to kill or even wound anyone. There hasn't been a Claiming and Maiming in decades."

"A what?" she asked, her face pressed to his bare chest. Even with him covered in sweat, stray bits of fur and some of Bloodbath's blood, Bernadette relished the sensation of Frank's embrace.

"We'll explain later," Luella answered, patting

her on the back again. "Frank, the scent of blood must be getting to her."

"Take her into the house." He quickly squeezed Bernadette, then relinquished her to Luella. "She's overheated, and after the jolt she gave Bloodbath, she's probably drained, too."

He rose, then pulled Bernadette to her feet. The world spun crazily, and she swayed. Catching her, he said, "Never mind. I'll carry her inside." As he passed Johnny, who brought two naked River Rebels out and shoved them to the ground, Frank ordered, "Get Hudson on his feet, if possible, and sit him in the kitchen. I want to find out what's behind this attack."

"Will do," Johnny said.

"If he gives you any trouble, Beastman will help you," Frank added. He spotted one of his other prospects and hollered, "Hey, Ass Crack! Check on Phil in the cab of Beastman's pickup, but make sure you announce yourself. He has a pistol with silver bullets."

The prospect jogged over to the Ford and rapped on the driver's door.

Snuggled against Frank's bare chest, Bernadette closed her eyes. In moments, she found herself in the living room. He placed her gently on a sofa.

Looking around, she gasped. "Oh, Frank! Your MC is destroyed."

"We'll deal with it," Luella said behind him. "I'll be right back, Frank. I want to grab some clothes."

"We have a lot to discuss, Bernadette." He swept a chunk of sweat-soaked hair out of her face. "But right now, I have to see who is wounded...or worse."

"I know." She smiled up at him weakly. Now the

attack was over, she felt as though she could sleep for a week, but she had the suspicion that the release of—dare she say magic?—was the main reason for that. "You do what you need to. I'll be fine."

"You need to rest and take time to absorb everything that has happened."

"I want to help—"

"Oh no you don't," Luella said as she returned from her bedroom. She finished tugging one of Beastman's tent-size T-shirts over her body. "You'll take it easy. You're not of the clan, honey. Humans aren't built to handle this kind of stuff. And there appears to be much magic packed into that little body of yours, so you need to take time to adjust."

Grudgingly Bernadette nodded. She did feel like shit. Her head pounded, her skin actually hurt, and she was trembling as if she were gripping a live wire.

"I'm going to see if I can find my cell phone," Frank stated, "which I think is somewhere around the workshop with what's left of my jeans, then I'll call Deputy Williamscot. Bloodbath's body will have to be turned over to authorities as well as any other bodies we might find."

"What do we tell the law?" Luella asked, her eyes round with worry.

He shrugged. "We'll say a new gang tried to take over our MC and as of yet, we don't know why."

Chapter Nineteen

"Why don't you go into the main bathroom and shower?" Luella suggested.

"Are you okay?" Bernadette asked. "You took a hard fall when Bloodbath dropped you."

"I'm a lykoi, so we take a lot more physical abuse than a human."

"Lykoi?"

"Greek for a wolf," Luella answered. "Our clan has a healthy dose of Greek blood."

"That's where the name Nightshade comes from too, right?"

"Yes." Luella smiled. "Frank told you his family is descended from healers?"

"Yeah."

"He's never told that to anyone outside of the clan." Luella helped Bernadette to her feet, then escorted her down a short hall off the living room and into the bathroom. "He seems to be smitten with you, and Frank doesn't let himself get close to any women except me, Myrinne, his mother and Galina. Now that you know what we are, you'll have a big decision to make soon."

"Such as?" Bernadette looked up at her much-taller friend. Something about the way Luella had spoken sent a little sliver of ice down her spine.

"That's something Frank will discuss with you," Luella said. "I'll find you some clean clothes. And when things settle down, we'll go shopping for some new clothes for you. What do you have? Only two outfits?"

"I travel light." Bernadette chuckled.

"You must be the only woman I know who doesn't have a huge wardrobe." Luella handed her two towels and a bottle of shower gel from a cabinet. "If you get light-headed again, sit on the toilet or sit in the bottom of the tub. I don't want to hear a thud in here and find you passed out and bleeding from the head."

"Yes, ma'am," Bernadette quipped.

Luella favored her with a warm smile that was part mother and part best friend. "Fighting for us was—unexpected. Thank you."

Clutching the towels and gel in her arms, Bernadette shrugged. "It was the right thing to do. I know I've only been here a short time, but you're like family to me."

"As I've been saying"—Luella grasped the doorknob.—"you're a keeper."

"What exactly is a Claiming and Maiming?" she asked.

"In a nutshell, it's when one clan decides to take over another," Luella explained. "It's a way to build one's clan, bring in new blood to a family and to build wealth. For lycanthropes, the practice goes back hundreds of generations. Now, it's not done often, but it still stands as law. For the Nightshade's people, it's been...oh, I guess nearly 80 years since the last time a clan tried to take us over through a Claiming and

Maiming." She thought for a few seconds. "I think the last one I even heard about was up in Canada, where things are a little wilder than they are here in the Appalachians." She shrugged. "Hudson's idea was clever, I'll give him that."

"Wait. Eighty years?" Suspicious, Bernadette gave Luella a once-over. If she were right, Luella was only about 35 years old, unless.... "Are you saying you've been alive 80 plus years?"

Her friend had the grace to blush. "Let's just say lycanthropes age slowly."

Incredulous, Bernadette could only stare at her. "Doesn't that cause problems with people who have known you a long time? They're aging and you're not."

"We have ways of handling that, and the longer you stay here, the more you'll learn."

"Oh, but I'm not—"

"Luella!" Ass Crack shouted through the house.

Beastman's bellow followed. "Damn it, woman. We need you out here to take a look at Phil's gunshot wound."

"I'm coming!" Luella tossed another smile over her shoulder as she left and shut the door behind her. Once the door was closed, she hollered, "I have lykoi ears, you two fucking idiots, so I'm not deaf!"

Despite her exhaustion, Bernadette giggled as she turned on the spigot.

* * *

Frank discovered his cell phone right where he'd thought it was—with his shredded jeans. He sighed. He went through more pairs of denims than a hundred men could wear in a lifetime, but biker boots were even more expensive. He frowned at the split sides and toes of his boots. And he'd just gotten this pair broken in well too.

He hit the button for Craig's personal number. After quickly relaying the matter to the deputy, he hung up and strode over to where Beastman was overseeing the River Rebels they'd caught and tied up. He approached him the same time Tom did.

"Hey, Beastman," Tom said. "Luella sent out some clothes for you." He handed the big guy the garments and a pair of tattered sneakers that looked as if they could be used as canoes. "She said she was tired of seeing your hairy ass wandering around the backyard."

"Fuck you, Tom," Beastman grumbled, grinning. "And tell my wife I'll fuck her later."

Tom burst out laughing as he walked over to help guard the prisoners, the lot of them all in human form now.

"Were you able to call down to the community?" Frank asked.

Nodding, Beastman pulled on briefs, then jeans. "The houses have all sustained a lot of damage, and there were reports of concussions, cuts and sprains. Tractor's wife suffered a broken wrist, but Tractor said if it hadn't been for the Stellarmi boys, things could've been much, much worse." He sighed heavily. "The youngsters' extra strength served to kick some major ass."

"Send Deputy Williamscot inside when he gets here," Frank said. "Has anyone found Puppy and the other women?"

"They showed up about five minutes ago and went straight down to the community."

"Thank God they're all safe." Frank let out a big breath. "I'm going to find some clothes and keep an eye on Hudson." He turned to go inside. "And no staring at my ass as I walk away."

Beastman roared with laughter. "But it's such a pretty ass."

After being attacked by the River Rebels, it was nice to be able to joke around with his men. He passed Hudson at the kitchen table. Luella stood smearing ointment on his face where Bloodbath's claws has raked him. The man groaned, keeping his eyes shut.

At Luella's questioning expression, Frank answered, "Clothes."

She smirked and resumed her task.

"Where's…?"

"Showering," she replied.

He padded barefoot through the house and upstairs to his room. After showering quickly, he dried off, donned fresh briefs and jeans and left his torso bare save for his spare cut. He pulled on socks and cursed again at the thought of having to buy yet another pair of riding boots.

He stepped out into the hall. The sound of movement from Bernadette's room stopped him. He could knock on her door, go inside and ravage her, show her how much he….

He couldn't fill in the blank. How *did* he feel about Bernadette? The idea that Hudson had tried to take her from him forced such strong jealousy to rise in him that he could almost taste it, but the fact Bloodbath had intended to rape, then kill her nearly pushed him into a murderous rage.

Those were all signs she was his mate.

But she was human.

He raised his fist to knock on her door and paused. Just days ago, he'd intended to send her home. Now he couldn't bear the thought of never seeing her again. A couple other human women already lived here, ones who had been taken as mates a few years ago. Maybe he could....

It was dangerous here if the River Rebels were still intent on taking over his MC. Someone would certainly want revenge. It was a code with one-percenters—avenge their brothers, whether they were right or wrong.

The door opened abruptly. Bernadette stared wide-eyed at him. "Oh, you startled me."

"Sorry. I was just going to...." He took in her still-damp hair, which she'd twisted and clipped to the back of her head. The short hairs around her nape and the sides of her face had twirled into curlicues. The aroma of citrusy shower gel and her personal scent tickled his nostrils. His cock stirred, but he willed it to abate. He couldn't afford to let her distract him. But oh how he wanted to kick the door shut, tear her clothes off and shove her onto the bed before sinking into her hot depths.... He gulped. What the woman did to him!

"Yes?" She blinked up at him, her expression innocent, lust shining in her eyes.

"Uh...I was going to say the heat will be here any minute. They'll probably want to question you too."

"That's fine." Exhaustion settled over her features.

Frank swept his gaze over her. The bruises scattered over her pale skin fired anger through him. How dare anyone touch her. But, just as quickly as it had arrived, his ire extinguished. She was, indeed, human. Few human women could handle a life with a lykoi man. She was soft, delicate, a writer...a white witch. This development mystified him. Had she been hiding her abilities from him? How could he even contemplate taking her as a mate?

"I'll see you downstairs." He turned to go, but she placed a hand on his arm.

"Frank? What's wrong?"

The way she stared up at him put his heart in a vise. Why did she affect him so profoundly? No other woman had ever inspired trembles in his limbs or left him breathless and wanting to spend more time with her.

Perplexed and a bit shaken, he threaded his fingers with hers, squeezed, then released her hand. "I just want this night over. It'll be hours of repetitive questions from the authorities."

"Are you sure that's all that's bothering you?"

"Come on, I'll walk you downstairs." He held out his crooked elbow, hoping she'd let the matter drop. Finally she wrapped her arm around his. "Just do me a favor and don't wander off," he said. "Stay in the house. We have no idea if any of Hudson's men are still lurking about."

"Oh!" Her worried gaze flew up to his. "What about Puppy and the women I went into the woods with?"

"They're fine." He liked that Bernadette was so selfless. But the instant the thought rose in his mind, he vanquished it. Living here wouldn't be easy for her. "Puppy led them back to the community."

Once they reached the ground floor, Frank led her over into the dining room, where many of the women had assembled. He grimaced at the cuts and bruises on most of them, but he also knew they were strong. Pulling a chair over next to the kitchen doorway, he placed it so Bernadette was out of the walkway but where she could also see and hear what was going on. He heard Craig's voice just around the corner as he discussed something with Beastman and Luella.

"This might take a while, so make yourself comfortable," he said to Bernadette. "Someone set out drinks and some sandwiches on the table behind you. You should eat and regain your strength." He leaned over and brushed his lips across hers. "You fought hard for us today." When she smiled up at him, he whispered, "By the way, we have a bet to settle."

At that, she blushed, but desire flared in her lovely, green eyes.

She would probably want to go home now, but maybe they could enjoy one more night together. "Until later."

As he stepped into the kitchen, he hoped like hell no one noticed the raging hard-on pressing against the front of his jeans.

The instant Deputy Williamscot saw him, he drew Frank out onto the sunporch. "What the hell happened here, Frank?"

"A Claiming and Maiming," he answered.

"A Claiming and…".Williamscot stared hard at him from beneath the brim of his black hat. "Who are those men tied up in the backyard?"

Frank righted the recliner he preferred to sit and collapsed into it. "The River Rebels."

As Deputy Williamscot looked around for a place to sit, he asked, "I thought they were in Steubenville?"

"Until recently, they were."

"Any idea why they decided to attack you—aside from a C&M?" The deputy tugged a straight-back chair out from under a broken stand that had once held an assortment of houseplants. "This doesn't make any sense."

Frank raked both hands through his hair. "You're right. It doesn't. And you're putting yourself in danger by being here, because Hudson and his men will know you're aware there are lycanthropes." He groaned and gripped the arms of the recliner so hard his knuckles ached. "But we had to call the law."

The expression on Craig's face almost made him laugh…almost.

"Are you telling me all the River Rebels are werewolves?"

Frank smirked. "Yep."

Taking off his hat, the deputy gaped at him. "Good God, Frank. How many of your kind are there in the world?"

"More than you realize."

His deputy friend sat quietly, staring through the tattered screens. A minute or two passed, followed by several more. Although Craig had long ago accepted that the Werewolves of Rebellion were truly werewolves, the knowledge more lycanthropes existed far beyond Rebellion would take time for him to process.

Still staring through the screens, Craig questioned, "And that guy with all the deep lacerations over his face and shoulder is the president of the River Rebels?"

"Yes, his name is Hudson Garsell."

"What made him think he had the gonads to come into your MC and take over? I thought there hasn't been a C&M for decades."

"I have no idea why he came here to do a Claiming and Maiming. All I do know is that Bloodbath, the dipshit who was Crow's bartender, was posing as a prospect in the Wraithkillers so he could be close to us to stir shit. Bloodbath is the one who murdered those people in Plainview and the white hat on the fracking pad."

"Shit." Craig swiped one hand over his face as though it would help clear his thoughts. "I don't know how we're going to explain this to the rest of the sheriff's department, let alone the feds."

"Let's talk to Hudson," Frank suggested. "I think Luella is finished patching him up, so the guy should be able to explain himself now."

Deputy Williamscot rose and entered the kitchen, stepping over broken crockery and the remains of chairs. Behind him, Frank looked over his head at Hudson, who still sat in the same chair. The swelling in his face has spread from the raked side to the ear of the unharmed side. His eyes were half-shut from swelling, his lips bruised and bloodied. Hudson's shoulder looked like it had gone through a meat grinder, and, despite Frank's hostility toward the guy, he still couldn't help feeling a little sympathy. Hudson must feel like he'd just fallen down a mountainside of glass shards.

Frank couldn't sit at the table. He was strung so tightly that he had to pace. Craig tossed him a curious glance, then flipped open the notebook he always carried with him and clicked the end of a pen.

"What the hell's behind all this, Hudson?" Frank asked. "There hasn't been a Claiming and Maiming for decades."

Luella moved between them and set a glass of water on the table in front of Hudson. "Here, this will help keep your lips moist." She moved out of the way and leaned against the counter.

"You should go to the dining room with the other women," Craig told her.

"I should stay right here and hear this, because I'm the one who takes care of the women, the ones his men"—She pointed a shaky finger at Hudson.—"tried to claim."

Craig nodded.

"Well?" Frank said loudly.

Hudson jerked slightly. "Money."

Frowning, Frank shook his head once. "Money? What the fuck, Hudson! You've heard my MC is struggling to get by."

"No." The word sounded as though Hudson had a mouth full of food. "Not your bank account." He drew in a long, shuddering breath. "Your gas and oil rights."

Like a lightning bolt, realization hit Frank so hard his knees nearly buckled.

"If we could Claim and Maim, make your MC ours…." Hudson grimaced, obviously breathing through pain. "If your MC became part of the River Rebels, we would have forced you to sign the deed over and we would've made hundreds of thousands of dollars off the energy rights to your land. After all, yours is one of the largest privately owned properties around these parts."

Frank jerked a chair out and sat, hard.

257

* * *

A collective gasp from the women erupted around Bernadette. Several of the men, outraged and encroaching on the kitchen from the dining room and living room entryways, were forced back by Beastman, who had entered through the back door. Bernadette looked from one person to another, waiting for someone to throw the first punch.

"Stay out of the way and just listen," the big man ordered, defusing the situation. He strode into the kitchen and leaned against the sink next to Luella, draping one arm possessively around her waist.

From where Bernadette sat, she could just see Frank at one end of the table, Hudson at the middle, sitting in front of Beastman and Luella, and Deputy Williamscot stood between Hudson and Frank.

"What about the three murders?" the deputy asked.

"I didn't have anything to do with those," Hudson rasped. "Bloodbath was supposed to pose as a prospect for the Wraithkillers. While there, he was close by so he could cause trouble for Frank's MC, stuff like planting pot in saddlebags and the odd unlicensed weapon." He paused, swallowed, then reached for the glass to sip some water. He set it down. "When I heard about the murders, I never dreamed it was Bloodbath who was killing those people. I figured it was some psycho until I heard how brutal the kills were, but even then—" He inhaled sharply. "—I figured it was a rogue werewolf, not anyone from my MC." He turned to look up at the deputy, his face twisting in pain. "Honest, Deputy, I didn't know it was Bloodbath until

I heard what he said to Bernadette in the backyard a few minutes ago."

"That's a lie!" Bernadette jumped up and stood in the threshold. "He told me things that proves he knew Bloodbath was responsible for the three murders."

"She doesn't know what she's talking about," Hudson said. "There was too much happening at the time. She's confused."

"I am not confused!" Bernadette's entire body vibrated with anger. "He told Bloodbath he'd killed enough and not to kill any of Frank's people unless it couldn't be avoided."

Frank rose and drew her back to her chair. "You'll get your chance to Deputy Williamscot everything, sweetheart."

She peered around the door at the deputy, who nodded with a wry smile.

"Why go after my MC for money?" Frank asked once he'd returned to his seat. "You've been running a"—he glanced at Deputy Williamscot—"lucrative MC."

"Easy money," Hudson replied, glowering at Bernadette through his good eye. "I'm tired of dodging the heat due to…other things. It's one main reason we moved the MC into this area. I want to sit back and relax, raise a family." He met Bernadette's gaze again from across the table. "I thought I'd found a mate, but I didn't realize you'd already claimed her, Frank." He picked up the glass again and muttered around the rim, spilling water down his chest.

Bernadette wanted to throttle him.

Stepping up to him with more ointment and gauze in her hands, Luella gently wiped the old ointment away, then applied fresh. The deputy pelted Hudson with more questions as she worked on his wounds. Frank, worried and looking exhausted, sat back in his chair, raking his fingers through his hair, a habit Bernadette found endearing. She looked around at the destruction inside the house. From the snippets of conversations she'd heard from the women, the community had sustained major damage, too. How would the MC ever recover when things were already on a day-to-day basis?

"All right," the deputy said. "I'm bound to honor my promise to the Werewolves of Rebellion." He looked directly at Hudson. "I'm the only person in any of the law enforcement agencies around here who knows lycanthropes exist, and that's because Frank saved my life. The sheriff's department doesn't need people around here going crazy with fear should they find out werewolves are real." He studied Hudson for a long moment, as if he expected the guy to protest. "If people knew the truth, they'd be shooting everything that moves. So…we're gonna give the rest of the department the story about the River Rebels wanting Frank's energy rights and Bloodbath working on his own as a serial killer, which should get the feds out of the picture, then we'll follow up with the River Rebels attacking the Werewolves of Rebellion, leaving the whole lycanthrope business out of it."

"Sounds good to me, Craig," Frank stated.

All around Bernadette, others voiced their agreement. She met Frank's gaze and nodded. He smiled.

"As for why all the men outside are naked—" Laughter burst from the deputy. "—I have no idea what to tell the sheriff or other deputies."

Everyone laughed.

"How about telling them it was some kind of club ritual?" Beastman suggested. "Like a hazing. All the guys we've tied up are young except for one or two. The law might buy it."

Officer Williamscot nodded. "That just might work."

Amused, Bernadette wondered if it could be that easy. After all the fighting, the trauma, the destruction and even the loss of a life, these people moved on and seemed stronger because of it.

And, she realized, she didn't want to leave them.

Chapter Twenty

For Bernadette, the rest of the evening passed in a flurry of activity, questions, more questions, and even more after that. She relayed the same details she'd given to Deputy Williamscot to the sheriff. By the time the coroner's van had motored away with Bloodbath's body, and the Monroe County Sherriff's Department had cleared out of the house and left the MC grounds, it was nearly midnight. Although what had happened to the people Bloodbath had so viciously murdered still troubled Bernadette, she felt a little better about them. At least now the victims' families would have closure.

Thankfully everyone was safe and sound, including Puppy, Callie May and the other women who had escaped with her that day. The River Rebels who had been tracking them in the woods had made the mistake of returning to the MC, only to be caught by a couple deputies and two of Frank's men. And, to her relief, Phil was already up walking around, his gunshot wound half-healed from Luella's homemade remedies, the antidote Frank had given him and the special healing abilities she was told all lycanthropes possessed.

Exhausted, Bernadette sat on the back stoop, her thoughts whirling, nerves still jangling. Inside, every Werewolf of Rebellion minus herself, the children, and two women to watch over them as they slept upstairs, had gathered for an important MC meeting. Rumbling and flashes of lightning in the west foretold of a nasty storm headed their way. Maybe a good rainstorm would clear the area of the heat and humidity. Better yet, maybe it would wash away all the bad energy from the farm.

She straightened. *Bad energy? Where did that thought come from?* She thought about it for a moment. Yes, it was true. The rain would cleanse the farm, and the lightning would recharge it with good energy.

Maybe she needed to spend some time with Scary Mary, find out exactly what her own abilities were all about. Perhaps her mom knew more than she'd told her. The fury she'd felt when Bloodbath had struck Frank and the release of that emotion had stunned her. If she could do that without really trying, what could she do if she concentrated?

That thought frightened her.

But she couldn't write any of what had transpired in her new manuscript unless she falsified information. Or, if she tried her hand at fiction, she could write the truth about her stay with the Werewolves of Rebellion and readers would be none the wiser.

It was a tantalizing thought, but she'd have to discuss it with Frank first.

She hadn't been with the MC long, but the idea of leaving tore at her heart. Until now, she'd never had supportive, caring friends like Luella and Puppy. She enjoyed working with the women in the clubhouse. The men were polite, helpful and protective, and Frank….

She drew in a deep breath, held it, then let it out slowly. She loved Frank. Loved him so fiercely that the fact he was a werewolf didn't bother her in the least. It seemed there were human women here who were in relationships with lycanthrope men, but would Frank want her? Would he take her as his woman and allow her to be a part of his MC? Especially now he knew she could wield magic?

A green-gold sphere of light caught her attention. At first Bernadette thought it was a cluster of fireflies or maybe ball lightning, but as it steadily progressed around the pond and up the path to the house, she finally made out Scary Mary's form. Once the older woman reached her, Bernadette marveled at the luminous ball of light the witch had conjured. It danced, depending on which way she moved, around the woman's hips.

"I'm glad to see you're safe and sound," Mary said. "Is all well with the rest of Frank's people?"

"Lots of damage to property, a couple broken bones and numerous cuts and bruises, but no member deaths or serious injuries," Bernadette replied.

"And the River Rebels have been taken into custody?"

Bernadette nodded. "Along with the 20 or so motorcycles the others rode in on."

"Have you considered my offer?" Mary asked, her dark eyes gleaming an eerie sapphire in the orb's light.

"I'll probably be going home soon, Mary. I don't

fit in here. I'm a human, and all but a couple others are werewolves."

"They prefer lykoi or lycanthrope," Mary said firmly, "and you won't be going anywhere."

"How do you know?"

"I see things." The woman smiled smugly, her teeth brilliant in the dim light. "You will be staying here a long, long time." She turned, waited for the sphere to illuminate her way, then said over her shoulder, "I'll be back in a couple days for your answer."

"But I can't write my...." Bernadette blinked a couple times to focus on Mary better, but the witch and her eerie ball of light were gone. She scanned the back lawn again, but the sorceress had vanished.

With a sigh, Bernadette rose and walked quietly past the last row of people in the living room, who were trying to hear Frank, Phil, Tom and Beastman speaking in the dining room. She hurried up the stairs and flopped down on her bed. For several minutes, she lay watching the lightning arc in the distance, her heart heavy, her brain a bundle of interwoven questions without answers. Fear of what she was, what she might become, finally tossed her into utter exhaustion, and sleep claimed her.

* * *

The next morning, Bernadette packed her belongings and headed downstairs to ask Luella to drive her to Columbus, or if one of the men would. In the kitchen, she found her friend in her usual spot at the counter, sipping coffee and chatting with her husband.

265

"Good morning," they both said almost in unison.

Luella dropped her gaze to the backpack hanging from Bernadette's hand. Her big blues widened. "I thought you liked it here?"

"I love it here," Bernadette replied. "But I don't fit in with the Werewolves of Rebellion." She shrugged. "Heck, I can't even write my book because it wouldn't be true. I'll have to call my editor and see if he'll brainstorm with me on an alternative true crime novel."

Luella set her cup aside and enveloped her in a big hug. "Oh, honey. I wish you'd reconsider. You're not afraid of us, are you?"

Shaking her head against Luella's shoulder, Bernadette answered, "Not at all. But I'm human, not lycanthrope."

"There are human women here," Luella stated, her voice rising to emphasize her point.

"Frank needs…." Emotion closed off Bernadette's throat. After a long couple of minutes, she finally managed to whisper, "Frank needs a stronger woman than I to make him happy."

"Beastman, do *something*," Luella said over Bernadette's head.

"What do you want me to do?" he asked. "Red has made up her mind."

"Don't you want to tell Frank good-bye?" Luella asked.

Bernadette stepped back out of her arms. "No, I think it's best I leave quietly. He has too much to handle now."

"But you paid a grand in rent and board," Luella protested.

"Keep it. It's a gift. If nothing else, buy everyone groceries or get some toys for the kids."

To Bernadette's surprise, tears shimmered in Luella's eyes.

"So," Bernadette asked, "will you drive me?"

"I'll drive her," Beastman said.

With a teary farewell, Bernadette followed Beastman out to the carport. Another storm had moved into the area, and light rain began falling. With the wind whipping her hair around her head, she climbed into Beastman's pickup. She'd miss everyone, especially Luella and Puppy, and never seeing Frank again punched a hole clean through her heart, but she was doing the right thing. Frank hadn't asked her to stay. If she tried to remain here, and even if she could harness her magic, she'd be a burden, another human to protect. The Werewolves of Rebellion didn't need another mouth to feed, either.

"Do you mind if I stop and pick something up in the community?" Beastman asked. "It'll save me a trip out."

"Sure, go ahead."

He started the struck and put it in gear just as a bolt of lightning struck somewhere behind the barns. Thunder immediately boomed, and the vibration of it traveled through the truck and into the seat beneath Bernadette.

"Damn," Beastman muttered. "That was close."

* * *

Frank dropped the hidden door with a loud thud. The storm had moved in faster than he'd thought it would, and standing near so many tall trees unnerved him. He was trembling after the last lightning strike.

Now that some of the River Revels knew the dugout's location, his MC would have to use it for storage and dig a new one somewhere else on the property for the women and children to hide. As he moved the sod back over it, he prayed there would never again be a need for such a hiding place. He stood for a moment, imagining what Bernadette and the women had felt when they were so close to sanctuary only to have Hudson's men catch them. For the thousandth time, anger sluiced through him. Frank reminded himself that Bernadette and the others were safe and unharmed, but it frightened him that someone had come into his MC so easily, undetected, and had lived among them for days bent on taking what was theirs.

But Hudson will be in prison for a while.

And someone would take Hudson's place at the River Rebels' MC. No doubt the River Rebels would avenge their president.

With a worried sigh, Frank headed up the trail toward the clubhouse. His cell vibrated, and he removed it from his pants pocket.

Bernadette is heading home to Columbus right now. If you hurry, you can catch her before Beastman reaches the gate.

His heart skipped a dozen beats, and he sucked in shocked breath. *What the fuck? Why is she leaving?*

He sprinted up the hill, using his lykoi strength to propel him. He reached the carport just as Luella shoved open the screen door he'd rehung that morning.

"Move your ass!" she shouted. "You can't lose her, Frank!"

He leaped on his Harley, started it, clenched the monkey bars and tore down the lane. A flash of lightning opened the sky and rain fell with a vengeance. Squinting against the downpour, his clothes instantly soaked, Frank fought the fear clenching his heart. It squeezed his chest so tightly he could barely breathe. Had he done something to upset Bernadette? Was she leaving because the River Rebels had frightened her so badly? Or was it because—he gulped—she couldn't handle the fact he was a lycanthrope?

He let off the throttle, almost stopping to turn around, but the need to have her with him, to make her his mate, overpowered everything else. He gunned the bike and rumbled down the hill and through the community so fast the wrecked houses were a blur.

Frank caught a glimpse of Beastman's truck through the orchard. He gunned the Harley, cutting over into the recently mown grass, and sped past the pickup, then back onto the lane to stop in front of it. Beastman slowed, then stopped the vehicle to let it idle.

Frank duck-walked the bike over to the passenger side. "I need to talk to you, Bernadette," he said. "But after we talk, if you still want to go home, I'll take you to Columbus myself."

She looked at him for a long time. Then she nodded at Beastman. After she'd gotten out of the pickup and had her backpack, Beastman turned the truck around by cutting through one side of the orchard and headed back to the clubhouse.

"How'd you know I was leaving?" she asked.

"Luella told me." He placed a hand on either of her shoulders. "Don't go."

"My life will never mesh with yours, Frank. I'm human. You're a…lycanthrope."

"Do we scare you?" he asked. "Do I?"

"No."

He stared into her vivid, green eyes and knew she spoke the truth. "Then why leave?"

"I can't write my book," she answered. "Telling the truth about your MC just isn't an option. No one would believe it, which would ruin my career, and those who did would be looking to hurt your MC." She stared at the muddy lane beneath her feet. "I'm human, weak. Although there may be a few humans in your clan, I'm not strong enough for your people, Frank,e not physically or mentally."

"You *are* strong enough." He pulled her into his arms. She dropped the pack and slipped her arms around his waist. Smiling, he looked into her eyes. "You're a white witch. You're powerful. All you have to do is learn to control your magic. Bloodbath was going to rape, then kill you, and you still fought to protect Luella. Few humans would do that. You stood up and told the truth about Hudson, something that could haunt you for a while if his MC decides to avenge him, but you still did it." He shook her gently to get her attention. "That takes more strength than you realize, so don't tell me you're not physically or mentally strong enough, because you are. And as for your book, maybe it's time you start writing true fiction, only no one will realize it's true."

She favored him with a soft look. "I didn't think you wanted me to stay. And your mom and grandmother don't seem to like me."

"My mom and grandmother like you plenty,

that's why Grandmother called you the flame to my fire. She was telling me that I'd met the one who would make me whole, happy. I haven't had a chance to tell you," he replied. "I've had one thing after another to deal with, then the River Rebels attacked...but, yes, I *do* want you to stay. I want that very much."

He dropped his head to hers and claimed her mouth as the rain fell harder, washing away his fears and indecision. She tasted sweet, her lips incredibly soft, yielding. She kissed him back, as though she were afraid if she didn't, she'd never have another chance. Just a simple kiss had him wanting to lay her in the grass and take her physically, to love her until she was exhausted by his kisses, his thrusting into her, his claiming her as his alone. There was no way he was letting Bernadette go, ever.

"You're the flame to my fire, the power that feeds my beast," he said, water trickling into his eyes, "and the delight of my soul. You're mine, forever. I love you, Bernadette."

* * *

Frank wanted her. He needed her to stay. He accepted that she was human, but he also believed she was strong for his people. Bernadette's heart sang with happiness and felt almost as if she could float into the treetops.

"I love you too, Frank." She kissed him back, sliding her tongue into his mouth. She tasted his personal flavor and the rainwater that coursed over their faces. He rewarded her with a needy groan and crushed her to him. Happiness filled her to the point she thought she'd explode from it.

Finally he broke the kiss and drew her against him so his arousal pressed into her and his heartbeat drummed so loudly against her ear that it sounded like the thunder above them.

"If we don't stop now," he said, "I'm going to lay you in the grass and take you right here for anyone to see."

"Well, I do have a bet to pay," she said.

His laughter rumbled in her ear.

"What are you going to do about all the damages to the MC?" she asked. "I don't want to be another mouth to feed when the club is already struggling."

He smoothed one hand over the back of her head. "Last night's meeting was about selling the gas and oil rights to my property. That way, the club will have a lump sum of money to repair everything and I'll give a percentage of it to each family. Plus, if I can set it up properly, maybe a quarterly amount will come into the MC as a regular income." He sighed and hugged her tighter. "I'm not sure how it all works, but one of the member's daughters is a great attorney. Pam has handled many gas and oil cases, and based on the MC's acreage, the profit should be around half a million. She's driving down from Pittsburgh tomorrow to get things started."

"But you were worried about tearing up the land." She snuggled against him, the rain feeling nice on her head and shoulders.

"I talked to Pam early this morning. She said there are ways to ensure the land is treated with respect. She explained a lot of the processes to me, so now I feel somewhat stupid for not looking into selling sooner. I could have saved my people a lot of grief."

Relief rushed through Bernadette. "That's wonderful news. I'm glad this is working out for you and your MC."

"So you'll stay?" Frank asked.

"Would my mother be allowed to live here?" she asked, praying he said yes. "My brothers have their own lives now, so Mom is alone if I stay here."

"Family means everything to my clan, Bernadette." He hooked his index finger under her chin, forcing her to look up at him. "She's more than welcome to move in with the Werewolves of Rebellion, but will she be able to accept what we are?"

She gazed into his onyx eyes and knew she'd love him forever. There was no way she could ever leave now. "I'm a lot like my mom, so yes, she'll be fine. After all, she must've known what I am to instruct me to hide my powers."

"Good, then we welcome her with open arms." He led her over to his Harley and helped her up onto the passenger pillion. "You do realize—" He nuzzled her ear, sending gooseflesh over her skin and heat to her pussy. "—that I want a big family."

"Then I suggest we get started," Bernadette replied, grinning. "After all, I do have a bet to honor."

Thunder rumbled overhead, and laughter burst from him as he straddled the seat and started the Harley.

She never wanted to leave Frank or his people. This was her home.

About the Author

Ana Lee Kennedy loves writing stories steeped in lore, history, mythology, and her wicked sense of humor, although she is known to pen hot paranormal and contemporary stories too. She is currently writing the final novel in the Werewolves of Rebellion trilogy.

After many actual dreams of traveling the world, Ana Lee hopes to do so soon with her husband and young son, and their first stop will be England. When she's not writing, she can be found in her flower gardens or at one of the local lakes playing with her son and their creepily intelligent Labrador retriever. She resides in the U.S. with her family, Sir Creepy Dog, two almost-as-smart felines, and a pair of pet ducks.

Other Riverdale Avenue Books By Ana Lee Kennedy

Seduced by the King
Volume One of the Valhalla Skies Saga

The Dragon God's Kiss
Volume Two of the Valhalla Skies Saga

The Sorcerer King and the Fire Queen

Invasion of Her Heart:
Book One of the Lovers of the Galaxy Series

Bounty Hunters of the Heart:
Book Two of the Lovers of the Galaxy Series

Raiders of the Lost Heart:
Book Three of the Lovers of Galaxy Series

Wrapped Around Your Handlebars

You Might Also Like

Passion of the Panther
By F. L. Bicknell

Whips, Chains and Candy Canes
by F. L. Bicknell

Collaring the Saber-Tooth:
Book One of the Masters of the Cats series
by Trinity Blacio

Embracing the Winds
by Trinity Blacio

Jeanne-Claude and Eugene's Magic Lamp
Book One: I Dream of Jinns
by Trinity Blacio